Selected Praise for

But Inside I'm Screaming

"An absorbing novel...this former reporter
writes a story that's hard to put down."
—*Oakland Tribune*

"An insightful, touching and, yes, even funny account
of what it's like to lose control as the world watches."
—*New York Times* bestselling author Mary Jane Clark

From the first page, Elizabeth Flock takes you inside the mind and heart
of a young woman of promise, about to be destroyed by her own past.
A riveting, fast-paced tale by a first-time novelist with a gift
for breathing life into her characters."
—Judy Woodruff, Anchor, CNN's *Inside Politics*

"[A] gripping story."
—*OK!* magazine

"Riveting, raw, painfully honest...Elizabeth Flock's well-written,
insightful, deeply emotional debut novel is a stunning portrayal...
an intense look at mental illness from the inside."
—*Romance Reviews Today*

"An insightful character study...[a] bleak, yet at times amusing,
well-written story...readers will agree that Elizabeth Flock
provides a powerhouse."
—*Midwest Book Review*

But Inside I'm Screaming

ELIZABETH FLOCK

HARLEQUIN®

entertain, enrich, inspire™

Recycling programs
for this product may
not exist in your area.

ISBN-13: 978-0-7783-1316-8

BUT INSIDE I'M SCREAMING

For questions and comments about the quality of this book, please contact us at
CustomerService@Harlequin.com.

www.Harlequin.com

Printed in U.S.A.

But
Inside
I'm
Screaming

It is almost impossible for me to properly convey my gratitude to the following people for their tremendous support—both professional and personal—throughout the years it took to complete this novel:

Laura Dail, Mary Jane Clark, Stuart Horwitz, Susan Swinwood, Amy Moore-Benson, Jodie Chase, Jill Brack, Tres Mills, Liz Flock… I could not have done it without all of you.

And to my parents, whom I love deeply—thank you.

"Come from the four winds, O breath, and breathe
upon these slain, that they may live...
and the breath came into them and they lived...
and they stood up upon their feet..."

—Ezekiel 37:9-10

One

Isabel

Isabel picked at the ragged threads that once hugged a shiny button on the front of her blazer. Hunched over her keyboard and sallow-skinned from too much fluorescent lighting, she had won computer solitaire three times before she bored of it entirely and listlessly reached for the mouse to click over to the wires to see what was not happening on this slow Labor Day weekend.

Staring at her flickering screen, either at words floating in front of her or at playing cards triumphantly dancing off a full deck, was a relief from the noise in her brain: angry shouts shifting into one another like a Rubick's Cube. "You disgust me," her husband called out as her father's voice interrupted with "You have no family" and "Why do you even bother?" Alex again: "You're nothing, you don't even register."

She shook her head to put the invisible squares back into place.

"Hey, Jack, check out AP wires. Princess Diana's been in a car accident," she called out across the newsroom to the assignment editor, her ring finger finding its way to her front teeth.

"Yeah, her Mercedes probably got a scratch and they're calling it a wreck," the overnight editor answered.

Isabel was filling in for the weekend anchor who wanted the holiday weekend off to spend with his family in the Hamptons.

"You think you can actually get away from this?" an unidentified voice snarled in Isabel's head.

She bit the skin around her fingernail.

"I don't know, Jack. Look how many 'urgents' they've entered. Why don't we call the London bureau and see what they know."

"Okay, *let's*," Jack replied bitterly, knowing that "why don't *we* call…" was a direct order for whoever was on the desk to carry out the task.

You disgust me. Did you hear me? You disgust me.

Isabel shook her head again. To an observer it might have appeared she was dodging persistent mosquitoes.

As Jack hit the direct-dial button to London, the phones started ringing. Isabel picked up the first line.

"Isabel, it's John. I'm on my way in. Who've you talked to?"

"Huh?"

"London just beeped me. You talked to Ted yet? I think he's making his way across town, too."

Jesus.

"What did London tell you? Jack's on the phone with them right now—I haven't heard." Isabel felt a knot tighten in her stomach.

"It's bad. They said they're going to coordinate with Jack to feed video as soon as the freelancer in Paris gets to the bureau. The car's all mangled, though. Should be good pictures."

"What about injuries?"

"London said they don't know yet. Listen, kid, we may need you to do a special report. You okay with that?"

No. Jesus Christ, no.

"Sure," she replied. She had tried to sound convincing but was sure she'd failed.

"You sure? Ted's made the call that it's you and he's on his way in to make it happen. But say the word and we'll get someone else in. You don't have to do it."

"I'm fine, John." Isabel corrected her posture and took a deep breath in. "Seriously. Don't give it another thought."

I can't do this. Not right now. Not tonight. Please.

But John was dubious. "Who else is in the newsroom?"

"No one. Just me and Jack and a couple of editors in the back—I don't know who."

"For chrissakes! Why hasn't Jack gotten backup in there? You're gonna need at *least* a couple of producers for now, until we can get our shit together and we know how bad this thing is. Lemme talk to Jack."

"Stand by." Isabel felt the thump of a headache gnawing its way to the front of her forehead. Her computer was beeping every two to three seconds with the same "urgent" wire report that Diana had been in a car accident. She signaled to Jack to pick up the phone. He already had a phone on each ear and was no longer sitting back in his chair but was pacing behind the assignment desk.

Calm down. This is my last chance. Last chance. Last chance. So let's dance…the last dance…to-oo-night. Yes it's my last chance….

"Buckingham Palace confirms that Diana, the Princess of Wales, was in a serious car accident earlier this evening in Paris. There is no confirmation yet on the extent of her injuries."

Isabel stared at the AP report on her computer. She squeezed her eyes shut, opened them again, and tried to pretend her peripheral vision was not narrowing.

"You think you can actually get away from this?" the voice asked again, its sinister laughter bouncing off the interior walls of Isabel's skull.

Not now. Please. Calm down.

Two seconds later the makeup artist backed away from her and then dabbed an extra bit of powder on her forehead.

"Okay." Ted Sargent was nervously arranging the two sheets of copy on the anchor desk in front of Isabel. "You got everything you need?"

"Yes, Ted," Isabel answered, her voice an octave higher than normal. "They're talking to me in my ear so, if you'll excuse me…" She was unaccustomed to having the president of the network news division looking over her shoulder.

"Stand by, Isabel," the voice came into her earpiece. "We don't know when we're cutting in. Stand by."

Isabel had never done a Special Report. She turned in her seat and scanned the newsroom. Within minutes it had come alive, desk assistants, producers, writers—many of whom she'd never seen before—were scurrying around, diving for phones, typing on their keypads, combing through hours of Diana footage for the best shots. She felt as if she were on a plane, taking off, the cabin pressure adjusting and popping her eardrums.

We are interrupting this broadcast to bring you an ANN Special Report. Just moments ago, Buckingham Palace confirmed that Diana, Princess of Wales, has been involved in what they are calling a, quote, serious car accident in Paris. The extent of her injuries and the nature of the accident are not yet known. Once again, Princess Diana was in a car accident roughly one hour ago in Paris, France. Buckingham Palace is characterizing it as serious. We will, of course, bring you more information as soon as it becomes available. Please stay tuned to your local ANN affiliate for further details. I'm Isabel Murphy reporting from ANN headquarters in New York.

Isabel's lips moved as she read the copy again to herself. Her heart was racing almost as fast as her thought process.

I'm anchoring a Special Report for the American News Network. Focus. I've got to focus.

"Chip?" Isabel spoke into her microphone at a whisper and barely moved her lips, which were now magenta, the blue fear freezing out the slash of her red lipstick. "Do I have five seconds to make a quick call? It's important."

"We're in standby mode so technically no, but since we're waiting for the break to drop out of programming...if you do it quickly...you've got about seventeen seconds until we're on alert. Go."

Isabel had already dialed the first nine numbers into the phone behind the anchor desk. She pushed the tenth on Chip's go-ahead.

"Hi, it's me," she said softly. "Just wanted to tell you two to watch ANN right now."

Her face fell as she listened into the phone. "But where is he? Oh. Okay. Well, bye."

Maybe he'll be home in the next few minutes. Then he'll catch it. Mom'll already have it on.

"Okay, Isabel." The voice in her ear was steady and commanding. "We're going live in one minute. Stand by."

You disgust me. You disgust me.

Isabel sat up straight in her chair and nervously touched her sprayed hair.

Calm down. Calm down.

"Isabel, you all set?" Ted was just behind the TelePrompTer facing the anchor desk.

Last chance. Last chance. For romance...to-oo-night.

"Yes," Isabel replied, looking down at her copy (a backup in case the TelePrompTer were to break down). There was already an imprint of her sweating hand on the printout.

Maybe he's walking into the house right now.

Isabel's heart pounded even harder when the voice of her producer came back into her ear: "Thirty seconds, Isabel. Stand by."

Oh, God. Please, God.

Isabel watched Ted hurry in to the control booth from behind the camera.

Last chance…

"In ten, nine, eight, seven—cue music—five, four, three, two." Good producers never say "one."

Last chance…

Isabel looked into the camera and, for the first time in her career, froze.

Chip's voice was urgent in her ear: "Isabel! You're on!"

Nothing.

Last chance…last chance…

Isabel was no longer at the anchor desk, she was in a parallel universe, one in which Donna Summers sang the same song over and over and Isabel was able to watch herself spiral down a dirty tunnel and yet was powerless to stop her descent, her arms frantically grabbing at the sides of the darkening cone, trying to catch hold of a slippery side. Viewers, alerted to the emergency cut-in by a fancy graphic and urgent music involving trumpets and French horns, were now turning to other stations.

Ted Sargent ran out of the control booth toward the anchor desk, just off camera. "Isabel!" he hissed angrily.

Nothing.

You disgust me. The voices had broken through—Isabel no

longer heard them as others but as herself. *Did you hear me? You disgust me!*

He ran back into the booth and yelled to the producer. "Throw up a graphic! Something! Cut to black! Jesus fucking Christ!" Ted looked up at the monitors running the other network broadcasts and saw that all were on the air with Special Reports about Diana. CBS was running video of her on an amusement park ride with her two sons. NBC had somehow gotten Tom Brokaw into the anchor chair in time. As precious minutes ticked by, ANN was missing the story. And with the evening news anchor out of town, all the network had was Isabel Murphy, who was spontaneously combusting on national television.

"Isabel, what the hell is going on?" Ted was one step away from reaching across the anchor desk and strangling his only hope. "Isabel! Jesus Christ, Isabel! Snap out of it!"

Isabel watched Ted's small calamari lips moving. His voice tangled up with others talking at her and confused her.

Chip, the man behind the voice in her ear, was in front of her. "Isabel? Do you need a doctor? What's going on?" Normally unflappable, Chip was nearly as frantic as Ted. This was the kind of thing that lost people jobs. Possibly the biggest news story of the year and Isabel was single-handedly wrecking the network's reputation.

"Isabel, you have got to listen to me." John Goodman, the senior producer on duty, was towering over her. His words were measured but powerful. "You have got to go live right now, do you understand? Whatever is going on, we can fix it when this is over. But right now, you have got to go live."

Isabel brought John's stern face into focus.

This is the man who hired me. The man who took a leap of faith in me when no one else would.

"Okay," she whispered through ventriloquist's lips. No one heard her but John.

"Okay? You'll do it? Okay?" he double-checked while nodding to Ted and Chip.

"Okay," Isabel said meekly.

I've got to do this.

Chip ran back into the booth.

He had left her earpiece on so she heard the voices thundering at one another in the control room. "This is a mistake, Ted. I *told* you I didn't want her in the chair tonight." Chip's voice.

"What, she's not used to *live television?* Give me a fucking break."

"Okay, Isabel, let's try this again." Chip had regained his composure. "In thirty seconds."

Please. Please.

"Nice and easy." Chip was trying to soothe her.

Please. Calm down. Please. Please.

"I have to protect my reporters, Sargent," Isabel heard John challenge Ted. "And I'm telling you, this is not a good call to make with Murphy right now! Where's Roberts? Get him in here."

"Fifteen seconds." The knot, ever-tightening in Isabel's stomach, threatened to erupt in vomit. "Ten, nine, eight, seven—cue music—five, four, three, two…"

Last chance.

With the camera trained on her, Isabel opened her mouth to speak but closed it when no words came out.

Please. Please no.

"No fucking way!" Ted shouted in the booth. "Go to a graphic." As Ted barked orders, Chip tried to coax Isabel one last time.

"Get her off the air!" Ted yelled. Isabel flinched at the volume of the words still piped through her ear. "Get her off the fucking air! She'll never make air again, if I have anything to say about it. Not on this network. She wants to go down, fine. But she's not taking this network with her, goddammit!"

So, let's dance the last dance...let's dance...the last dance...

"If you threaten her, I swear to God I'll make your life miserable," John warned Ted.

To-oo-night...

"She's over. She's finished," Ted ranted.

"If she is it'll be *her* choice, not yours," John volleyed back. "You hear me?"

"Do I need to remind you who you're talking to, Goodman?" Ted's voice a decibel lower.

"Just give her some room right now. Agreed?"

Look at you. You disgust me.

Ted looked through the glass door into the newsroom. His assistant was running across the room to him.

He opened the door. "What? You reach him?"

"He's five minutes away," she panted.

He turned back to John. "She's lucky Roberts is in town or I'd wipe the floor with her. Okay, Chip, let's get the desk ready for him. The computer's all booted up, right? Melissa, go down to the lobby and hold an elevator open for him. We got some water by the desk in case he's thirsty? Good."

Move. You have to get up now. It's over. Move.

TWO

It's so thin and small it seems impossible that it can end a human life.

Do it.

Two long, quick slices and the pain bleeds away.

So why am I hesitating? Do it.

Isabel knows that she is scared to slit her wrists. She'd rather find a painless solution. To her it sounds like something Yogi Berra might have said: *I'd kill myself but it'd hurt too much.*

The white porcelain feels cold to her as she climbs, fully clothed, into the tub.

This is it. This makes the most sense. Do it.

Isabel looks from the metal blade balancing on the edge of the bathtub to the sink counter where her sleeping pills are neatly arranged. Plan B. The last time she tried swallowing pills she did not take enough and woke up with a stiff tube snaking down her throat, pumping charcoal into her belly. For hours she vomited up the black coal as unsympathetic interns scowled and mixed up more of the pitch-black concoction that's meant to absorb the poison.

Maybe I'll try the pills again. That's much easier. And this time I'll take the entire bottle and throw in some Tylenol PM for good measure. That'll work.

She pulls herself up and out of the bathtub. After pushing down and twisting the prescription bottle open, she turns on the faucet. Then she finally gives in to the magnetic pull of the mirror facing her. She had resisted it until now, knowing her face, however exhausted, haggard or gaunt, would betray her fear.

Look at me. Jesus. Who is this looking back at me?

She looks back down to the running water.

Thirty-five years of living, thirty-five years packed with classes she excelled in, jobs she succeeded at…Isabel's thirty-five years all boiled down to one moment, an image she pulled out and focused her inner eye on whenever she despaired.

In the image is five-year-old Isabel, pretty and shy, quietly curled up on the floor alongside the family dog, a huge Saint Bernard named Violet. The two slept together almost every night, the enormously fat Violet providing enough body heat to warm the tiny child nestled against her. Isabel's parents took many photographs of this scene, but it is Isabel's own recollection she relies on in times of confusion. When she needs to feel comforted, to feel safe. Lately the image was becoming mentally frayed with overuse.

Thinking of the warmth of Violet's belly, the steadiness of her breathing, the softness of her thick coat, Isabel is once again momentarily transported away from her pain.

How did that little girl end up alone and desperate in a cold New York City bathroom trying to decide whether to slash her wrists or swallow a fistful of pills?

What else is there? What else can I do?

Three

Isabel

Isabel gingerly touches her upper chest and winces at the pain. Her throat feels sore from the plastic tubing, her stomach raw from being angrily pumped the day before.

"Hi." Isabel's mother, Katherine, is waiting on the sidewalk in front of the freshly washed SUV.

She holds out her arms for a hug that Isabel returns perfunctorily. Isabel studiously avoids meeting her mother's eyes.

"Let's go" is all she says as she climbs up into the black Range Rover.

"I've got the directions, so we're all set," Katherine says, trying to fill the awkward silence that descends once both are buckled inside. "You don't have to worry about a thing." She pulls into busy Manhattan traffic.

Isabel stares out the window, watching her apartment building disappear into the distance.

"Do you want to listen to the radio?"

"Huh?"

"The radio. Do you want it on or off?"

"I don't care." Isabel never breaks her numb stare. She is fighting to keep her eyes open.

"What's that station you always used to listen to?" her mother asks. "You know the one. You and your brother used to call in all the time."

"Mom." Isabel turns her weary head. "I just got released from the emergency room. I'm exhausted. I don't care if the radio is on. Put it on if you want to. I don't care."

"Watch your tone, Isabel," her mother warns. "I'm your mother and I'm just trying to make conversation."

"Do we have to have a conversation right now?"

"Your father and I don't know why you didn't call us last night. We could have talked to you, cheered you up. You're always giving up so easily."

"So even in this I didn't do the right thing? The thing you and Dad would have wanted? Sorry to disappoint you once again, Mother."

"Well, I don't understand why you always give up. Like ballet, for instance. Whatever happened with that? I'll tell you what happened with that—you weren't any good so you dropped it. Instead of sticking it out you dropped it."

"Thanks, Mom. This is making me feel so much better."

"And then there was volleyball…you couldn't get that ball over the net no matter what you tried…so what'd you do?"

"*Mom.*"

"You dropped it. I'm sorry, Isabel, but someone has to help you see the truth here. Maybe it's tough love…."

Isabel closed her eyes, her mother's familiar lecture a sad lullaby for the rest of the ride up the interstate.

There is no sign for Three Breezes, just a discreet number expensively etched into the low stone pillars flanking the wooded driveway. Katherine slows as she makes the turn, anticipating the speed bump just inside the entrance. While they ease over it, Isabel catches sight of a groundskeeper raking a few errant leaves underneath a magnolia tree. As their car passes, he glances up and ever so slightly tips his head to Isabel. She looks away.

Everything is in slow motion.

Within forty-five minutes her belongings are spread out on the floor of the nurses' station. Everything she has brought with her to Three Breezes is out of her suitcase and on display for all to see. Her underwear, her raincoat, her nail clippers, needlepoint, tweezers. Everything.

What the hell is going on?

"You don't have to stay here while we do this, Isabel." The nurse is sitting cross-legged on the floor among Isabel's things, Isabel's own hairdryer in the nurse's lap. "We explained to you when you checked in that everyone's suitcase has to be inspected. It's nothing personal. Some people find it easier to let us do this and then we bring them the things they're allowed."

"What do you mean *allowed?*"

"It's for your own protection," the nurse answers. "We just go through here and take anything that might be dangerous and we set it aside. After the inspection, we take all the things we set aside and we put them into a bin marked with your very own name on it...."

Why the hell is she talking down to me as if I'm in kindergarten? Can't she see I'm nothing like the people here?

"...that bin then goes into the sharps closet," the nurse continues, "and any time you need to use something from your bin you just need to come find one of us and we'll help you out. You might find it easier, though, to let us do this by ourselves."

The hell I'm leaving when she's going through my stuff. Why is my hairdryer going into that pile with my pack of Lady Bic razors? I understand the razors—I'm not a complete idiot—but what'm I going to do…blow-dry myself to death? My needlepoint, too?

"Why are you taking my needlepoint?" Isabel asks through gritted teeth. "I'm making a pillow for my niece." *She doesn't care what the needlepoint is for…why did I say that?*

"It has a needle?" the nurse answers in up-speak. "You can work on it only if you're supervised."

Even the Oil of Olay moisturizer is confiscated. "It's in a glass jar?" Up-speak again. Before Katherine can regain her own composure, Isabel catches her mother's mouth gaping open—mirroring the horror Isabel feels closing in on her, suffocating her.

Her Hammacher Schlemmer sound machine is set in the "no" pile.

"Okay, that's it. This is ridiculous." Isabel feels the fury beginning to unleash. "Give me back my sound machine. It's not sharp. It's not dangerous."

"Um, well, we need to run a test on it."

"My ass you're going to run a test on it." Isabel's voice is an octave higher than usual. Katherine puts a hand on her shoulder.

"Get your hand off my shoulder, Mom." Isabel whips around to face her mother. "I know what that's code for. That's code for *Shut up, Isabel. Mind your manners, Isabel.*"

Katherine withdraws her hand quickly and takes a step back.

Astonished, Isabel asks, "What, Mom? You think I'm going to hurt you?"

Katherine, with eyebrows stretched across her forehead in mock fear, addresses her reply more to the nurse than to her daughter. "I just don't know you anymore, Isabel. How do I know what you're going to do next?"

Oh, this is rich. This is just perfect. Now she's making them think I'm dangerous.

"What I'm trying to say, Isabel—" the nurse goes from friendly to firm "—is that we simply run a quick electrical test on it and we'll return it to you by tonight. Tomorrow at the latest."

I can't take this. I can't take this…

Isabel steadies herself in the doorway.

"We'll get it right back to you."

It's not just the sound machine, you idiot. It's everything. It's this whole place. It's this whole snake pit.

Isabel slides down the door frame, collapsing into a heap at the base of the doorway.

"All right, that's enough, young lady." Katherine is standing over her crumpled daughter. "Let's go outside for a minute."

"Ma'am?" It's the inspection nurse again. "Um, she can't go outside the unit anymore? She doesn't have her privileges? She has to stay inside at all times."

Isabel is stunned. The tears that had just begun to flow stop immediately.

"What?" She stares directly at the nurse, the fog that had enveloped her briefly dissipating.

"Um, you have checked in so you cannot go outside. Your caseworker will be here any minute to explain all this to you," the nurse says as she returns to her inspection.

"Mom?" Isabel's breathing becomes shallow as she reaches for her mother and tries to stand up at the same time.

"Yes?"

"Let's go," Isabel says simply. "Let's get out of here. Do you have the car keys?" Katherine looks from her daughter to the nurse, unsure of what to do.

Another nurse, who until then had been sorting through files, turns to Isabel.

"All right, hon." Her voice is craggy but gentle. Her tone betrays a hint of resignation, as if she has seen a thousand Isabels come and go. "Let's go sit down for a second." She tries to lead Isabel into the single room she has been assigned. Isabel pulls her arm away and focuses on her mother.

"Mom? The car keys?" Her stare is intense. Her lips are pursed and her throat is trying to choke back vomit. She sees, for the first time, that she is here to stay. Her mother is not even reaching into her cavernous bag to hunt for the keys.

Oh, my God. Why isn't Mom doing anything? Why is she looking at me like that?

"Mom? Mom? Please, Mom. Please take me home." Isabel is crying again as the nurse helps Katherine lead Isabel to her stark room with an ominous stain on the industrial wall-to-wall carpeting. "No. No, Mom. I've changed my mind. I don't want to come here, Mom. Seriously, I've changed my mind. Mom, do you hear me? Mom?"

When she sees that yelling is not advancing her case, Isabel begins to beg.

"Mom! Please, Mom…"

Isabel sees the same mix of dread, shock and disgust on her mother's face she had seen two nights before in Manhattan. On that night Isabel had announced to her parents that she had decided to follow her doctor's advice and was checking into a psychiatric facility in upstate New York, "before they check me in involuntarily."

"Just give it twenty-four hours, Isabel," the nurse is saying as she guides Isabel to the bed by the elbow. "Just twenty-four hours."

As she tries to unscrew the cap of her water bottle, she frantically scans the room and sees she is surrounded by the dregs of society. Losers, both literally and figuratively. Literally because they lost the battle to end their lives. Figuratively because, collectively, they look like the rejects from a *One Flew Over the Cuckoo's Nest* casting call.

Isabel's hands are shaking so badly she gives up the thought of hydration. Her pupils are so dilated by fear her green eyes appear black.

Across the room a woman with short, thick jet-black hair is staring at her. Slowly, still staring at Isabel, the woman brings her own bottle of water to her lips and sucks, like an infant, through the sport spout.

Jesus. Where am I? What is this place?

Isabel shrinks into herself when, moments later, a large man stumbles into the room. The only free seat is next to her. He lumbers toward it and loudly exhales as he squeezes into one of the mismatched Naugahyde armchairs. His fat pasty-white thighs begin to melt uncomfortably into the chair. The hot weather has intensified his body odor and the only thing separating Isabel from the man's stinky armpits is a useless polyester mesh jersey that adds a gamey scent to the sweaty giant.

"I know exactly what I'm gonna talk about today," he gleefully declares to his miserable neighbor. He resembles a puppy with huge paws and baby fat that he hasn't yet grown into. He appears to have the mentality of a six-year-old.

Isabel continues to stare straight ahead, knowing that looking at him will only encourage his conversation. She is willing the day to be over, willing the clock to tick faster.

This is a nightmare.

"Barbecued chicken wings!" shouts the smelly man-child. She thinks he meant to whisper to her, but he is too excited to regale the group with this topic that he forgets to adjust the volume and instead loudly blurts it out. It doesn't seem to bother him that Isabel is pointedly ignoring him.

These people are freaks and this is a nightmare.

"Shhh," everyone in the bedraggled group hisses. Everyone but the black-haired sport-spout girl, who is laughing disproportionately hard at the outburst. And another, younger woman with long, stringy hair, who is staring off into space. Two people over on Isabel's left sits an older woman in restraints because, the smelly man loudly whispers to Isabel, "Yesterday she tried to hit the group leader when he asked her what she was thinking."

Isabel takes it all in, frozen in her sleek black gabardine slacks and Barney's New York black T-shirt, her arms tightly wrapped across her chest in an invisible strait-jacket, her legs tensely crossed, her thick blond hair dried out and brittle.

How the hell did I end up here?

Hours later, Isabel has not changed out of her clothes and is lying on her back, wide awake, her purse still on her shoulder so that if tipped upright, she could walk straight out. Through the cinder-block walls, Isabel hears something slamming into the wall and strains to identify the sound.

Slam!

After five more minutes trying to block it out, Isabel sits up. With her heart beating rapidly, she inches off the bed, which is several inches higher than a normal one, so, upon sliding off, she is startled when it takes her feet longer to find the floor. After waiting a few seconds she swallows hard and takes a few steps to the doorway, following the crack of light beaming from its edges. The hallway is deserted. She waits while her eyes adjust to the bright overhead lights. The sharp sounds next door echo her panic and amplify her fear.

She moves silently toward the sound, her body pressed up against the painted concrete wall like a cat burglar. Again she swallows hard. Her heartbeat is now pulsing in her ears. She jumps when she hears something crash to the floor several feet away from her around the corner.

Maybe I should go back to my room. This is stupid. I'm going back to my room.

After several seconds of silence, Isabel peeks around the corner and in through the doorway of the adjacent room.

Inside, the dark-haired sport-spout woman is a blur of activity ripping apart her room. Drawers are pulled out, sheets untucked, closet emptied. Every twenty seconds or so the woman kicks the wall.

Just as Isabel is about to turn and creep back to her room the woman whips around and sees her.

"Are you spying on me?" she asks, her eyes darting from side to side. "What do you want?"

"Huh?" Caught off guard, Isabel panics. "Um, want help or something?"

Goddammit, why did I just offer to help? I don't want to help her...she's crazy.

The woman has already turned away and is dumping the contents of her purse onto the floor in the middle of her bright room. "My name's Melanie," she says breathlessly.

Isabel backs up and looks up and down the hallway.

Shouldn't an orderly be in here calming her down? Doesn't anyone else hear all this noise she's making? Hel-lo? Nurse Ratched? Anyone?

"Hey?" Melanie shouts. "You helping me or what?"

"Uh, okay." Isabel cautiously kneels down just inside the doorway and, not knowing where else to begin, delicately picks up Melanie's lipstick.

Get me out of here....

"What're you looking for, anyway?"

Melanie breaks into a sob. Her hair is angrily pulled away from her face with a simple barrette. Her pajamas are splashed with primary colors, exaggerating the sense of chaos. Melanie must have been told she's arty and eccentric and then capitalized on the compliment.

"My beaded bracelet," Melanie answers in an annoyed tone that suggests Isabel should have known the object of the search. "I made it in art the other day and now I can't find it." More sobbing.

Isabel looks up to see someone else joining in the hunt.

"Hi. I'm Kristen." The woman cheerfully introduces herself to Isabel as though she's in a sorority meeting. "What's up, Mel? Want help?"

Isabel is still holding the lipstick. "Okay, well...I'm going to go now," she says to no one in particular.

The night nurse comes barreling through the door with her flashlight even though the lights in the room are on. Her nameplate reads "Connie."

She is the nurse who just hours before talked Isabel into staying at Three Breezes for at least one day. Isabel takes a closer look at her. Connie's face is wizened from years of sunbathing. Her voice is raspy from years of smoking.

Finally! Somebody cart this woman off to solitary confinement.

Instead, Connie casually plops down on the floor and helps

look for the bracelet. Melanie starts shaking. Her whole head vibrates and she starts hyperventilating. No one can calm her down. She's talking so fast even she is tripping over the words and thoughts pouring out of her mouth.

"She's only two months old. Elwin is never gonna deal with me," Melanie chokes in between breaths, "he's put up with so much. I have the baby. I get the postpartum thing and stop taking my meds and now he's taking care of her all by himself. Of course he's got his parents. They love this. They love the fact that they were right about me. I'm not good enough for their son. I hope he remembered to get the lamb-and-rice dog food. Coco hates the beef flavor. When I was little I used to love running through sprinklers. Wasn't that fun?"

This is unreal. If I saw this in a movie I'd think it was heavy-handed.

Connie pulls Melanie up and takes her over to the nurses' station to give her a sedative. Kristen and Isabel remain on the floor, Kristen still searching for Melanie's bracelet, Isabel listening to Melanie's disturbing chatter echo from down the hall.

Isabel steals a glance at Kristen's right arm, bandaged because, as Isabel will later find out, her obsessive-compulsive disorder leaves her clawing at her skin until it starts to bleed. Perhaps sensing Isabel's stare her hand flutters to this spot and quickly withdraws. There is an awkward silence between them.

Isabel looks back down at the floor.

How do I extricate myself from this one?

Melanie returns just as Kristen spots a cigar box and opens it. Voila! Among some pictures and letters is the bracelet. Melanie grabs it and shrieks with happiness.

"Good night, everyone," she says as she crawls into bed,

the shot Connie gave her a few minutes ago taking hold of her tiny, troubled frame. "Thanks for helping."

When no one moves she adds, "That's all I have to say."

Kristen and Isabel file out and head back to their respective rooms. The bed crinkles as Isabel climbs up into it: instead of soft mattress covers there are thick sheets of plastic under the paper-thin sheets in the unlikely event someone becomes incontinent on top of everything else.

Every fifteen minutes the door opens and a flashlight shines in Isabel's face. Directly into her face. So even if she manages to fall into a light sleep the beam wakes her up just enough to toss and turn all night. Isabel is on suicide watch. The flashlight checks are a status symbol. Everybody seems to know who's got checks every fifteen minutes and who has the more desirable thirty-minute variety. Isabel wouldn't have known this except that Kristen asked her point-blank about her checks while they were on Melanie's bizarre scavenger hunt. When Isabel told Kristen that the nurse checked on her every fifteen minutes Kristen looked relieved. Kristen had been at Three Breezes for some time now, but she was still, apparently, a "fifteener."

Four

The ant is neatly marching along the mortar line on the cement block wall alongside her bed. To Isabel, it appears he is as frantic as she is to leave the hospital. She tugs once more at the lower lip of the window but it will not budge. Windows are nailed shut at Three Breezes. So instead of freeing the insect, Isabel, with miserable resignation, watches it make its way down the wall.

Isabel avoided anthills. In the spring- and summertime, when nature was busy reinventing itself, those telltale signs of ant industry—miniscule pyramids of dirt—multiplied in cracks of buckled pavement, between bricks and along fence posts, and Isabel always stepped around them. She had ever since she was a small girl growing up in Connecticut.

Her brothers, on the other hand, went out of their way to step directly on them.

"Don't!" she yelled at Owen, who was twisting his foot on top of the fourth of twelve anthills along their short front walk. Isabel ran over and pushed her seven-year-old brother away. Too late. Isabel imagined hundreds of suffocating ants under the cement gasping for air.

"I'm telling Mom if you do it again." She was on her hands and knees frantically trying to clear a passageway so that the ants could find their way out of the rubble. Her nine-year-old mind realized this was futile so she grabbed a tiny stick to drill a hole into the ground so the ants could get some oxygen.

"I'm telling Mom if you do it again," mimicked her brother. "You're such a tattletale."

He was right.

But Isabel didn't think of it as telling on her brothers, she just couldn't stand to see anything or anyone hurt. Even ants.

"What's going on out here?" Isabel's mother called through the top screen of the porch door.

"Nothing," her brothers called out, disappearing into their fort in the backyard.

"Isabel? What're you doing?" Katherine asked as she approached her hunched-over daughter.

Isabel was furiously drilling, pausing only to wipe her tears out of her eyes so that she could continue her rescue mission.

"Is it the anthills again?"

"I don't understand why they do this," Isabel cried as she squatted over the fifth flattened mound. "There're families under here. Whole families. And they're dying!"

"Oh, for God's sake. This is ridiculous. Look at me for a second."

Isabel obeyed as she wiped her nose on her sleeve.

"They're going to be okay, the ants. We've been over this. They like to burrow out. They'll be okay."

Isabel looked back down. No ants were crawling out of her manmade holes. She looked back up at her mother.

"You've got to let it go. You think this is sad? Wait'll life kicks you in the rear a few times. No one's out there drilling holes for all of us, you know. Now, come on inside. Help me sort the Girl Scout cookie orders."

As she stood up to go, Isabel looked back at her doomed friends. But she swallowed her tears and forged ahead.

As her childhood advanced, Isabel's empathy for creatures of all shapes and sizes morphed into a sadness that was difficult to shake. Sadness gave way to isolation. Isabel constantly felt as if she were on the outside looking in. As if she wasn't quite a participant in everyday life, but a sleepwalker. While she maintained the polished front of an oldest, overachieving child, her true personality had yet to emerge, and that only added to the disconnected feeling she wore like a bulky shroud.

As Isabel floated numbly through elementary school, her physical appearance was taking a very definite shape. She began to hear over and over again that she was pretty, and soon, perhaps because she felt so empty, the compliments at least temporarily filled her up. Isabel began to crave the attention that was paid to her looks. No one wanted to hear about her sorrow, no one wanted to see her sad.

She was becoming an expert at reading people. She soon learned that humor got more results than anger or tears, that attention was paid to the attractive, and that people were inherently egotistical. Everybody likes to talk about themselves. So she honed her listening skills. Isabel was learning to survive by playing roles: the curvaceous beauty, the class clown, the intense listener. She was excellent at being whatever someone else wanted her to be.

"Isabel. What can I do for you?"
Isabel cleared her throat.

"Um. Mr. Clulow? Um, I was wondering if I could have another chance."

The high school drama teacher slightly cocked his head to the side. "Another chance." It was a statement, not a question.

"Yeah. I mean, yes. I know I froze up there last week. I totally froze. I blew it. I just wasn't prepared. For improv. But I'm ready now. I can do it. I'll act out anything you want me to act out. If you'd just give me one more chance."

Mr. Clulow looked down at the papers on his desk. Then he looked back up at Isabel.

"Why do you want to join the drama club, Isabel? What is it that's drawing you to drama?"

"Drawing me?"

"Yes. You see, some people feel it's the perfect way to tap into their creative side. Others find it's the perfect form of self-expression. I'm just wondering what's driving you."

Isabel looked down. Without looking back up she answered.

"I guess it's that…well, I suppose I just like the idea of being someone else," she mumbled.

Mr. Clulow raised his eyebrows as if he'd caught her in a trap.

"So you don't like to be yourself?"

"No!" she said, too loudly. "I mean, I do. What I really mean is that…" She stammered, aware that he was prepared to pick apart her next sentence. "It's…um…"

"Miss Murphy," the teacher scolded, "I have a class to teach in five minutes. I suggest you get to the bottom of what it is you would like to say."

"Please. Just give me another chance to try out. Please?"

He tapped his pencil impatiently and looked out the window.

"Hmm."

"Please?"

"All right. One more chance. But this is hardly fair. I don't do this for other students who buckle under pressure. If you get embarrassed in an audition, how on earth will you be able to act on stage in front of hundreds of people? Don't…answer. It's a rhetorical question, Miss Murphy. Tomorrow after school meet me in the gym and we will try it one more time."

"Thank you! Oh, thank you so much, Mr. Clulow," she said, backing out of his tiny office.

It was eight o'clock on a school night and Isabel's mother was furious.

"I thought rehearsals were never more than two hours after school."

"Mom, we've got a play coming up and no one knows their lines yet. We *had* to stay late. Mr. Clulow said—"

"Mr. Clulow said. Mr. Clulow said. That's all I ever hear— Mr. Clulow said this, Mr. Clulow said that. Well, *Mr. Clulow* said rehearsals wouldn't take time away from homework assignments on school nights!"

"I don't have that much work tonight. I have history and English and that's it."

"No math? No science?"

"No. And for English all I have to do is read one chapter and I can do that in fifteen minutes."

"Your father's home and he hasn't seen you in a week. You missed dinner and he's got a conference call at nine, so I don't know when you two will have a chance to visit."

"He's coming to the play, right? Please tell me he's not going to miss the play."

"Of course he's coming to the play."

"It's just…" she trailed off.

"What?"

"Nothing. It's nothing."

"What were you going to say? I hate it when you do that."

"Nothing! Seriously. I forgot what I was going to say. He's just…like…he's just never here."

"Don't be silly, Isabel," her mother said sharply. "Your father has to work, you know. He loves you, but his job—"

"I know, I know. His job calls for a lot of travel. I've been hearing that since I was born. I get it."

"But he tries."

"But he tries," said Isabel.

Five

"Fuck! Fuck, fuck, fuck!"

Isabel slowly follows the sounds of the shrieks, unsure whether she wants to find out who or what is behind them.

"Get your hands offa me, you motherfucker!"

Through the front window of the unit, Isabel watches as two aides try to pin down a young, wiry newcomer. Just as they seem to get her under control enough to slip her lanky frame into restraints, she lets out a piercing scream.

"I'm gonna fuckin' kill you! You hear me? I'm gonna kill you."

Because she is young-looking and breakably thin, it startles Isabel to hear this come from the girl's mouth.

The restraints are finally in place. The new girl is sapped of all her angry energy and is sobbing on the ground, her head twisted to the side, her face shiny with sweat.

Isabel looks down the winding driveway and, as the black girl is hauled past by two hospital aides, stares at her only way out.

I'll walk down the driveway, wait for a truck and step in front of it.

The thought calms Isabel. It soothes her to plan her fatal escape.

First I've got to get privileges.

Kristen, the girl Isabel had met the night before, chirps "good morning" and walks past Isabel out the door of the unit. Isabel watches Kristen's hand shake as she attempts to light her cigarette from a box on the wall that contains what appears to be something resembling a car lighter. Matches and lighters are confiscated on arrival.

The blubbery man she sat next to the day before lumbers past and joins Kristen just outside the door to the unit. Isabel turns her head and hopes her ear can bionically pick up their conversation through the pane of glass. It's so riddled with greasy fingerprints that Isabel is careful to keep at least one inch of space between herself and the disgusting barrier.

"What's up with that new girl?" Kristen asks him. "Did you see her yesterday?"

It's disconcerting for everyone on the unit to see someone in restraints. In the jacket. To hear someone resist. The new girl will provide conversation material for the entire day: Did you hear the new girl this morning? Did you see how long it took the orderlies to get the jacket on her?

"Her name's Keisha," the giant tells Kristen in a conspiratorial voice. "She was gang-raped."

"She was gang-raped?" Kristen repeats it slowly, as if it's a spelling bee and she has to use the vocabulary word in a sentence.

"Yeah," he answers, pleased to have Kristen's undivided attention. Isabel, inside the unit but off to the side where they can't see her, feels her head butt up against the slimy window. "She was raped for four hours or something. And she was baby-sitting her nephew or something, and the guys? They killed the kid. They killed her nephew she was sitting for. Then they took off. She lost it. Completely fucking lost it. They found her wandering in the middle of the street."

Isabel jumps when the quiet is broken by a voice coming from behind her: "Asshole don't know what he's talkin' about."

"Oh, my God." Isabel steps back. "You scared me!"

Keisha calmly turns her eyes from Kristen and Ben through the window to Isabel right in front of her.

Keisha could be the poster child for the inner city. She looks about fourteen, with long, skinny limbs and a head full of short nappy dreadlocks. Her entire outfit consists of sportswear: Air Jordans, five years old but pristine, nylon Adidas sweatpants that would make a swish sound if her lanky legs ever rubbed together, which they don't, and a hooded sweatshirt about four sizes too big. It's her uniform. She takes a long time to look as if she hasn't taken any time at all.

"Listen to them goin' on and on like they know." Keisha juts her chin in the direction of the smoker's deck, Kristen and Ben.

Isabel knows Keisha wants to be asked about herself but cannot summon the energy it would take to enter into any conversation, much less this one. She turns and looks out the window and hopes nothing will be required of her in what is threatening to be a social interaction.

"That ain't it!" Keisha says to the window, after hearing another fragment of Ben's prattle. "Okay, you want to know what happened?" She is addressing Isabel.

Did I say I wanted to know what happened?

But Isabel is finding herself begrudgingly drawn to the edgy teenager.

"I wasn't walkin' in the street, first of all," Keisha begins without encouragement. "The police came and got me from my sister's place when neighbors called 911. Hours, my ass. It wasn't no hours passed. A few minutes, sure. Maybe, and this I'm not sure about, but *maybe* half an hour. But no *hours,* Lord. They talkin' shit out there," she says, again motioning with her chin to the gossiping patients outdoors.

"Wow," Kristen says, exhaling smoke and looking down. "Hey, Ben? How do you know all this?"

"You think I'm a freak, Kristen." Ben pouts. "You think you're the only one who's got a clue. You're not, you know. I know stuff, too."

Isabel looks over her shoulder and past Keisha toward the nurses' station to see if anyone cares that they are eavesdropping.

"Ben," Kristen says, trying to soothe him. "We're buddies, right? It's just...well...I'm a little surprised that you know all about this girl. I just want to know what you know, sweetie."

Isabel marvels at the fact that both Ben and Kristen are missing the point. She looks longingly at the driveway.

"You teasin' me now, Kristen? Huh? You a fuckin' tease now?" Ben is getting red in the face. He stomps toward the door to the unit and Isabel busies herself with the old *National Geographic*s stacked on a corner table next to the window in case he is headed her way.

Kristen throws what little is left of her cigarette to the ground and steps on it just as a nurse with a clipboard brushes past Isabel and opens the door to the outside.

"Hi, Kristen," she says, making a mark on her notepaper. "Just doing the check."

Kristen smiles and shakes out another cigarette. "Hi."

The nurse lets the door close and sees Isabel and Keisha. More marks on the clipboard.

"Hi, ladies. I'm just making the rounds."

Isabel and Keisha turn their attention back out to Kristen, who is now talking towards Melanie.

"He said her name's Keisha," she is telling Melanie, "and she was raped for hours and hours and hours. They found her naked in the street. The police. That's how she ended up here. I guess she was on some kind of suicide watch...."

"See you later," Isabel says as she slips past Keisha, who is emphatically shaking her head. As Isabel crosses the room Keisha mutters, "Bitch don't know what she talkin' about."

A few minutes later Isabel is willing sleep to visit her in the little airtight room at the end of the hall.

Six

"Erin Hayes has exhausted all her appeals and now waits for a last-minute reprieve from the Texas governor. Her legal team is not optimistic, given the state's well-known record on stays of execution. Crowds have already begun to gather here outside the state penitentiary in Huntsville. Some will hold candlelight vigils, others say they'll cheer if and when Hayes goes to the electric chair."

Isabel Murphy, ANN News, Huntsville, Texas.

An overripe banana was the only health food in the Huntsville 7-Eleven. Isabel picked it up, felt the oblong bruise running along its backside and wondered if she could make herself eat around it.

"Is that it?" the cashier asked.

"Yes," Isabel replied while putting the brown banana back into the basket by the register. "That's it."

"Three seventy-eight."

Isabel picked through her change purse for quarters but

remembered she'd used all of them for laundry. "Cigarettes sure are cheap here."

"Where you from?" the cashier asked politely, though Isabel thought she saw a bit of a sneer.

"New York."

The cashier smiled as if she'd won a bet and made change from the five-dollar bill. "Have a nice day."

"Thanks," said Isabel, shaking her Snapple. "By the way, could you tell me how far to the Motel 6?"

"It's about four miles from the prison gates. Two stop lights." She was already ringing up the next customer.

Before getting back into the rental car Isabel popped the safety seal on the Snapple and took a long swig. She balanced the glass bottle on the roof of the car while she opened her Marlboro Lights, turning her back to the highway to block the wind from passing trucks. After several failed attempts, she finally managed to light her first cigarette of the day.

Breakfast.

"This is one remote outpost," Tom said, barreling out of the 7-Eleven, his camera equipment rattling against his back. "How does a 7-Eleven not have a Slurpee machine?"

"I think the better question is, Who wants a Slurpee at 6:00 a.m.?"

"Says the girl with the Snapple and cigarettes."

"At least I've gotten my fruit in."

"Ex-squeeze me?"

"It's *raspberry* iced tea Snapple. And raspberries are a super food. High in vitamin C. Or maybe it's A. Vitamin A. I'm pretty sure it's A."

"Guess you should be a personal trainer instead of a reporter. You're one healthy chick."

"Says the guy choking down a ninety-nine-cent heart attack. I'm guessing there's some sort of sausage ingredient in it, judging by the hieroglyphic grease markings on that waxed paper."

"That's affirmative. Sausage-cheese biscuit," Tom said with a full mouth. "Want a bite?"

Tom lowered himself into the car and Isabel stepped on her cigarette and got back behind the wheel.

"Tom?" Her tone serious.

"Isabel?" His tone joking.

"Seriously. About last night." She shifted uncomfortably.

"Forget it."

"No, I want to say this." Isabel cleared her throat. "I drank way too much. I know that. I just…I mean…I just really… oh, God."

"Hey. Colonel. It's me."

"I know, I know. It's just that my life is going way too fast. And then I feel this pressure thing up here at my temples and I see spots and I go blank. It's like I'm spiraling or something. Do you ever feel that way? Don't you ever want to slow it all down so you can think, really *think* for a minute? I never mean to get out of control like that. I don't *plan* it. God, listen to me. I just want you to know that I'm really grateful to you for taking such good care of me. I don't know what I'd do without you."

"There'd be no one for the bartender to call to carry your ass home, that's what you'd do without me."

Isabel winced with the memory.

"I've been there, believe me," Tom said. "I'm no one to talk. But you gotta be more careful, Iz. A woman passing out in a bar isn't exactly cool, you know?"

"I know, I know." Isabel knew she was sounding defensive. "I'm just going through a phase."

"Yeah, yeah, yeah. You say that every time."

I do?

"This phase of yours is gettin' old and dangerous, know what I'm saying?"

Isabel looked as if she'd been slapped.

"Hey, listen." Tom softened. "What goes on in the field stays in the field. Copy that? You read me? I'll always cover you."

Several minutes later Isabel looked at Tom.

"Hey, Tommy, the nineties called. They want all *Wayne's World* references back."

"Huh?"

"I haven't heard 'ex-squeeze me' in years."

"Very funny. Let's go, huh? I want some fries to go with my biscuit. Get it? Fries? Execution? Get it?"

Five minutes later reporter and photographer were inching their car back into the prison parking lot jammed with news vans and satellite dishes smiling up at the sun. Overworked generators crowded parking spaces alongside the trucks. Worried producers scurried into and out of their makeshift offices while reporters scribbled on notepads and talked to whomever was speaking in their ears.

"How long till the magic hour?" Tom asked.

"Six hours. Long enough. Why? You in a hurry to get to the hotel?"

"Motel 6? That's a negative."

Seven hours later she collapsed on the top of the natty motel bedspread, too exhausted to undress.

Beep, beep.

"Mom, wait up!" Isabel called out from across the congested street. "Dad? Wait for me!"

Beep, beep. The cars demanded attention. Beep, beep.

Isabel's parents glanced over their shoulders at their daughter, who was waving frantically from nearly a block away. Unfazed, they kept walking.

Why aren't they listening to me?

Beep, beep.

"Mom!" Isabel was now shouting to them. "Dad!"

Beep, beep.

The honking was so close her head snapped from the parental dots in the distance to the car speeding directly toward her. Isabel's eyes widened in fear but her body was immobilized. Swerving, the car was feet away and showing no signs of stopping.

Ten feet. Beep, beep. Eight feet. Beep, beep. Two feet.

She shrieked and bolted upright in bed. It took Isabel a few moments to realize it had all been a nightmare. She put her hand over her heart as if she could stroke the beat back down.

Beep, beep.

Startled again she looked over at the hotel night table and saw that the insistent car horn of her dream was the deceivingly harmless-looking tiny black pager.

She reached for it and instantly recognized the number screaming at her through the neon green glow of the LCD display. She picked up the phone and dialed.

"Hi, it's Isabel returning my page." She tried not to sound as panicked as she felt.

"We've been calling you but your ringer must be off," Rob, the assignment editor, said.

"Oh, God." Isabel remembered turning it off when she came in hours earlier. "I haven't slept in three days and I wanted to get a—"

"We do need to be able to get a hold of you as quickly as

possible," Rob scolded. "We need you to get to Atlanta as quickly as possible. Can you call the airlines and call me back to let me know what flight you're on? You don't have a fax, right, so I'll fax wire copy to the Avis counter at the airport in Atlanta. That's the only way I can think to get you this stuff without holding you up."

Rob paused as though he were trying to come up with a better solution.

"What's the story?" Though she was fairly new at the network, Isabel was almost certain it wasn't asking too much to inquire after the subject of the trip.

"Oh, geez," Rob sighed. "I've been burning it on both ends tonight. Sorry. Um, we've gotten a heads-up that we could get a verdict in that police brutality case first thing in the morning. We want you in place so we're covered if it comes down."

"Okay. I'll call the airlines and let you know."

It would be only a matter of months until the excitement and intrigue Isabel felt upon hanging up the phone this night shifted into a howling bitterness, an exhausted dread that slowly ate away at her until she was nothing but a hollow shell mechanically moving through her formerly full life.

"Isabel! Time to meet!" The rapping on the door, coupled with the shrill announcement, cause her stomach to twist with dread.

Seven

"I love chicken wings," says Ben, looking quite earnest. "Any kind, but in particular I love the barbecued ones at Bobby D's near where I live." Ben does not seem to care that there is a huge smudge of a chocolate-like substance in the middle of the right side of his thick glasses. He is wearing baggy camouflage pants and another tank top that barely covers his wiry chest hair. "If I could take you to Bobby D's you'd see what I mean." Ben is staring so intently at Isabel she cannot make eye contact with him without feeling uncomfortable. Her eyes dart alternately from his wide face to her lap.

This is hell. I'm in hell.

"Thirty seconds are up," the nameless nurse excitedly announces. "Everyone on the B team get up and move to the right and sit with a new A partner. Remember, the A group stays put and lets the B group shift partners around the room so by the end of the exercise we'll all have had the chance to visit with one another."

Isabel seethes.

They explained the concept of this asinine group exercise four min-

utes ago. Is everybody so zoned out on tranquilizers they'll forget what we're doing here in four fucking minutes?

"The new topic is pets. Remember, no interruptions from your partner. Go!" The group leader seems orgasmic.

Ben lumbers away and a sad-looking woman named Lark lowers herself into his place. Lark is a forty-something woman who, because she always looks as if she's one sentence away from bursting into tears, seems much older. She is too young for osteoporosis but she seems to know its calling cards: she hunches over and looks brittle, like if you hugged her too hard she'd break.

Pets. Hmm. Buck. And my little kittens.

Isabel's mind is a slide show of the pets she shared with Alex.

You disgust me.

Stop it. Just stop.

Isabel is concentrating so hard on quieting the voices she is not able to explain that she has lost custody of her two cats and dog to her soon-to-be ex-husband. The group leader tells them to shift partners again.

Great. I now know that Ben loves Southern barbecue and that I never miss the chance to cry in public.

Lark looks straight at Isabel before she gets up to continue on. As Isabel blows her nose she realizes Lark is looking straight through her and as she stares, a single tear falls down her bloated face. After a moment and with considerable effort, Lark silently hoists herself out of the chair, making room for Isabel's next partner.

"We haven't met yet." The woman who on Isabel's first day had been in the jacket is smiling at her—extending her hand to be shaken. "I'm Regina."

Isabel looks from Regina's face to her hand and back to

her face. Unfazed, Regina withdraws her hand and sits down across from Isabel.

"Fish."

"Huh?"

"Fish." Regina repeats the word and waits for it to make sense to Isabel.

"I don't follow."

"I have pet fish," she says in a tone of exasperation. "They like to ride with me on my bike. Well, in the basket on my bike, actually. I keep a leash around their bowl just in case..."

Two weeks ago I was covering the Middle East peace summit at the White House. Two weeks ago.

"...people don't stop at stop signs anymore so I say—you can't be too careful. That leash gives me peace of mind, let me tell you."

"Excuse me. Regina, is it?" Isabel asks. Regina nods her head, eager to hear her partner's comments.

"Regina, I want to tell you something."

Regina shimmies up to the edge of her seat.

"I don't care about your fish," Isabel says.

Not only do I not give a shit about your goldfish but I think you're a freak. Everyone here is a freak—come to think of it. I don't want to hear about everyone else's pets or whether the barbecue sauce here can compare to some shithole in some godforsaken town in Minnesota or whether someone's mother neglected them in early childhood—which, I'm sure, is a topic we'll be covering in great depth in group therapy.

"I really don't care about your fish," she says again.

Regina stiffens in her seat.

Isabel continues. "I just want to get out of here, okay? I'm only here because I screwed up and didn't take enough Tylenol PM—not because I want to talk about my childhood or my pets."

Exhausted, Isabel sinks back into her chair and looks out the window.

Unfazed, Regina shuffles over to a free chair across the room.

"Sukanya, I notice you haven't taken part in this exercise." The nameless nurse is looking at a young woman with long, dirty hair who has remained silent in the corner of the room. "Can you tell us why you have decided not to participate?"

Isabel looks at Sukanya, who has been catatonic since she arrived at Three Breezes.

The only thing she has uttered, to Isabel's morbid fascination, is "I'd prefer not to say." And, right on cue, Sukanya fixes her stare on the overenthusiastic nurse and quietly repeats her mantra: "I'd prefer not to say."

The nurse pauses for a second, clearly trying to decide whether to pursue Sukanya's cryptic reply or cut her losses and proceed on with the group.

"Well, it looks like time is up for this session." She directs her attention to the rest of the room. "You'll gather here again in two hours for another group. That's two hours, people."

She definitely dots her i's with smiley faces. And does that annoying sideways smiley face on her e-mails.

Everyone files out of the makeshift living room on the unit. Everyone except Sukanya. She stays in the same chair all day long. Group therapy sessions may come and go around her but she just sits there.

I wonder if there are such things as bed sores for people who sit. Chair sores.

Isabel, who has just learned that she can indeed go outside the unit for fifteen minutes at a time during breaks pushes the door open and lines up at the box lighter to smoke.

Kristen is already out there, sucking the air out of her cigarette as if her life depended on it.

Lark is there, too, even though she has been warned by her doctors not to smoke because she has extreme asthma.

"So what's the deal with Sukanya," Isabel asks Kristen as she inhales. Isabel and Kristen seem to recognize in each other an unspoken similarity, perhaps in background or in mentality. They look alike—both are thirty-something, career-types, and their social skills mirror each other's. To Isabel, Kristen seems like someone she might have been friends with outside of Three Breezes, had the circumstances been different.

"I don't know," Kristen answers. "I can't even imagine what must've happened to her. Or what's wrong with her."

"Does she ever have visitors?"

"I saw her parents once—at least I assume they're her parents. They brought her Beanie Babies. Like twenty of them. They were all wrapped up in tissue—each one individually wrapped—in this beautiful gift bag, and it just sat on Sukanya's lap until they opened each one for her. Like a baby or something. Then they oohed and aahed over each one like they'd never seen them before, like she would like them if she saw they liked them. I don't know, it was weird. Sad."

"What'd they look like—the parents?"

"Normal. Like you and me—or like our parents, I mean. You know," Kristen replies in an insider tone.

Isabel knows exactly what Kristen means. She knows that clubby tone.

"I guess you could look at any of our parents and think they looked normal, though, right?" Kristen says. "My parents look totally cool. My mother's a whack job but she looks normal."

Kristen laughs nervously, afraid that she has crossed the line and has shared too much too soon.

I'm supposed to jump in here and save Kristen from feeling embarrassed. I know the drill. I can't do it.

Isabel feels a wave of exhaustion that brings the social interaction to a screeching halt. She musters a smile and walks away, knowing Kristen is offended.

On her way past the living room, Isabel sees Keisha nodding her head to the beat of the music funneling into her ears from headphones the size of fluffy earmuffs.

With those headphones on she looks like a black Princess Leia.

Eight

Isabel

Isabel and Kristen are sitting next to each other for the evening session. All the patients on the unit are seated in a circle and in the middle is an empty chair.

"What's the deal with the chair?" Isabel whispers to Kristen, who is still wounded by Isabel's snub earlier in the day.

"You'll see," she answers curtly. "He does this every once in a while."

Isabel is smart enough to know that someone is going to have to sit in that chair in the middle and, whatever it entails, she does not want it to be her.

"My name is Larry," a large man says after quietly closing the living room door. If Larry were a state he would be Vermont: earthy, self-sufficient, nonthreatening, easy to overlook. Almost entirely gray, his beard appears to be aging faster than the rest of him. His clothing is eclectic and, Isabel notes, hemp in spirit if not in reality.

"Because I see we have someone new in our evening session I want to start tonight by quickly going around the room. Let's start to my right, here."

Isabel's heart races, knowing she will be second.

Oh, God, I hate these things.

"Um, I'm Kristen. I'm here for a lot of reasons. I'm bipolar and I have obsessive-compulsive disorder. Among other things."

All eyes settle on the newcomer: "I'm Isabel," she says, her voice an octave higher than usual.

"Why are you here, Isabel?" Larry prompts.

"I don't know," she says, feeling her blush deepen. "I mean, I guess I'm here because the doctors thought I should be here."

Please move on to the next person.

"Well, welcome, Isabel," Larry says. "You'll get the hang of this pretty easily."

"I'm Ben." The giant can't wait until it's his turn. "I'm here because the judge ordered me to be here."

"I'm Melanie. I'm manic. I mean manic-depressive. I mean, I'm bipolar." She directs this to Isabel. "People aren't quite used to the whole 'bipolar' diagnosis yet so I always start by telling people I'm manic-depressive. Which is really the same thing. People say 'bipolar' isn't a proven diagnosis yet but, you know, it really is. Doctors know that but people, like the general public, I mean, don't realize that yet. And that's all I have to say about that."

"Okay, Melanie," Larry gently interrupts. "Thanks. Next?"

"I'm Lark."

"Lark? Do you want to tell Isabel why you're here?"

"No."

"Okay, then."

Larry politely waits for Sukanya to introduce herself. When it appears she is not going to speak he moves on. Leaning on the empty chair in the middle of the circle, he surveys the group, noting that Keisha is absent. He checks a small notepad and nods to himself.

How'd that girl Keisha get out of this?

As she realizes that her facial expression is mirroring her dread, Larry points directly at her.

They can always smell fear.

"Isabel," Larry begins, "you're new to the group so let me explain what we do here. The purpose of this meeting is to get more intensive work done. We set aside two hours for the session because we've found that extra time allows us the freedom to dig deeper.

"The chair here represents someone or something you would like to address. Maybe it's someone you're angry with. Maybe it's something that has caused you pain or suffering. Only you can know what it means, this chair."

Larry stops talking. He waits patiently for Isabel to begin.

"Um," Isabel clears her throat. "I don't know. I don't have any anger," she lies.

"You don't?" Larry asks with mock incredulity. "No anger? That's a bit unusual. Not to generalize, but most people wouldn't exactly be here at Three Breezes if they had not experienced some form of anger. Hmm. Let's see." He consults a file that until then had been sitting on the table next to him.

"Isabel, why don't you begin by telling the group why you took all those pills."

Isabel feels like her cheeks are on fire. Her stomach is in her throat and her throat is rapidly closing up. She hears a rushing sound in her ears.

I can't believe this man I've never met wants me to talk about this personal thing in front of these people. Plus, he looks like Obi-Wan Kenobi.

Isabel stares at Larry's Birkenstocks.

"I don't really feel like talking about that right now," she manages to say, fighting to keep her voice from cracking as she chokes back her tears.

"When do you think would be an easier time to talk about it, do you think?" Isabel knows Larry is asking a rhetorical question.

"I get your point, okay? I get it," she says. "It's just that I don't really feel angry at the moment and I don't have much to say."

Why can't you just move on, you big hippie.

"I know it's tempting to retreat when you first get here, Isabel." Larry sounds kinder. "It's just that in the beginning, when everything is still pretty raw, pretty fresh, it's usually a good time to talk about emotions in general, anger in particular."

"I don't feel like talking," Isabel repeats herself, adding a tone of warning. "Just go on to someone else." She clenches her jaw.

"Isabel, what are you so angry about?"

Goddammit.

"Isabel?"

Goddammit.

"Right now I suppose I have anger toward you, Larry." Isabel tries to mimic the group leader's controlled tone of voice.

"Why me?" Larry asks, a sardonic look on his face.

"For starters, where do you get off reading something from my personal medical file to this entire group?"

"This is group therapy, Isabel," Larry soothes. "That's what we do here. We talk about the tough stuff in front of one another."

Isabel swallows hard.

A moment later, giving in to her exhaustion she says, in a whisper, "I couldn't do it anymore."

"Couldn't do what?" Larry softly urges her on.

"I was on one of those Habitrail wheels they have in gerbil's cages, you know?" she starts, looking back up at Larry. "I couldn't keep running on the wheel. I couldn't live anymore, disappointing so many people like I was."

"Who? Who were you disappointing?"

Isabel pauses once more and then slowly begins bailing out the water that is sinking her.

"My marriage is over so I'm sure my husband's disappointed with me. My parents have been disappointed in me for as long as I can remember, I screwed up majorly at work so I *know* my boss is disappointed in me..." She trails off, knowing she hasn't scratched the surface.

"Keep going, Isabel. We're listening."

"It's hard to explain."

Isabel turns her head from Larry to the empty chair. She stares at it for a long minute.

"For me that chair represents all that I expected of myself," she says sadly. "I was supposed to be perfect."

Nine

Isabel

Isabel had been friends with Casey since the third grade. They were close in the way a rose befriends the stake that is meant to help it stand tall. As time passes stalk and stake become interchangeable: they take turns propping each other up, bending into each other with every gust of wind.

When Casey found a lump in her breast it was Isabel she called first.

"Will you come with me for the biopsy?"

"Of course." Isabel stifled her tears and nodded into the phone.

"You're crying, aren't you?" Casey asked.

"No," Isabel lied. "I think I have a cold."

"You can't cry. You're not allowed to cry right now. I need you to be the strong one. If you cry I'm gonna start freaking out. And you've seen me freaking out. It ain't pretty."

"Okay, okay." Isabel sobered up. "When's the appointment?"

"Tuesday. I've got to be there at eight in the morning. I think they said it'd only be a couple of hours."

"You're staying in the hospital, right?"

"No. It's outpatient. I'm going to need you to drive me home and put me to bed. They said I'd be really groggy."

"Tuesday. No problem. I'll be there with bells on. Where are you having it done, by the way? UCSF?"

"Yeah."

"So, what're you doing tonight? Want to go to a movie? Your pick, Lumpy."

Casey laughed. "No, thanks. I think I'm just going to take a nice long hot bath until my fingers get all shriveled."

"I'm coming over."

"Okay, bye."

"Bye."

"Isabel? I'm assuming you're on your way. It's 7:50. If you're not on your way, you're in big trouble. I think I just heard a car door slam. That's probably you. Bye."

"Okay, it's 8:05. Where *are* you?"

"I've called a cab. I hope you were in an accident or something. That's the only thing that's going to keep me from killing you later."

"After the crash of TWA Flight 800, the FAA intensified its scrutiny of center fuel tanks, not only in 747s but in other, older, aircraft with similar design. Then, an alarming discovery. On Sunday, Boeing notified the FAA that recent inspections had turned up a high degree of wear and tear on wiring in and around fuel tanks in three 737s. Now, airlines have a seven day deadline to inspect and replace wiring and conduits in certain pieces of equipment. Sixty days for others."

Isabel Murphy, KXTY, San Francisco.

"Okay, great job, guys," Isabel said, rubbing her cold hands together. "I'm heading back to the station for the conference call."

"Fine," said Mike, her cameraman. "But you'll have a lot of time to make it there. The conference call isn't till tomorrow."

"What're you talking about? It's always on Wednesdays. When did they change that?"

"Since today's Tuesday they didn't have to."

"Today's Tuesday?"

Oh, my God. Casey.

Ten

Casey

Casey was propped up in bed.

Isabel, shamed, buried her head in her hands. "Casey, I'm so sorry. Words can't express how sorry I am. It's just…"

"You got called to do a story," Casey sighed. "I know the drill by now. I never should have asked you to take me."

Isabel shook her head emphatically before her friend had finished the thought. "Don't say that! I feel terrible, okay? Nothing you can say would make me feel worse. Tell me how I can make it up to you."

"How can you make it up to me? Jesus! I went to have a lump removed from my breast and you weren't there and now you wonder how you can make it up to me? You blew me off for *my own biopsy*. What else am I going to think but that you don't give a shit about your friends? You've always been Miss Career Woman and I understand that. I've been your biggest supporter. You know that. But this was important. This was a goddamn *biopsy*. And you totally forgot. And it's not like this is the first time that's happened. Every week you're standing one of us up. I talked to Nancy last week and she said she was waiting at the café for forty-five minutes before she finally gave up and left. And Paula went to the movies alone three weeks ago, after buying you a ticket and waiting outside the theater through the first half of the film practically. At the rate you're going you're not going to have any friends left! Are you even listening to me? Furthermore, you haven't even asked me about the surgery."

"That's because you laid into me the minute I walked in the door."

"Can you blame me?"

"No. No, I can't."

They looked at each other.

"How was the surgery?" Isabel asked.

"It sucked, if you must know. And now *both* my boobs are sore. I don't know why they both are since they only worked on one. But thanks for asking."

"Casey, I know I screwed up. It kills me that I let you down. You have every right to be pissed off at me. *I'm* pissed off at me, too. I don't know why I'm such a terrible friend. I don't mean to be. I love you like a sister. I would do anything for you—don't make that face. I would. Something happens when work calls me. I can't explain it. It's like work overrides everything else in my brain. Like I don't have room for anything else but work. I wish it weren't true but it is."

Isabel started to cry but continued through tears.

"I am so sorry. I hate that I let you down. I will never forgive myself for this. For all of it. Please forgive me. Please?"

"Aw, Iz. Don't cry," Casey said from the bed. "I'd hug you if I could but I'm afraid I'd ooze pus."

Casey had wanted her to laugh but she couldn't. On the contrary, Isabel's sobs became three-dimensional.

"I know you're sorry," Casey sighed. "I'm sorry I was so

tough on you just now. I understand how important your job is to you. I've always known you're really kick-ass driven. You get that from your father, if you want my opinion. You've always tried to work as hard as he did. That's your model. And your mother. Well, let's just say that I get where your perfectionism comes from. And I respect that, don't get me wrong. But somewhere you've got to take a break and have a life outside of work. That's something you didn't see your dad do so maybe you don't know how to juggle it all. But try, okay? For me?"

"I promise. I will. I love you, Casey."

"I love you, too, kid."

Eleven

"What are you thinking about?" Dr. Seidler was assigned to Isabel when she entered Three Breezes days ago. Though her perfect posture and severe haircut suggest an aloof personality, Dr. Seidler's hands more than cancel out the implication of cruelty. They are long delicate hands punctuated with ribbons of veins that add to their character and grace. Isabel can do nothing but stare at them.

"Isabel?"

Silence.

"I realize it's been quite an adjustment to get used to life here at the hospital and I've chalked our last two sessions up to being quiet times for you to be contemplative," Dr. Seidler continues. "But we do need to work together—you and I— if you'd let me help you. I guess what I'm saying is, you have to let me in, Isabel."

"What do you want from me?" Isabel asks, reluctantly looking up from the hands.

"I don't want anything from you. I want to help you. Let's start by looking at why you're really here."

Jesus. Why are you here? Why are you here? I'm so sick of that question! I don't know why I'm here. I don't belong here. Look at me: do I have bandages on my arm to keep me from scratching? Do I babble incessantly about bullshit? Do I sit all day staring into outer space? I don't belong here. Just give me my privileges and let me go down the driveway, for God's sake.

Dr. Seidler's stare is unwavering.

Okay, I'll blink first if that's what you want.

"I'm here because I want to kill myself," she shrugs.

"Why? Why do you feel you can't live any longer?"

"Um, I don't know." Isabel feels like a third grader.

"This isn't a quiz, you know. It's not like there's a right or wrong answer to the question. I'm just curious." The therapist looks at Isabel's file and reads from it.

"You mentioned when you first got here that you felt like you were disappointing everyone in your life. Like you couldn't stay on the treadmill at work and keep everyone else happy. Is that how you feel? You couldn't make everyone happy so you might as well kill yourself?"

"When you say it like that it sounds ridiculous," answers Isabel. "Which, I assume, is your point. But it's not that simple. I feel like I'm being pulled in every direction."

"What about today? Do you feel suicidal?"

Grounds privileges. The driveway.

Isabel is torn between telling the truth and risking a doctor's recommendation that she stay hospitalized, or lying in order to be free of this place. "Um, well, no. Not like before."

"What does that mean exactly? 'Not like before'?"

"Well, I don't think about it like I did a few days ago. When I got here," she continues the lie. "I mean, I can actually think about next week, whereas before I couldn't see that far into the future. I figured I'd be dead by then."

Tell her. Tell her how you only buy single rolls of individually wrapped toilet paper. Buying in bulk would be a waste. Tell her.

"So now you can see living? At least another week, or a few days or what?"

"Yeah, I guess so. A few days…"

Tell her.

"What about Christmas?"

"As in Christmas of this year?" Isabel knows where this is going and is confronted with the truth dilemma again.

"Yep. The Christmas that comes in a few months. Can you picture yourself celebrating Christmas?"

She's got me.

"No."

"You can't picture Christmas?"

"No."

"It's okay, Isabel. You don't have to feel crestfallen about that. You've only been here a short time. We don't expect miracles. Patients aren't expected to go from suicidal ideation to long-range planning in that short period of time. It's okay."

Isabel begins to cry.

"Can you tell me why you're crying?"

Through her tears Isabel's voice cracks. "I want to get out of here."

"I hear this is highly upsetting to you," Dr. Seidler says, trying to soothe her. "But as I told you yesterday, I am going to recommend to my colleagues that you stay with us a little while longer. That will help you in the long run."

Isabel can barely hear her. Her depression is floating away, disappearing like an airline tray neatly folding back into its cave underneath the armrest, patiently waiting to again emerge for the next flight. She has stopped crying.

"Isabel? Isabel, what are you thinking right now?"

"I don't know. I'm just blank."

"Try. Try, if you can, to tell me what is on your mind right now. You've got a strange look on your face. You look scared."

"Huh? Oh. No, I'm not scared."

"What's the first thing that pops into your mouth when I ask you to speak?"

Isabel's eyes settle directly on Dr. Seidler's face. "There's no way I'm living until next Christmas. No way."

"Why? Isabel? Stay with that thought...why? Can you hear me?"

Isabel is already gone. In her mind she sees the truck speeding toward her. She hears the screech of the brakes, the truck's tires locking up too late. She closes her eyes imagining the impact, the feel of the pavement beneath her bloody body, the relief.

I refuse to be someone who's in and out of institutions. I will not be Zelda Fitzgerald.

"Isabel. Listen to me for just a minute." Her therapist is trying to get her attention. "While you're here we need to work on your coping skills. I see you get a little overwhelmed with life. We need to teach you how to deal with the stuff that's thrown at you. That way you won't need to dissociate yourself from it, like you seem to be doing right now."

"'A little overwhelmed'?" Isabel snaps back and is crying again. "'A little overwhelmed'? I'd say it's a little more than that."

"Okay, tell me."

"Well, first of all, I have absolutely no control over my life and what I do with it. ANN has me on call twenty-four hours a day, seven days a week. They'll beep me at three in the morning and tell me to get to the airport and sometimes I don't even know where I'm going until I call from the back of the taxi. I have to have a bag packed at all times so that I can just walk away from whatever I'm doing and go to work. I'm in the middle of getting divorced. I don't even have time to go to couples counseling—not that that's any big loss, though...."

"Before you go any further," the therapist interrupts Isabel, "let's look at these things one at a time. You bring up some very good points. Let's start with the divorce. What happened in your marriage?"

Isabel softens and slumps into her chair.

"My marriage?"

"I think that might be a good starting point for us."

"Alex. That's his name. Alex." Isabel is sobbing again.

"Tell me about Alex."

Twelve

"What can I get you?" the bartender asked as he slapped the paper cocktail napkin in front of Isabel.

"A greyhound, please," she answered while rifling through her purse for her cigarettes. "Actually, could you make that a double?"

"No problem," the bartender said. But he looked as if it were.

"Where's Stu, anyway? Tuesday's not his night off."

"Yeah, well, it is tonight." The bartender talked as he surveyed his cage of bottles. He tentatively picked one out, looked at the label and slid it back into its dusty cell. "He's sick."

"Is it too late to change my mind and order a gin and tonic?" She knew it wasn't, as the bartender was looking up "greyhound" in his bartender's guide.

"Nope," he said, looking relieved. "That I can do."

Isabel took a long drag of her cigarette. "What's your name?"

"Alex."

"I'm Isabel."

"This is on the house," he said as he delivered the drink. "For going easy on me with the order."

"Not necessary but thank you." Because she had an audience she decided to sip not gulp her drink. "Slow night, huh."

"Kind of. I'm not complaining, though. I'm not used to bartending, in case you hadn't noticed."

Isabel smiled. "I knew it."

"How'd you crack the code?" he asked.

"Well—" she fiddled with the swizzle stick poking out of her drink "—first of all you aren't studying a quartered-up section of the want ads. You must not have heard it's required reading for all barkeeps."

Alex laughed.

"Whoa! You've got Kennedy teeth," she said.

"Kennedy teeth?"

"It's like you have more in there than the rest of us. It's really quite amazing. Open up, let me see them again."

Alex clamped his mouth shut.

"Come on," Isabel mock begged. "One quick peek."

Careful to cover his teeth with his lips, Alex shook his head and said, "Good Kennedy or bad Kennedy?"

Isabel laughed. "What's good Kennedy and what's bad Kennedy?"

"You know: JFK Jr. or Chappaquiddick?"

"Uh-uh. I'm not falling into that trap…." Isabel took another sip of her drink.

"What trap?"

"If I say JFK Jr., you'd get a big head and then I'd have to spend the rest of the night breaking your spirit…"

"Yeah, 'cause my spirit is flying so high here behind the bar…"

"…and if I said Chappaquiddick I'd have to spend the rest

of the night hearing a laundry list of things that make you a swell guy…"

"It'd be a short list since my only competition would be an adulterer who let his date drown…"

"…so I'm damned if I do and damned if I don't."

"And to think this all started because my dad's a dentist…."

"Aha! So you do have an unfair advantage over the rest of us, dentally speaking, I mean."

"You saw right through me."

There was a brief pause in the banter.

"What do you do normally? I mean," she laughed and corrected herself, "what do you normally do?"

Isabel knew she was flirting, but she was sinking into her comfortable buzz and didn't care.

"I wait tables. How come I've never seen you here before? You I would have noticed."

"I don't eat here. I just come for liquid nourishment."

"Always this late?"

"I just got off work. So, yeah. Always this late."

"We're both night owls, then."

"Guess so."

"Excuse me." Alex left to serve a couple who should not have been served. Isabel watched him put napkins in front of them.

The drink was settling her stomach, filling it with warmth.

"Sorry about that," he said as he leaned back against the space of mahogany in front of Isabel. "Duty calls."

"Let me ask you something."

"Shoot."

"Seriously."

Alex forced his smile into a frown. "Go ahead."

"How do you like your job?"

"You mean tonight? Bartending? Or serving?"

"Serving."

"It's fine, I suppose," he answered, and gave the question more thought. "I like the fact that I have complete control over my life. I don't have to answer to anyone, really. I can make my own hours, more or less. Like I have the days to myself, I can do what I want, and then I can come in, serve and make a killing with tips. I think it helps that I'm not always going to be doing this."

"Why? What are you going to be doing? Could I get a re-fill while you answer?"

"Sure." He cleared away her empty glass. "Another double?"

She paused as she decided whether the look he gave her was judgmental or just inquisitive. She decided it was inquisitive and she nodded.

"I'm going to open my own place."

"Wow. That's cool."

"I know what you're thinking."

"I'm not thinking anything."

"Yes, you are. You're thinking 'Just what San Francisco needs, another restaurant.' Don't worry—I'm used to it. And I agree with you."

"I wasn't thinking that."

"Yes, you were. But that's okay. Because my place is going to be different."

"Seriously, I wasn't even thinking that."

He leaned into her as he replaced her drink. "So…what were you thinking, then? That you wanted to go out to din-ner with me? Saturday night?"

Isabel smiled as she gulped.

"That's what you were thinking, wasn't it?"

Isabel felt emboldened by the booze. "You hit the nail on the head."

"Meet here? Eight?"

"Right again."

Alex smiled as he went to check on the couple a few seats away from Isabel.

"Case, he's so amazing," Isabel said as she spread out the blanket for their picnic.

"There's a rock in the middle, pull the blanket your way," Casey said. "Good. Okay. Back to Mr. Amazing. What's so amazing about him?"

"He's so *there*. You know? He's a little intense, but after my last two fiascos I think I can handle intense. He's a great listener. He's a hold-doors-open, walk-me-to-the-front-door, call-the-next-day kinda guy."

"Wow. I'm impressed. Michael hasn't held a door open for me since...come to think of it I don't think he's ever held the door open for me. Wait! That's not true. I carried lumber in from Home Depot. He held the door for me then. And they say chivalry's dead." Casey lifted the foil on one of the sandwiches and handed it to Isabel. "That's yours. Pass me mine."

"I think he might be the one, Casey." Isabel held her friend's sandwich hostage so she could command her full attention.

"Right now *I'm* the one...who's about to have a hypoglycemic attack if I don't get some food in my stomach." She grabbed her sandwich, peeled the foil back and took a huge bite.

"How on earth did you ever get Michael to marry you with eating habits like yours? Look at you. I didn't think your mouth could hold that much food. Then again you do have quite a big mouth, missy."

"My big mouth is exactly what Michael likes the best about me, if you know what I mean," Casey chortled in between bites.

"Speaking of which," she continued, "how's the sex with the one?"

Isabel took a dainty bite of her sandwich and looked away.

"Oh, no." Casey was watching her. "That bad, huh?"

"I think…it's just…well, I think we're both so nervous," Isabel said. "It's kind of like when you get a haircut and you don't like the way they've blown it dry at the salon? You know the cut's good, it'll look fine, you just need to work on the styling at home."

"Cut the bullshit. It's either good or bad. And I'm guessing from this salon simile that it's bad."

"The jury's out. And for the record, I disagree. It's not just black or white, good or bad. There's plenty of gray-area sex out there. You just don't realize it because you and Mr. Macho have such raging hormones."

"Don't underestimate raging hormones. Raging hormones are what keep me from becoming a single mother. If I leave you with nothing else, know this—if the sex ain't good, he ain't the one. Trust me. The sex's gotta be good if he's going to go the distance. By the way, does The One have a name or should I just hold up my index finger every time I refer to him?"

"Alex. His name's Alex."

Thirteen

Isabel

"Isabel? It's Alex. If you're there, pick up. Isabel? Okay, well, call me when you get in. We're still on for tonight, right? I got reservations for us at that new place you mentioned last week. I'll pick you up at seven, okay? Okay. Well, I can't wait to see you. I've been thinking about you all week. Call me."

What's wrong with me? He's a great guy, but I just wish he'd leave me alone.

"Isabel, this is your father. I, ahem, ah, want to apologize for what I said the other night. Perhaps I did have a bit too much to drink. I may not understand what you do for a living but that does—"

"Isabel, this is your father. I, ahem, ah, want to apologize for what I said the other night. Perhaps I did have a bit too much to drink. I may not understand what you do for a living but that does—"

★ ★ ★

"Isabel, this is your father. I, ahem, ah, want to apologize for what I said the other night. Perhaps I did have a bit too much to drink. I may not understand what you do for a living but that does—"

Isabel replayed the message countless times, wondering what her father would have said if her answering machine hadn't cut him off.

A bit too much to drink.

She winced at the thought of her father back off the wagon. She had thought her father would have been proud of her dogged reporting, of her dedication to this, her first network job. She had been unprepared for his disdain. Television was bullshit, he had said. Cars are *tangible.* Everyone wants to see the new lines. Dealers from all over the world were lined up to meet with him, he had slurred.

She had not taken a shower in four days. The boxers and T-shirt she wore to bed had started to smell because she hadn't changed out of them for two days.

She had lost her appetite and all her energy. Her shades were drawn and her heart was closing up. She lay in bed listening to Alex leave yet another message on her machine—his voice booming throughout her tiny San Francisco apartment like a foam life preserver a drowning man can't quite reach.

I'm so tired. There's no way I'm going out tonight.

"Isabel? Hi, it's me, Alex. Um, should I be paranoid, here? If you don't want to see me again just tell me and I won't keep bothering you. It's just, well, I just thought we really hit it off. Tell me if I'm wrong. Your answering machine is probably going to cut me off—and that's probably a good thing since

I'm sounding like a real loser here. I'd like to see you again when you feel better. Call me whenever. Bye."

"Isabel? Hi. It's Alex. I promise I'm not a stalker, but I just thought I'd call you again. Listen, I have tickets to the Giants game this weekend. If you're feeling better, wanna go? You can't live in San Francisco and not go to a Giants game. It's just not allowed. Okay. Well, call me when you get this message. Bye."

"Hi! It's Alex and I got your message. I was just calling— hello? Oh. I thought I heard you pick up. Anyway, I was glad to get your message. I'd love to get together tonight. You know that. I mean it's not like I haven't called you practically every day for the past three weeks or something. Okay. So. Call me when you get this message and we can talk about where to go and what time. Hey, Isabel? Thanks for calling me back. Bye."

"I just don't know, Alex." Isabel couldn't look him in the eye.

"What? What don't you know?" His pleading tone depressed Isabel even more. "You love me. I love you. Why *not* get married?"

"It's just so soon," Isabel ventured. "We've only been dating six months. And I don't even know where I'm going to be working. I'm just coming out of this funk—"

"Aw, man! Not the 'my life has no purpose' speech again. I'll tell you what your purpose is, it's to be with me. *I'm* your purpose."

They were married six months later.

Fourteen

"Amid partisan squabbling on the hill, Inauguration Day seemed the perfect opportunity to mend fences. At a congressional luncheon, House Speaker Newt Gingrich presented the president and the vice president with flags flown in their honor over the Capitol Dome. The president is wasting no time getting back to business. He's scheduled to meet with the Democratic National Committee on this first day of his second term. After fifteen balls stretching into the early morning hours, it looks like it'll be another long day for President Clinton."

Isabel Murphy, ANN News, Capitol Hill.

"Alex, I told you—" Isabel held her head in her hands "—I'm exhausted. You knew I wouldn't have any time with you. I told you—I'm here to cover the inauguration."

"The inauguration's over, in case you hadn't noticed," he said as he smoothed out his sport coat and carefully hung it in the hotel closet. "You don't have to be back in New York until tomorrow."

"I haven't slept in twenty-four hours. I'm incredibly hungover. I just want to sleep."

"You can sleep on the shuttle back tonight. There's a media brunch in an hour I thought we could go to. Silent partners don't exactly grow on trees, Isabel. Jennings just signed that fat contract: he might be feeling flush enough to invest in my place."

"I've been with these people for a week straight—I have absolutely no desire to hang out with them today. I just want to sleep, pack and go home."

"You're seeing someone."

"Here we go…"

"You're seeing someone. That's it, isn't it? You don't want to go to this thing because he's going to be there. Who is he?"

"We've been over this and over this, Alex. I'm not going to do it again."

"For the life of me I don't know who would have you. You disgust me. Look at you. You're a fucking mess. You're disgusting."

"Alex…"

"Why do you have to lie? Just tell me the truth." The vein on Alex's forehead was starting to look like a blue river line on a map.

"I *am* telling you the truth. I want to go home."

"No." He was too measured. "That's not what I want the truth about. Are you or are you not cheating on me?" He stood up from the edge of the hotel bed.

"I am not cheating on you Alex," she said. "But you never seem to want to believe me." Isabel backed up toward the minibar.

"Oh, I want to believe you. It's just that I don't. Believe. You."

Fifteen

Isabel

"Isabel? Could you come to the nurses' station with me?"

It's the nameless nurse who works the early dawn hours. Isabel follows her in. "What's up?"

"We wanted to tell you—" the nurse eyes something on a clipboard as if double-checking her information "—you have been approved for grounds privileges."

It's about time.

"So, what does that mean exactly?" Isabel pictures the stone gates at the edge of the driveway.

The nurse puts the clipboard down, tilts her head down and looks over the rims of her glasses at Isabel. "Up until now you've only had access to the deck adjacent to the unit. From now on you may go anywhere on the compound but—" she emphasizes "but" as though Isabel is the birdman of Alcatraz "—*but,* you are required to check in here at the nurses' station and update the dry erase board ev-er-y thir-ty minutes. Is that clear?"

"Yes, that's clear," Isabel answers with more than a trace of sarcasm. She is careful, though, not to push it too far for fear that her privileges will be taken away.

"To reiterate. You may go anywhere on the grounds but you must check back in here at the unit every thirty minutes. On the dry erase board you must account for your whereabouts. This also means that you no longer have to wait to be accompanied in to the dining hall—you may meet the group there and you may leave when you're finished eating, if you choose to. *But...*"

Jesus.

"...your mealtime remains the same. You need to eat when the unit eats. This is a big facility and units have allotted times in which to use the dining area. Am I being clear?"

"Got it," Isabel nods, already backing away. "Thanks."

She goes immediately to the dry erase board and signs herself out, carefully writing the word *walk* in big letters with the *k* backward, mocking the nurse's childish instructions.

Outside the air feels warm and sticky and, to Isabel, heavenly.

Freedom.

She follows the steep driveway that curled into her unit and pauses at the top of the hill.

Only an idiot would rush down and do it right away. They probably have cameras all over this place...at the driveway especially.

Mindful of her thirty-minute limitation she continues on past a low building resembling her own called Southgate. A few yards away she notes another identical structure. Medical Care Unit.

Three Breezes is a blend of ugly fifties-style units thumbing their noses at the centerpiece of the acreage: an enormous turn-of-the-century Tudor mansion that houses the administration and admissions office. The rambling estate fools newcomers into thinking that they will be housed in similar luxury: the boxy one-story units litter the land behind the manor, though, rendering them invisible to new arrivals.

"Okay, everyone, line up." Isabel is woken out of her thoughts and follows the sound of the command. There, not fifteen yards away, filing out of yet another unattractive out-building, is a group of small children. "We can't head over to lunch until everyone is in a straight line. Ramon? Get in line!"

Isabel ducks behind a huge oak tree and watches the children take their positions.

Jesus, they're so little. They must only be about seven or eight. What on earth are they doing here?

"Okay, guys. Off we go."

Isabel's eyes fall to the end of the line. A little blond boy wearing glasses is studying the ground ahead of him.

"Come on, Peter, hurry up," the nurse calls over her shoulder.

The boy named Peter is mumbling to himself.

The nurse stops the group to wait for him to catch up. "Peter! Wake up! Let's go!"

After a moment Peter calls back, his tiny voice quite clear. "Could you please tell Ramon to stop stepping on the ant-hills?"

Isabel is astonished.

Anthills.

She watches with tears in her eyes as little Peter trails the group, carefully picking his way around the pavement.

Sixteen

It is eleven o'clock and most everyone has gone to sleep. But not Sukanya. She is still sitting in the common room and staring straight ahead. At first glance it looks as though she is watching television because she is staring in that direction. But a closer look proves that Sukanya is looking through the TV, past it.

Isabel stands in the doorway of the same room.

"Topping tonight's news, a five-alarm fire is finally out this hour." The earnest tone of the TV anchor coaxes Isabel a few steps into the room. "It was a grueling day for firefighters, some of whom are being treated for smoke inhalation tonight at St. Luke's hospital...."

Isabel eases into the wing chair alongside Sukanya's. The plaid upholstery is tattered but soft. Sukanya gives no indication that she is even aware of Isabel's presence. Minutes pass.

"And now, in our continuing series called 'Taking Back the Neighborhood,' a profile of a little boy—" the anchor cocked her head ever so slightly to the left, coordinated perfectly with a hint of a smile: clues that a heartwarming story was moments from unfolding "—who took on a giant...and won!"

Isabel lets the sounds of the television wash over her. She looks at Sukanya. Then, as she turns back to the screen, she relaxes all the muscles in her face, her neck, her back and legs and finally exhales into a stupor.

The pictures of angry neighbors picketing in front of city hall, once clear, blur into a comfortable kaleidoscope of color. The voices, once a cacophony, blend into a symphony of sound, and become a waking lullaby for the two women, side by side, late at night in a mental institution.

Night after night Isabel and Sukanya sit immobilized in front of the television. To Isabel the newscasts that just months ago were precision Swiss timepieces are now melting clocks that litter barren dreamscapes. The stories that once implied competitive edge are now superficial jumbles of words tied together by nursery school segues.

"Isabel?" Connie the night nurse calls into the room half-heartedly, assuming Isabel is elsewhere. But the twin wing chairs intrigue her. "Isabel? You in here, hon?"

Go away.

Isabel feels the spell of the stupor being broken as the nurse calls her back into reality.

No. Go away.

Connie peers around the chair and looks surprised to see Isabel sitting there.

"You must not have heard the call for meds," she explains to her mute patient. "I brought them in for you."

Wordlessly Isabel turns her palm upward and watches as the small pills roll out of the white Dixie cup and into the center of her hand. She takes the cup of Hawaiian Punch from Connie and stares at it with an equal amount of blankness.

"You okay, hon?" Connie's face crinkles up. Isabel watches her mouth move. "Do you feel all right?"

Isabel looks back and forth between her two hands and, in one smooth motion, brings the pills to her mouth. Slowly she follows with her Hawaiian Punch and swallows the sleeping pills. Connie hesitates before moving away and, eventually, out of the room.

Isabel turns back to the TV. Sukanya has never looked away.

There is comfort in being left alone. Something about the numbness hugging her feels familiar.

Seventeen

"What I mean is, they just want to take you over, know what I'm saying?" Keisha says. "They want to control you and make it so they own you or something."

"So just opening up to someone, just talking to someone, would make them control you?" Larry asks her. Isabel sits forward on her chair and stares intently at Keisha.

Let her finish.

"Yeah, kind of." Keisha scratches at her head. "But it's more than opening up. I'm talking about *talking,* really flapping with someone."

"Flapping?"

"Flapping. Flapping gums. Talking. You know? Like about all your *stuff.* They think they got you in their hand, you belong to them and you can't belong to yourself anymore. I hate that. Like the tribes who think if you take their picture you're taking a piece of their *soul.* It's like that. You tell yourself to someone and they steal your soul. That's why I don't talk to anybody. I wanna keep my soul, man."

"Go on," Larry says.

"No one wants to hear about all my shit, anyway," Keisha continues. "Who am I supposed to go to—my sister? Ha." And she looks genuinely amused at such an apparently bizarre notion.

"Why do you always have to do that?"

"Do what?"

Alex looked down at the comforter on the bed and traced a line of quilting with his finger.

"You're always calling Casey when you've got a problem." He calculated a sulking look. "You even call your mother…"

"And?"

"And you never come to me with the problem," he said. "You won't let me have a crack at it first. I *am* your husband after all. That's what husbands do."

Isabel crossed the room to the spot right in front of Alex on the edge of the bed. "I am so sorry," she said, kissing his cheek, "how about," *kiss* "I promise," *kiss* "to come to you," *kiss* "first next time." *Kiss.*

Alex pulled his head away and looked her square in the eye. "Only me," he said.

"Only you?" Isabel was smiling, leaning to kiss his cheek again.

"*Only* me," he repeated. If Isabel had been paying attention she would have noticed his emphasis was on the first of the two words. And he wasn't smiling back.

"We all have to have someone to talk to," Larry says.

Leave it to Birkenstock Boy to paraphrase Dylan.

Keisha is shaking her head. "Not me, man. Not me." She looks proud of her stoicism. "No one I know talks about all this deep shit, anyhow. All we talk about when we get together is who sleeping with who, who wearing what, who got what CD...all that shit. No one sits around talking about how bad they had it with their mama."

Amen to that.

"Have you considered that you might need more than that?" Larry asks her. "Especially now?"

"I tell you what, Larry," Keisha says, her childish face suddenly somber. "I don't see any black folk here, in this place. Not a one. I'm the only one I see. And black folks, the ones I'm talking about, not talking about all this psycho-shit. And they ain't here. So that tells me that maybe there's something to that, know what I'm saying?"

She's exactly right. Exactly right.

"What are you saying?" Larry asks.

"I'm saying maybe that's the key," she says proudly, "that's the secret. Talking about the shit's what makes you psycho. You don't talk about it, you don't have the problems. The problems start when you start digging all around them." Keisha is triumphant with her theory.

"Or—" Larry follows her theory with his own "—or, the digging leads us to a deeper understanding of what we're all about and therefore moves us to a deeper appreciation for life."

I like Keisha's philosophy better, dude.

"I like my philosophy better, man," Keisha says. If Keisha had been paying attention to Isabel she would have noticed the startled look on her washed-out face.

Eighteen

The woman uncomfortably perched on the edge of the Adirondack chair has not opened up in group. Unlike Sukanya, though, Lark is very "present," very aware of what is going on and very sad. Her brown hair is unkempt and badly cut, as if she had done it herself. Her face is reddened and swollen.

Lark's whole body is bloated: her wedding ring is surrounded by fat flesh and shows no sign of ever leaving her finger. Lark is a mess by anyone's definition.

The only time anyone speaks with Lark is when she is smoking on the deck. There, the nicotine softens her hard defenses, loosens her tongue.

"Can I ask you something?" she addresses Isabel.

"The doctor confiscated my carton of cigarettes," she confesses, not without a sneer toward the unit, "and I was wondering if you would do me a favor." Lark has a thick Brooklyn accent. "Favor" is "fay-vah."

Isabel has just finished lighting her own cigarette and pulls her plastic chair closer to Lark.

"What do you want?" Isabel asks.

"It's gonna sound weird, I know," Lark begins in what constitutes, for her, an apologetic tone, "but this happened to me before I was here. When you take a drag and exhale… just blow it my way and I'll suck it in." This is the most Lark has spoken and Isabel is hooked.

"I'm not sure I follow," Isabel says.

"I'll show you." Kristen has pulled up a chair. She takes the smoke from her own cigarette into her lungs, and as she prepares to exhale, Lark leans way in, as though she were about to kiss Kristen. When Kristen exhales, Lark inhales.

"Do you actually get anything from it?" Isabel asks, slightly disgusted.

"Yep." A fragment of a smile creeps into Lark's face. "But more than secondhand smoke I get the satisfaction of not letting anyone tell me I can't smoke."

Lark's asthma and a raging case of bronchitis have put her on the danger list at the hospital so the staff had to take drastic measures to get her to stop, at least while she is a resident.

"So, you said you've been here before?" Isabel starts slow.

Lark senses an interview but can't withdraw if she wants to inhale any of Kristen's or Isabel's smoke. She's stuck.

"Yeah." Lark's addiction takes precedence over privacy. "This is my fourth time."

"Oh." Isabel is the one stuck now since she has learned it's an unspoken rule to let others tell you why they've checked in, not to push it out of them. But Isabel is a reporter at heart and knows how to interview. "Is it difficult coming back?"

"Naw." Lark is looking her straight in the eye. "This time I'm trying to be proactive," Lark confides. "Father's Day is tomorrow. That's my hardest day all year."

They look at each other for a moment. Kristen gets up to light another cigarette and Lark looks down into her lap.

The eyes of the cat planter gleamed like marbles.

"But why?" Isabel asked, tracing the line of the tail.

"You're just too young." Her mother briskly moved Isabel's hair out of her face. Still, wisps stuck to the tears on her cheek.

"He said I could come. He said."

The plastic fork was stuck in the soil, the card still in its three prongs. "Sorry, kiddo. I'll see you soon. Love, Dad."

"I know that he said you could go, but Dad has lots more meetings than he thought he would. They like the new line of cars Dad is showing them. Isn't that great? Anyway, he told me on the phone that you can definitely go on the next business trip with him."

"But I wanted to go on this one," she sobbed. "Why? Why can't I just go? I can wait in the hotel room for him till he gets finished with his meetings. I can just wait there."

"Stop whining, Isabel. Now, I've about had it with this conversation. You're only eight. You're too young to stay in a hotel room all day alone. And you'd get hungry...."

"I could order room service. Like Eloise. I could order something to eat and wait for him."

"What did I just finish saying? Next time you can go with him. The next trip he has that doesn't have too many meetings you can go on."

"He always has too many meetings," she said miserably. She stood up to go.

"Don't forget your new plant. It's so pretty in this planter." Isabel reached for the cat with the shiny eyes.

★ ★ ★

"Dad, I'm trying to help you up to bed." Isabel's legs were buckling under his weight even as she tried to distribute it more evenly by pulling his limp arm tighter around her shoulders.

"I'm so sorry," he was mumbling repeatedly to his teenage daughter.

"It's okay, Dad," she lied. "Just try to walk up these stairs. Six stairs, that's all you got."

"One father, that's all you got," he muttered.

"Lucky me," she said, more to herself than out loud. "Come on, Dad. Three more stairs. Here we go. You can do it."

"Why do you even bother?" he asked, trying to stand up on his own for the first time since his daughter shoveled him off the bar stool in the living room.

"Huh? Come on, Dad, two more stairs." Isabel looked down the long dark hallway to her parents' bedroom and then focused again on the remaining stairs.

"Why do you even bother." This time it wasn't a question. "You know you have no family."

A sharp pain radiated down her back. "What did you just say?"

"You have no family," her father said, his tone mean and cold, his words no longer slurred.

"You don't know what you're saying," she said, hoping she was right and that her drunk father was babbling about nothing again.

"You have no family."

Isabel stood on the top stair and flinched.

"You have no family."

Isabel would never know that her father was speaking to himself and not to her.

★ ★ ★

"Dinner's in ten minutes," Lark mumbles. "Want me to sign you out?"

Isabel shakes the memory away like a wet dog coming in from the rain. She looks at Lark.

"Yeah, thanks. We can walk over to the cafeteria together if you want."

A friendship forged over carcinogens. Lark walks back into the nurses' station where the dry erase board hangs.

Kristen calls out to Lark: "Lark? Will you sign me out, too?" Then to Isabel she says, "Do you guys mind if I walk with you?"

We're back in elementary school and we're forming a clique.

"Sure, whatever," Isabel replies as she steps on her cigarette.

"Where're you from, anyway?" Kristen asks as she puts out her unfinished cigarette. "It just occurred to me that I don't know where you live."

"Yeah," Isabel said. "I don't know anyone's last name. I grew up in Connecticut but I live in Manhattan now."

"I grew up in Connecticut, too! Where in Connecticut?" Kristen asks excitedly.

"Greenfield."

"I grew up in Winsford." Kristen is beaming. Winsford is only minutes away from Greenfield.

Please let's not play the name game.

Isabel takes a couple of steps back and looks toward the unit to see if they are to start lining up for their meal march. She hopes her body language will quiet Kristen.

"Where's the dinner nurse, anyway?" Kristen asks, picking up on Isabel's signal. "I'm starving. I hate it when they're late taking us over."

"Want another cigarette?" Isabel asks her. Kristen nods gratefully.

Isabel smiles as she pulls out her pack of Marlboro Lights. "We are one sick group," she says, heading over to the wall-mounted lighter. "One sick group."

Behind her Lark's mouth turns upward, forming a slight smile.

"You got that right," Lark says.

Nineteen

"Okay, guys, grab a magic marker!"

Larry the group leader is sick today and his substitute is a therapist who looks like she is fresh out of graduate school and hasn't yet had her spirits trampled by life. Her name is Rita.

No one moves. They all stare at Rita.

"Come on, people." Rita is now batting her eyelashes in what Isabel thinks is a pathetic schoolgirl attempt to get everyone to do what she wants.

She has no experience. She'd never waste the eyelash-bat for a group of nuts if she had half a brain. Besides, this is shaping up to be an artistic venture, and if so, I am outta here.

"What we're going to do tonight..." Rita is now trying to reason with the group. "What we're going to try to do is make a mural on this piece of poster board. I want everyone to take a magic marker and go and draw a picture of how you see yourself."

Still no action from the group.

This is embarrassing. Like watching someone on stage struggle to remember her lines.

"Seriously, you guys." Rita is plugging away. It's as if there's a competition among the mental health care workers to come up with the breakthrough group activity. Rita seems convinced that her activity will beat them all. "Just try it out. If you don't want to continue that's fine."

"That's fine?" Lark croaks. "If we don't like it, then what? We get to leave the session for the night?" She challenges Rita. Everyone turns to Lark. Even Sukanya.

"Um, well, no, Lark. But we can try something else if everyone decides they don't want to do this. But I really think you ought to give it a chance."

"Yeah, well, what do you know?" Isabel is staring at Lark, who, for some reason is taking Rita to the mat. "You just don't want to hear about the hard stuff. The shit. The things in our lives that've fucked us up. Right? Am I right? You just want us to draw pretty pictures." Lark's voice goes high to mimic Rita's.

Rita is literally cringing. Lark has the entire group transfixed.

"My father raped Lark when she was eight, Rita. My mother watched him do it. Want me to draw a picture of that? She never said a thing. Not a word."

What the hell is going on? She never says a word at these things. Now she's spewing all this stuff in the third person?

"You know what dear ole dad did when Lark got her period? Stuck a hot curling iron up her, that's what. Said he'd burn it outta her. Said she wasn't pure anymore. Little fucking Lark is such a fuckin' crybaby," Lark continues, Rita staring along with everyone else. "She asked her daddy to stop. You believe that shit? She actually asked her father to stop...like that would work or something. She's unbelievable."

Lark has now pulled a pack of cigarettes from her shirt

pocket. Isabel is surprised to see that they are her cigarettes—Lark must have taken them from the bureau in her room. She lights one up—verboten inside the unit—using matches she must have stolen from the nurses' station when no one was looking. Rita has absolutely no control over the group.

"Lark, I don't think you're supposed to do that," Ben says nervously, looking at Rita for approval.

Melanie starts to laugh. Keisha tilts her chair back and looks as if she's enjoying the conflict. Sukanya maintains her catatonic stance.

Lark inhales and drapes one arm over the back of her chair while crossing her legs…a difficult undertaking since her thighs are extremely fat. She has to force her right leg to stay poised across her left.

Rita looks panicked. She stands up, and instead of directly approaching Lark, she announces to the group that she's forgotten something outside the room and will return momentarily. She bolts out of the living room.

Lark turns to address Isabel and Kristen. "Scared little Rita," she laughs. Then she inhales again. "I think I scared her off!"

The person talking bears no resemblance to the quiet woman who inhales secondhand smoke out on the deck.

Seconds later the evening nurse and two orderlies burst into the room followed by Rita, who at least had the intelligence to realize she was in over her head. Lark looks at them expectantly, like she knows the routine, and she slowly drops her cigarette in to her half-empty can of Diet Coke and stands to greet them as if she is at a cocktail party.

"Boys, good evening." Lark stands jauntily with one hand on her hip.

Isabel watches as the orderlies pin Lark's arms behind her back and escort her out of the room. As they do, Lark spits on Rita's astonished face. "Fuckin' baby!" she yells at Rita. "Asking Daddy to stop…"

As she leaves the room, Lark breaks into uncontrollable laughter.

Once the double doors are closed behind her, a visibly shaken Rita, who has wiped her face clean with a balled-up Kleenex fetched from her pocket, looks at the group and says, "Okay. Now. Where were we? Magic markers for everyone. Come on, guys." This time Rita makes it an order.

After a minute or so Melanie rises and goes to the bin and picks a violet marker. Ben watches her, heaves himself up and chooses yellow. Kristen exhales and follows suit. Isabel looks at Keisha, who rolls her eyes, shrugs, stands up and stretches.

Who are these people?

Isabel stands up and quietly walks out of the living room.

Without anyone stopping her, Isabel returns to her room and climbs up onto her uncomfortable bed.

Twenty

"A nationwide manhunt is intensifying for this man: twenty-seven-year-old Andrew Cunanan. Police believe Cunanan could be the serial killer responsible for four killings that stretch from Minneapolis to Chicago. They are requesting that anyone with information about the man you see here on your television screen contact your local police station. He is considered armed and dangerous."

Isabel Murphy, ANN News, Chicago.

"But why?"

"They haven't found this guy yet. I've got a great lead that he might be heading south. I've got to go, Mom. I'm sorry."

"It's your father's birthday, though. Can't you just take one night off?"

"I'm sorry, Mom. I just can't. Tell Dad I said happy birthday. I'm really sorry. Really."

"Just come for coffee."

"I don't drink coffee, Mom."

"Since when?"

"I never have. Nice of you to notice."

"Who doesn't drink coffee?"

"Some people don't. Anyway, they're boarding my flight now. I've got to go."

"Where are you going again?"

Isabel sighed. "Miami."

"Nice work if you can get it. I bet it's eighty degrees and sunny there."

"I'm not going on vacation, Mom. I'm going to work."

"I know, I know. You're always going to work. Don't you ever take any time off?"

"Not really."

"What am I going to tell your father? It's his birthday, after all."

"I don't know," she said, and then paused. "Wait. Tell Dad his boy turned out just like him. Like in the song."

"You're talking gibberish now, Isabel." Her mother sounded annoyed.

"The Harry Chapin song. You know the one. 'My boy was just like me. He turned out just like me.'"

Twenty-One

"This is about the last sorry-ass-excuse-for-a-meal I'm gonna have, suckers!" Keisha is smiling so hard her face resembles the center of an overgrown farmer's market sunflower.

"What're you talking about?" Isabel asks, her mouth full of salad.

"I am leavin' this hellhole!" Keisha surprises everyone at the lunch table, including, it appears, Sukanya, whose fork pauses for a moment before piercing the next bite of her special-order kosher meal. "I got my walkin' papers today and I am outta here."

Isabel feels a knot in her stomach.

How come she gets to leave? She's barely opened up in group.

"I gotta hand it to my insurance company. It's like they read my mind or somethin'. Just as I'm getting sick and tired of this place, they send my doctor a letter sayin' they ain't coverin' me anymore. So I get to go home, baby. Home sweet home." Keisha says this so loudly that a group at the next table stops eating. It is very disturbing for patients to hear about someone going home from Three Breezes. Many are patients for extended periods of time, so to see that someone in their midst is leaving is like restless soldiers hearing of someone going AWOL.

"Keisha, okay, I know what you're going to say but just hear me out." Isabel isn't quite sure what she's going to say. "Group's just now getting good and maybe your insurance company will go eighty-twenty with you on coverage. I'm sure your doctor can talk to them about it."

Keisha gives Isabel a mournful look, but Isabel knows immediately that Keisha is too young to know that even a horrific thing like a mental institution can turn out to be the best thing for you. She knows Keisha is homesick, tired of her fits of rage and her subsequent restraint. She wants her mother and her own bed.

"No way, baby, I'm outta here. No more salad bar that's been sittin' here since I was in diapers. No more sharps closet. No more padded cell. Freedom, baby!"

Isabel slumps in her chair. Her bitterness at being left behind is palpable. "How're you getting home? When are your parents coming?"

"To-morrow night." Keisha split the word in two. "I just left a message with my sister, Mo, and she's going to tell my mama to come up right after she gets out of work."

"What time's that?"

"'Bout nine. What're you, the human dry erase board or somethin'? That reminds me, after tomorrow I ain't got to sign out no more."

"Okay, okay. Give us a break for God's sake." Lark speaks for the first time since she was released from the soft room following her psychotic break.

"I got to go to the art studio to pick up the vase I made my mama." Keisha turns to Isabel. "Wanna come?"

"No, thanks." Isabel avoided the art studio. Her first day at Three Breezes she had been appalled to learn that there really was a place you could weave baskets. She would never sink that low, she told herself. She wanted no souvenir of this place.

"See ya back at the ranch," Keisha called over her shoulder.

"I know how you're feeling," Kristen comforts. "It's tough when people you like leave. Feels like I've been here forever, I've seen so many people go."

You don't know a thing about me. I don't give a shit about any of you, that's how much you know how I feel. You think we're friends.

Isabel walks on in silence.

"It gets easier, if that's any consolation." Kristen pats Isabel's shoulder. "It gets easier."

The following day Kristen approaches Isabel, who is reading and smoking on the deck.

"Hi," she says.

Isabel looks up. "Oh. Hi."

"What're you reading?" Kristen is twisting her head to the side in order to see the cover of Isabel's book.

"Anna Karenina," Isabel answers.

Kristen looks like she wants to talk, but the Russian novel is a dead end to her, conversationally. Sensing this, Isabel closes her book and asks about Kristen's bandaged arm.

Kristen does not know why she likes to bleed, she tells Isabel. She loves to pick at her cuticles until they are ragged and bloody. She loves to let her hair get dirty so she can scratch her scalp until it bleeds in different places. She has one area at the very top of her head that she has kept from healing for two years. Every time she makes up her mind to stop, the scab will itch and she will pick it off, usually pulling several hairs out at the same time. It hurts so much that it feels good.

Even at a young age, Kristen says she knew this was not normal. Then, her first boyfriend in high school confirmed it. Billy was more than six feet tall, almost a foot taller than Kristen, so he could literally see over the top of her head. He spotted the bloody sore along the part in her hair.

"What happened to your *head?*" asked the fifteen-year-old, sounding disgusted.

Kristen quickly ran her hand through her thick hair and repositioned her part so the sore was covered up. She had just picked at it so the blood was vivid red.

"I told him it was a mosquito bite," Kristen tells Isabel. "I was embarrassed when he saw it so I told him I'd scratched it because it itched."

"Ew" was all he said and the conversation was dropped. Kristen was careful to move her part from then on so Billy would not notice that it was not healing.

"Did your parents like him?" Isabel asks.

"Yeah. At first they *loved* him," she answers with a weary smile that fades too quickly. "Until they found out we'd been having sex."

Twenty-Two

"I think we have a lot to talk about tonight so let's get started." Larry starts talking as he shuts the door to the living room. "I'd like to begin with what happened at last night's session. Lark? Can we start with you?"

As Larry turns the empty chair in the center of the circle to face Lark, she shifts in her seat.

"What was on your mind yesterday afternoon, before the session began?"

Lark looks at Larry.

"Lark? Could you talk to us? Tell us what you were going through yesterday…"

"I'd like to talk about it, Larry." It is Ben.

"All right, if Lark doesn't mind yielding the floor then Ben, why don't you start us off."

"I was very upset, Larry, that Lark smoked in here. I mean, smoking's not allowed inside. I think you should know that Lark smoked in here, Larry."

Silence.

"Hmm. You're right, Ben. Smoking is not allowed inside

the building. Matches aren't allowed, either. Lark? Can you hear that Ben had some concerns about your smoking inside?"

More silence.

"What did that call up for you, Ben?"

"Huh?" Ben looks confused by the question.

"Why did that upset you?"

"There are rules, Larry. There are rules about that and I don't like that she broke that rule."

Can we please get to the point, folks?

"You're right again, Ben. Lark? Care to jump in? Why did you feel compelled to smoke inside this room?"

Lark looks drugged. *She probably is.*

"What do you want me to say, Larry?" She slurs her words, but her tone is unmistakably confrontational. "You want me to apologize or something? Is that what you want?"

"What I want, Lark, is for you to talk to us about what was going through your mind yesterday. Were you feeling upset or anxious about anything in particular?"

Lark looks out the window and appears to be mulling over the question.

"What interests me is what led up to your break last night. Because that is exactly what happened here. Who was talking to Rita last night, Lark? Who was that?"

Lark turns back to face the empty chair.

"I don't remember."

"Oh, I think you do remember. But just in case, let me help you out. You talked about your father touching you when you were a little girl. Remember? You talked about the curling iron. Who was that talking about young Lark?"

Silence.

"Lark?"

"Donna," she says quietly.

"Donna? Who is Donna?" Larry asks this as he surveys the group. "Lark? Who is Donna?"

"She sticks up for Lark. She tries to protect Lark sometimes," she says in a childlike whisper. "But sometimes she can be a bully."

"Like when?"

"Larry?" It is Keisha.

"Yes, Keisha?"

"I was thinking that maybe Donna comes in when Lark can't defend herself."

"An interesting observation. Tell me more about that."

"It's like, um, maybe when Lark gets pinned down or somethin', like with her daddy, Donna comes in like a wrestler to try to be strong for her when she can't be strong for herself."

"What made you think of that, Keisha? That's a very good point."

Keisha tips her chair back so far that it is teetering precariously on its two back legs.

"I don't know."

"You don't?"

"Ain't nobody gonna hold my arms down, know what I'm sayin'? Nobody. When I leave here? Ain't nobody gonna ever hold me down again. Uh-uh."

Me, neither.

"I know you're leaving, Keisha, and I want to address that in a little bit. For now, though, let's stay on this topic. Why does it bother you to have someone hold your arms?"

Keisha turns to look out the window. "That's what they did to me," she says. "I don't really remember it, but my therapist here told me that's what the police report said. That they held me down."

"When they raped you?"

"Yeah."

"Do you remember anything about that afternoon?"

"Naw," she says, turning her attention back to the group. "Thank God for that, know what I'm saying?"

Lark is still staring at the chair.

"Lark? What do you think about what Keisha just talked about?"

"I wish I couldn't remember," she says.

Silence.

"Keep going," Larry gently urges her on.

"That's it. I wish I couldn't remember."

"Do you think about it a lot?"

"No."

"No?"

"No."

"Do you think that when you *do* think about it someone else comes in and sticks up for you so that the memory can't hurt you? Like Donna? Maybe she comes in when you start thinking about it and she takes all the bad out of it for you? Lark, do you know what yesterday was?"

"Yesterday?"

"Yesterday was Father's Day, Lark."

Isabel looks at Lark, who is nodding her head.

"I know."

"Maybe that's what was so difficult for you. Maybe the fact that yesterday was a day for all of us to think about, to honor, our fathers was upsetting for you. It's not an easy day for you, I know."

More silence.

"It takes a lot of fortitude for a woman—for anyone—to overcome abuse at the hands of a man," Larry says. "That abuse colors everything we are and everything we will encounter. It's incredibly difficult to move past it, to trust again. And even then it's an incomplete trust. So patterns develop. We repeat them because they're familiar. In your case, Lark, the abuse started with your father and since then—and correct me if I'm wrong—you have continued in other similarly destructive relationships."

"What's that?" Katherine pointed with her triangle of toast at a mark on Isabel's leg.

"What? Nothing. I don't know," Isabel said, brushing off the inquiry.

"It's a huge welt, Isabel." Her mother continued chewing. "You don't know how it got there?"

"Mo-om," Isabel whined, knowing it wouldn't be too difficult to deflect her mother's probe since her parents had become quite accustomed to her adolescent mood swings. They were quick to back off and give her space when she started turning their names into two syllables.

"I told you, I got it somewhere…I don't remember. What's with the third degree?" Isabel knew the bruise was ugly. But she thought it looked far worse than it was. The accompanying cut and scab turned the black-and-blue mark into special effects material.

Isabel and David had been dating for six months—since the first week of freshman year in high school. One night he began pressuring her to have sex, and what began as a gentle rebuff while kissing turned into a fight and, before David stormed out of the truck he drove, he punched the seat in frustration. But he missed the seat and caught Isabel's leg instead. Later, when Isabel was alone, she tried to reconstruct the scene to figure out how it was that he punched the side of her leg instead of the seat and couldn't. So she bought David's explanation of a misdirected right hook and let it go. The mark had been easy to cover up, since her school uniform hit her just below the knee. But her mother noticed the bruise on this particular day because she had a tennis match and her game uniform was short.

Dating David was like being caught in a light spring drizzle. At first the infrequent drops of water are cool, refreshing even. Isabel had never had a man wanting, almost needing, to know everything about her. She reveled in this newfound attention. It no longer mattered when her father missed a play—David was there. When her father canceled dinner plans, David was there, ready to whisk her out for pizza. But the drizzle that had been light ultimately soaked Isabel to the bone.

David told Isabel his father had given his mother six stitches on their honeymoon. Though it horrified her, Isabel was strangely drawn to this troubled guy who had had to grow up so fast. She loved feeling needed: his insatiable fascination with the wholesomeness and stability she represented was intoxicating for her. It became an addiction for both of them. David's sad stories about his family, the hardships he had to endure, and the pain he was in as a result, touched Isabel in a profound way. To David, Isabel's home life was idyllic and dangled in front of his desperate eyes like a carrot in front of a hungry rabbit.

But love only fed the flame on the slow burn that was David's anger. Over time he tired of having his face pressed up against the glass and his anger turned to bitter resentment. She began feeling the heat of David's hate directed at her. Isabel began to represent all that had been denied him.

Isabel was shocked the first time he hit her, but David was sufficiently apologetic and all was soon forgotten.

The next time the slap was backhanded, with more force.

And then, mixed in with apologies was subtle blame: I'm so sorry, I'm so sorry, I love you, I'm sorry, but you *did* twist my wrist backward when we were wrestling and it hurt like hell. But I'm sorry. Please forgive me.

It was ingenious: slowly but surely David was making Isabel feel she deserved to be hit.

Isabel withdrew from her friends and allowed her relationship with David to consume her. The bruises became a part of who she was and she made an unsettled peace with it.

"Now, Keisha, I know you are getting ready to leave and I want you to know that we here in the group support you and wish you well. Does anyone have any parting words for Keisha?"

"Bye, Keisha," Ben dutifully replies.

"Yeah, good luck," Regina says.

"We're all pulling for you," Kristen chimes in.

Isabel doesn't say anything. Instead, when the session ends and before Keisha stands up to go, Isabel moves to the seat next to her.

"I wish you didn't have to go," she says.

Twenty-Three

"What are you thinking about, Isabel?"

She looks up.

"Nothing."

"Nothing?"

"Yeah. Nothing."

"Your mind is blank, then," Dr. Seidler prods.

"No." Annoyed, Isabel answers as though she is explaining something to a child. "I'm thinking of *nothing*. I have nothing. There's nothing in my life, not one living thing. My plant was the only living thing in my life that was still mine and I came back from my last out-of-town trip and there it was, all shriveled up. Dead. The perfect metaphor, really. When you think about it."

The tears that had been balancing precariously on her lower eyelids finally push past the dam and make tracks down her hot cheeks.

"Are you thinking about suicide, Isabel?" Her doctor looks earnest, concerned.

"Yes. If you must know, yes. There. I've said it. I know

that means I'll never get out of this place, but shit, yeah I'm thinking about it. I could walk down to the end of the drive-way and step in front of an oncoming car."

"There are other options, you know." Dr. Seidler's tone is urgent. "You have a lot to live for—"

"Before you go on and on about how many people would miss me if I died you can just save it," Isabel cries. The thera-pist lets her continue. "It would be a relief."

"A relief for whom?"

"For me, first of all. I wouldn't have to figure out each and every single goddamned day how I am going to haul myself up and into this meaningless world. I wouldn't have to fight the silent scream—you know that painting? Actually, I think it's called *The Scream*—the one where that person has its hands on either side of its scary face? People look at me and they see this happy face, but inside I'm screaming. It's just that no one hears me."

Dr. Seidler waits for her to continue.

When Isabel doesn't she asks, "You don't think anyone would be sad if you killed yourself?"

"Who?" she challenges. "Who? My parents? I haven't been close to them in years."

"Can she call you back, Katherine?" Alex took a sip of his cappuccino. "She's taking a nap and I hate to wake her since she's been so tired lately."

Sip.

"I know, I know," he said, trying to make his voice sound as if he were smiling, "she's terrible about returning calls. But I'll make sure she calls you back this weekend, okay?"

Sip.

"Good to talk to you, too. I will, I will. Okay, bye!"

"Who was that on the phone?" Isabel rubbed her eyes as she shuffled out of the bedroom. She yawned.

"Oh, no one." Alex turned toward his sleepy wife. "Telemarketer. How'd you sleep?"

"Like a rock. What time is it?" Isabel turned Alex's wrist so she could see the face of his watch. "Why'd you let me sleep so long? Damn! I have so much to do today."

Alex stroked her hair. "You need your sleep, Isabel."

She curled up on the couch alongside her husband. "You take such good care of me," she purred. "I don't know what I'd do without you."

"You won't have to find out," he said somberly. "You won't find out."

"Plus, my parents have two other children to think about. My brothers are healthy and successful and happy. No. They'd be sad for a while but they'd go on."

"That's depression talking, Isabel," the doctor says. "It's hard for you to see beyond your feelings right now, I know that, but a lot of people would be sad, very sad, if you killed yourself."

Silence.

"I just want to go." Isabel is exhausted. "Just let me go."

"I can't do that and you know it."

Why? Why can't you just let me go?

The next morning it is impossible for Isabel to pull herself out of bed. She lies on top of the covers and stares at the acoustic-tiled ceiling, focusing on the mess of holes punched in each square.

Someone has the mind-numbing job of running a machine that pokes the holes into each of those perfectly measured squares. How can they live with themselves?

A knock on the door breaks the embryonic whoosh of her sound machine. "Yes?"

"Isabel, you've got to take your meds." The nameless nurse pokes her head in the door.

"Okay, okay," she sighs, not moving from her bed. "I'll be there in a minute."

Here we are, scurrying around like ants: "You have to take your meds, Isabel"; "Line up, kids"; "It's time to file your income tax returns"; "Would you like this for here or to go?" Each person has their little job and they do it, then they go home, then they eat, then they sleep and then they get up and do it all over again the next day. What's the point? We're all just filling up space. Why do people want to reproduce? So they can bring more children into this already overpopulated world so they can fill up space with some meaningless job and then go home and do it all over again the next day? Like those ceiling tiles.

The knock comes again. "Isabel?" It's the nurse again and this time she looks annoyed when she sees that Isabel hasn't moved. "You have to come get your meds, Isabel. After that you can get back in bed for a little while if you want, but you have to come take your medicine," she says emphatically.

I wonder what she thinks of her job. What does she do when she leaves here? Does she talk about all of us to her husband?

Isabel hauls herself out of bed and puts shorts on over her boxers.

"Okay, okay," she says to no one in particular as she heads down the hall to the medicine distribution window. After swallowing the controlled substances that will beat back nature until the next dispensation—all have foreboding names packed with too many late-alphabet consonants like Serzone, Zyprexa, Trazodone—she shuffles back to her room and crawls back into bed, this time assuming the fetal position.

Doesn't anybody else see how meaningless this is? How we are all consumed with our chores, which are ultimately useless because with the swipe of a broom we can all be swept away into the abyss. Here I am in a mental institution, trying to get better so that I can go back into the world and rush from job to job, killing time until I die of something other than suicide. I take medicine to help me deal with the nothingness of my life. Millions of us have to take pills to distract us from the sheer boredom of it all. We hurry from thing to thing like ants when we're all going to end up suffocating, anyway.

"Isabel." The voice on the other side of the door sounds like Kristen's. "We're getting ready for the morning meeting. You coming?"

Isabel looks at her watch. An hour has passed.

Twenty-Four

Another sign of failure.

Isabel is out of clean clothes. She has been out of clean clothes for two days but has doubled up on dirty underwear instead of admitting to herself that she has been in the hospital for so long she has cycled through her hospital wardrobe twice.

She bends over and starts gathering her clothes together in a bundle and trudges down the hall to the communal laundry room. The door is closed. Balancing her laundry on her hip, Isabel opens the door and is startled to find Sukanya.

Sukanya stands, wedged in between the dryer and the washing machine—which, Isabel notes, is in use—holding an open book and mumbling what sounds like a prayer. In front of her, on top of the dryer, is a single lit candle.

Before backing out the door Isabel watches the sixteen-year-old girl.

Sukanya looks up, sees Isabel and looks back down, without interrupting her prayer.

Isabel closes the door and thinks how nice it is to hear Sukanya say something other than "I'd prefer not to say."

She dumps her laundry back in her room and grabs her pack of cigarettes.

"Kristen? Patio?" Isabel has started the question on her way around the corner into Kristen's room but stops short when she finds Kristen immersed in paperwork spread out on her crinkly bed. "Oh. Sorry."

Kristen looks up for a split second and then races on with her paperwork as if she is in the middle of taking SATs.

"What is this stuff? What're you doing?"

"Application forms! Can't you see? I'm trying to fill out application forms. I'll talk to you later…" She trails off as she flips over the side of one form. On it is an unmistakable logo. A huge *M* formed by two golden arches. McDonald's. Next to Kristen is a stack of what appear to be a hundred more.

"Seriously, what's up? Everything okay?"

"Yeah," Kristen answers distractedly, not looking up from her work. "I love to fill out forms. Any forms, really. These are the best, though. McDonald's. They're the best because you have to fit each letter in its own square; it takes concentration. Other forms give you a line to fill in. That's not as challenging. I love these forms." Kristen is hunched over a fresh application and is carefully squeezing her name, letter by letter, into the appropriate boxes.

"You do this often?"

"Yeah. I have hundreds of the same forms. I take them everywhere with me. Want to do one?" she asks hopefully, as if these are *New York Times* crossword puzzles.

Um, yeah, Kristen, we're so alike.

"Ah, well…no, thanks," Isabel says. "I guess I'll go, then. I'll be outside if you want to come out."

But Kristen does not seem to hear her.

Isabel goes out to the smoker's patio and sits alone in an

Adirondack chair flanked by two pots of fatally dehydrated geraniums.

A half hour later Kristen pushes through the door and looks relieved to find Isabel.

"There you are!"

"Hey." Isabel is tentative in her greeting. She watches Kristen light her cigarette at the wall, noting her shaking hands.

"I'm glad you came and got me," Kristen says as she pulls a chair up alongside Isabel. "I can get a little obsessive about my forms…"

No kidding.

"…but it calms me down when I start thinking about my mother," she is saying. "After we talked about Billy the other day I talked more with my shrink and I guess that's what got me going."

Isabel feels Kristen looking at her, studying her. She knows Kristen wants to talk but does nothing to encourage it.

That does not dissuade Kristen.

"It sounds corny, but I feel like you get it," Kristen says. "You understand me."

"All I did was ask if you wanted to come smoke." *Don't do this, Kristen. Don't drag me into your personal hell.*

"It's more than that." Kristen is insistent. "No one else understands me. You remind me of this girl I used to know. Laurel. That's her name."

Kristen told only one other person when she had had sex with her boyfriend, Billy. From Laurel she sought reassurance and advice. Laurel gave it in the form of a ten-page letter passed to Kristen between classes.

But one night, while Kristen was out with Billy, her mother, Nora, went into her room to straighten up. When Kristen got home she found her mother in the master bedroom, an ashtray overflowing with cigarette butts next to her on the bed.

"What's going on, Mom?" Kristen was worried. "What happened? Did something happen?" Her mother smoked, but not this much. Kristen could not take her eyes off the ashtray. A couple of half-smoked cigarettes had not been fully extinguished and smoke was spiraling up. She knew, in the pit of her stomach, something was terribly wrong.

And that is when she noticed the letter lying on the bed in front of her cross-legged mother.

Suddenly her mouth was very dry.

"Tell me it's not true." Her mother looked intensely at Kristen. "Tell me you have not had sex with Billy. Tell me."

"What?" Kristen was buying time. "What're you talking about, Mom?"

"*This!*" Nora grabbed the letter in her fist and waved it angrily. "This letter is what I'm talking about! Tell me you were just trying to show off to a friend, this *Laurel* person. Tell me you made the whole thing up just to impress an older girl. *Tell me*, Kristen."

Kristen knew she could tell her mother what she obviously wanted to hear and tiptoe to safety or she could tell her mother the truth. She took a deep breath and tried to swallow, but her mouth was so Communion wafer-dry that her tongue stuck to the roof of her mouth and she had to take another deep breath.

"It's true," Kristen whispered. She couldn't look her mother in the eye.

Nora let out a guttural moan that seemed to go on forever. She was doubled over as if to get more vocal power. Kristen had never seen her mother like this. She felt alternately sick and scared.

"Mom, I'm sorry—" was all she could think to say.

"How long?" Her mother was talking in a different voice.

"Huh?"

"How *long* have you and *Billy* been having *s-e-x?*" Her mother didn't actually spell the word *sex,* but said it as if it were poisonous.

"Um. Well." Once again the truth prevailed. "Three months. Something like that. I'm not sure, exactly. Maybe less. Probably less. Less for sure. Two months. I don't know."

By now her mother was rocking back and forth on the bed while trying to light another cigarette. She was so mad, though, that her hands were shaking, making it nearly impossible to unite the tip of the cigarette with the Bic lighter.

Nora reached for the phone.

"Mom? Who're you calling?" Kristen was panicked. She had no idea what to expect.

"Bob?" Her mother had called Kristen's father, who had stayed in a company apartment in Manhattan for the night because he had an early breakfast meeting.

"Come home right away" was all Nora said into the phone.

"Mom? What're you doing? Dad's going to think someone died or something! Why does he need to come home now? It's ten at night. He's going to freak!"

"Too bad." Her mother was completely still on the bed. She looked Kristen in the eye. When Kristen looked into her mother's eyes she felt nauseous. Something in her mother's stare was violently frightening.

Nora swung herself off the bed and stormed out of the room. Kristen followed, not saying anything, just watching in horror as her mother stood in front of the bathroom mirror and screamed. Not a high-pitched scream. A wail of such sad frustration and anger that Kristen moved in to try to hold her mother.

"Get away from me!" she shrieked, pushing Kristen out of the bathroom. *"You make me sick!* Get away from me!"

"Mom?" she called through the bathroom door. "Mom, I'm sorry. I'm so sorry. Please, Mom. Please come out. Let me explain…"

The door flew open and Nora was in Kristen's face.

"I told you. Get out of here! I don't want to see you. I don't want to hear your voice. *Get out of here!*"

With a vise tightening in the pit in her stomach, Kristen crouched outside the now-closed bathroom door and waited, listening to her mother's sobs.

After about a half an hour she heard her father's key in the front door and two seconds later she saw his worried face as he ran up the stairs.

"What on earth is wrong?" He still had on his coat. "Kristen? What's happened?"

Kristen flew into his arms and, for the first time since this incident began to unfold, cried.

"Dad, I'm so sorry," she sobbed. "Please remember that. No matter what happens…I'm so sorry."

Her father was apoplectic. "Where's your mother? *Nora?* Nora!"

The bathroom door opened and standing in front of her frantic husband stood Nora, with clumps of her thick hair wadded up in her fists.

"Oh, my God," her husband said. "What happened? Will someone please tell me what in the hell is going on here?"

"I'll tell you what's going on here," her mother said as she pushed past father and daughter and made her way down the stairs into the living room. The two followed her as if sleep-walking.

"Your daughter *fucked* Billy." Nora was rocking in the middle of the living room floor. Kristen stood at the entrance to the living room and stared at her disheveled mother.

"Is that what this is all about?" Her father was incredulous.

"Dad, I'm so sorry." Kristen ran over to kneel at her father's feet. "It's my fault. I'm so sorry."

He pulled her up alongside him on the couch and hugged her. And, before he released her, he whispered in her ear. "We'll get through this," he murmured.

Kristen looked back at her mother and addressed her, through her tears. "Mom, please forgive me. I'm so sorry."

"You're sorry," her mother mimicked Kristen, putting an emphasis on a different word each time she repeated it. *"You're* sorry. You're *sorry. You're sorry!"*

"Honey." Kristen's father spoke gently to her mother, as if trying to soothe a child. Kristen had never seen her father talk to her mother this way. "Sweetheart, let's go upstairs for a minute and talk. Okay? Let's go up to our room."

But before he could reach down to try to pull his wife up from the floor she moaned again, the way she had when Kristen first told her the truth. The moan was the spookiest of the entire display. It was full of such pain and suffering that Kristen vowed she would never again do anything to hurt or disappoint her mother.

And she kept that promise for many years. Kristen began to dance as fast as she possibly could.

Isabel looks away from Kristen, down the rambling driveway.

One step. That's all it would take. One truck and one step.

Isabel's eyes are fixed at the space between the two stone pillars.

One step.

"That's when I first tried it," Kristen is saying as she lights another cigarette.

"Tried what?" Isabel asks.

"Suicide."

For a week following her mother's discovery of Kristen's sexual secret she was under what amounted to house arrest. The first night of what Kristen would come to think of as the Incident, Nora slept on the floor of her room. She demanded to know every detail of Kristen's and Billy's first encounter.

Kristen did her best to answer her mother, even though she was petrified to talk about such a personal, and apparently horrific, thing with her angry mother. She told her mother the truth: that she and Billy had decided together that they were going to make love. That Billy had not forced himself on her in any way. That Billy used a condom. Kristen was humiliated, recounting what she had presumed was a wonderful experience to her disgusted mother. Kristen had no idea what she had done was so terrible, but now, seeing her mother react the way she had, she began to see sex as a shocking, dirty, humiliating act.

When her mother asked her where they were when they lost their virginity, Kristen lied. She knew she was forbidden to be alone at Billy's house (she had also promised that the two would never be alone in Billy's room) so she told her mother they had been in Billy's car.

A few nights later, Kristen snuck into her room when her parents were distracted and called Billy. Whispering into the phone, Kristen sketched out the situation for him and told him that she had lied about where they had lost their virginity ("I just want to get our stories straight so if she asks you..."). Kristen heard a thump outside her door.

The vise that still had a grip on her stomach tightened and Kristen got off the phone within seconds.

She opened her bedroom door and there was her mother, crumpled up on the floor at the threshold of Kristen's room.

"Mom?" Kristen was sick to her stomach. "Mom?"

Her mother pulled herself up off the floor and headed to the master bedroom with Kristen on her heels. Quietly, her mother faced the mirror in the bathroom and again started to pull clumps of her hair out. Kristen grabbed her wrists.

"Mom! Stop it."

"Quiet!" her mother spat like a feral cat.

"Okay, okay." Kristen didn't know if she had any more strength left for her mother's volatility.

"Go away!" her mother snarled, shoving Kristen out of the bathroom.

Kristen stared at the wood-grain patterns of the closed door. She turned and went into her own bathroom.

Once the door was shut and locked, Kristen opened the medicine cabinet. She scanned the shelves. There was a bottle of Tylenol, but Kristen knew there were more options in her parents bathroom. Options that could release her from the guilty hell she was living in as a result of her repulsive behavior.

She was caught between hope and dread. Between the allure of escape and the danger of deeper trouble.

She decided to wait until her mother came out of her bathroom.

Kristen shuffled back to her room to listen for her mother's bathroom door opening. She would put an end to all the pain swirling around inside her. The decision made her feel calmer than she had in days.

When Kristen finally heard her mother emerge from her bathroom, she steadied her queasy stomach and opened her bedroom door. Silence. Her mother was nowhere to be seen.

"Mom?"

Kristen timidly walked downstairs to the kitchen, to find her mother who was busying herself by peeling back the tiny square of tin foil that covered the dessert section of the Swanson frozen dinner.

"Mom?" Kristen whispered.

Her mother carried on with the frozen-dinner preparation as if she hadn't heard a sound.

"Mom?" Kristen's whisper was slightly louder this time.

Again, no reaction from Nora.

Kristen left the kitchen and went back upstairs, this time to her parents' bathroom.

She reached for a prescription bottle that had her father's name on it. He had blinding headaches from time to time so Kristen reached for what she was sure was a painkiller. The bottle felt huge in her hand. She was mesmerized by the orange-tinted plastic.

She let the faucet run for a minute to get the water really cold.

Twenty-Five

"We need to discuss your medication."

"What about it?"

"For one thing—" Dr. Seidler looks concerned "—it doesn't seem to be working. You are trying to battle severe depression."

Oh, God.

Isabel has been switching from pill to pill for most of her adult life and knows that changing medication is a traumatic event. "But," she stammers, "I don't think about killing myself as much as I did when I first got here. We talked about that, didn't we? I don't think I need to change."

Side effects. Jesus, shaky hands. Upset stomach. Plus they won't let me out while I'm still "adjusting to new medication."

"I hear that this is scary for you but it doesn't need to be. Recently we've discovered ways to work with older methods in order to reduce side effects. I want to talk with you about something that I think could be extremely effective for you."

Isabel knew what was coming. Her therapist in Manhattan had told her about it. Three Breezes is known for successfully treating suicidal depression with a mix of antidepressants. Patients call it the "cocktail." Individualized to meet different needs and bodies, it consists of combining the two or three most powerful antidepressants on the market in order to boost their effectiveness.

"I know all about the cocktail." Isabel wants to beat her therapist to the punch.

"Ah, the cocktail." The doctor laughs awkwardly and then clears her throat. "Well, no, actually. That's not what we've discussed in reference to your case. We are considering what's nicknamed ECT…electroshock therapy. It sounds like the Dark Ages, I know." The doctor moves quickly to explain since Isabel's face has fallen into a long look of horror. "But it's not at all like you would imagine. In many cases it can be the single most effective way to combat severe depression. It has little to no side effects and we happen to specialize in it here.

"I can see from the look on your face that you are thinking about something. Why don't you share what's on your mind, Isabel."

"Frances Farmer." That is all she can say. All she sees is Jessica Lange portraying the old film star.

"Heh, heh." Another throat clearing. "That movie did more damage to ECT than anything before or after. I get your point, though. The image of electroshock therapy is quite scary if you're not familiar with it. Is that what you mean?"

I think she ended up having a lobotomy, a frontal lobotomy. Frances Farmer. That's what did her in in the end. Wasn't it a lobotomy?

"Oh, my God." The implications of the doctor's suggestion are starting to sink in. "Oh, my God, you think I need shock therapy?" Isabel starts taking in deep breaths.

"I think I'm going to pass out," she says while she slips

down farther into the club chair she always chooses for her private sessions.

"All right. Okay. We don't have to talk about this anymore today." The doctor is looking alarmed. "Take it easy. I'm sorry I upset you, Isabel. I didn't mean to—"

"Do you ever get any takers for that? For E–C–T?" she asks in angry disgust. "I mean, does anyone actually say 'Hey, yeah! Let's stick some electrodes to my temples and then crank some electricity into them! Cool!'?"

"I hear that you're upset."

Isabel starts to cry.

Hold on. Just hold on until you get out of this office. Don't cry. Don't cry.

"Isabel? You can cry in here, you know. You don't need to hide your tears."

"I'm going now," Isabel says sharply. "I want to take a shower and forget this conversation ever happened."

Dr. Seidler looks at her watch, notes that they still have fifteen minutes to go in the session, pauses, and thinks better of urging her patient to stay. "Okay. That's fine. I'll see you tomorrow. If you want to talk before then you can ask the nurse to page me."

"Fine."

Before Isabel walks out of her doctor's office she takes a deep breath and pulls her shoulders back, a posture meant to show determination. On her exhale, though, her shoulders fall forward and her body collapses into itself, deflating her defiance completely.

She retreats to her room, gathers up her shampoo and soap and heads to the nurses' station.

"Yes, Isabel. What can we do for you?"

"I need to get into the sharps closet for a second."

"Sure," the nurse says while reaching for the big ring of keys attached to her white belt. Isabel follows her over to the closet. "What do you need?"

"Ah, well…I'm needing to shave, actually. I'll bring the razor right back when I'm done."

The nurse had started shaking her head halfway through Isabel's tentative request. "Has anyone talked to you about shaving?"

"No."

"If you want to shave you need to be supervised. It's not as bad as it sounds. One of us has to be there when you do it. Did you want to do it now?"

Isabel had known that there was probably a rule about shaving, but she hadn't imagined a nurse would have to watch her do it. She tries to seem unfazed. "Um, sure. Okay. If that's good for you?"

"Yep. Let's get your razor first."

The bathrooms at Three Breezes are large enough to accommodate a toilet, a sink and a long, narrow plastic shower stall. Inside the shower Isabel lets the water get hot before balancing her leg parallel to the floor to begin shaving.

"Okay, Isabel. Here's your razor." Before Isabel can reach around the mildewed vinyl shower curtain, the nurse pulls it back altogether and cheerfully hands the Lady Bic to a horrified Isabel. She tries to pull the curtain closed to maintain a semblance of dignity but the nurse catches her wet arm. "Nope. It's got to stay open while you shave. I need to watch you."

"Never mind! Just take the razor and go!" Isabel yells, her face already burning in shame and embarrassment, tears about to flow. The nurse looks bewildered for a moment, but then takes the razor gently from Isabel and leaves.

Twenty-Six

Maybe sleep will make this day go faster.

Several hours after falling into a restless sleep Isabel wakes with a jolt of the kind of nausea that signals something tremendously important has been forgotten.

"What time is it?" she asks the first person she runs into outside her bedroom door.

"Eleven o'clock," the orderly answers.

"A.m. or p.m.?"

"P.m." His tone is sympathetic, as if she has just come out of a coma.

"Oh, my God, Keisha!" Isabel rushes over to the nurses' station.

"Well, hello, Sleeping Beauty." Connie the night nurse is on.

"Connie! Where's Keisha? Did she leave already?"

"Nope. She's still here. Ready to go. Her parents haven't gotten here yet." Connie exchanges a look with the other night nurse.

"Where is she? In her room?"

"Um, honey, no." Connie sounds apologetic. "Keisha was supposed to leave earlier tonight before bedtime and so they gave away her room. We had a new arrival tonight and we needed Keisha's bed."

"So where is she?" Isabel is still waking up but is alert enough to know that something is amiss.

"The kitchen."

Isabel turns the corner into the tiny kitchen. There, with her nappy head resting on her crossed arms sits Keisha.

"Keisha? I'm so glad I didn't miss you. I fell asleep…." Isabel realizes that Keisha, too, has been sleeping. "Oh, sorry."

Keisha sits up and Isabel sees that she is back in her street wear: the Nike swoosh emblazoned on her hooded sweatshirt, the baggy Adidas sweatpants in a matching navy blue. Keisha's packed suitcase sits alongside her, as if she is at a Greyhound bus terminal. "Izzy—" Keisha smiles groggily "—what time is it?"

"It's eleven. Your parents call? They running late or something?"

Keisha looks upset and defensive and Isabel wonders if Keisha's parents are going to turn up at all. She looks down.

"Want to watch TV with me? We could just hang out for a while until they get here."

"Yeah, whatever."

She stumbles as she stands up from the table, rights herself and follows Isabel into the living room. Sukanya is, of course, planted in the armchair that faces the television so Keisha and Isabel take the couch. Keisha curls up and resumes sleeping.

Isabel watches her and suppresses the urge to pet her, to pat her back, to reassure her that everything is going to be okay.

★ ★ ★

Keisha's mother looks just like her but fat. She is hunched over a clipboard at the nurses' station when Keisha and Isabel walk into the unit from breakfast.

"Mom? Mama?" Keisha runs up to her obese mother and gratefully throws her arms around her.

"Hi, baby." Her mother seems weary and wary of her daughter. Isabel thinks she does not seem as happy to see Keisha as Keisha is to see her. "You 'bout ready to go?"

Keisha is so elated her whole body looks like it is shaking. "Ready? I was *born* ready to leave *this* place. Lemme get my bag." On her way past her sad mother, Keisha eyes the two men who appear to be accompanying her mom but she does not ask who they are. She runs back to Isabel's room, where she had stowed her suitcase before leaving for breakfast.

Isabel is standing off to the side of the nurses' station and is taking in the scene. As soon as Keisha bounds off, Isabel approaches Keisha's mother.

"Mrs. Jackson? Hi, I'm Isabel Murphy. I'm a friend of Keisha's." She smiles, extending her hand.

"Hi there, sugar, how're you?"

Why is she looking to these guys for permission to talk to me?

"Fine. Keisha's so excited to be going home. She's been talking about it nonstop."

Who the hell are these guys and why are they looking me up and down…? Take a goddamn picture, it lasts longer.

Isabel pretends she has not seen Keisha brush past the two men without a greeting. "Are you guys friends of Keisha's or something?"

No response.

Mrs. Jackson looks miserable.

The reporter in Isabel worries.

Finally, Keisha returns, dragging her bag and heading straight for the nurse on duty. "I almost forgot the sharps closet! I need to get my stuff from in there." Because Keisha had been brought to Three Breezes involuntarily she does not have much in the way of belongings.

The two burly men move in to either side of Keisha. The nurse, on her way to check the sharps closet for Keisha, tries to whisper, "Can't you wait until she's in the parking lot?" but Isabel picks it up.

"Keisha? What's going on? Who are these guys?" Isabel asks Keisha, who is still smiling.

"Them? Oh, I dunno. All I know is I'm goin' home with my mama!"

"Oh, baby." Her mother looks like she is about to cry. "Oh, my baby."

"Why you cryin', Mama? I'm comin' home!"

"Keisha Jackson?" One of the two men steps forward; his patience has run out. "You are under arrest. You have the right to remain silent. Anything you say can and will be used against you in a court of law…"

As he is reading Keisha her rights in front of the nurses' station, Mrs. Jackson begins to wail loudly and wave her hands in the air around Keisha's head. Keisha is frantic.

"Mom? Mama, what's happenin'?" she cries. "What's goin' on here? Why they arrestin' me?"

Chaos erupts on the unit. The nurse who had, moments earlier, urged the police to wait to arrest Keisha, rushes over to comfort her. The police are loudly, as if on a dare, reading Keisha her Miranda rights while handcuffing her wrists behind her back. Mrs. Jackson is wailing and chanting "my baby" over and over again and a bewildered Keisha is asking everyone who catches her eye why this is happening. Ben has joined the fray and is peppering the police with excited questions about their guns.

"Is that a .45 or a .22? I always get them mixed up....45s and .22s. How much ammo you carry with you? You have some stored in your cruiser, right? Am I right?"

Melanie, returning from breakfast, skips up to Keisha and tries to hug her goodbye.

Doesn't she see Keisha's a little tied up for the moment?

"I didn't get a chance to say goodbye at breakfast!" she squeaks. *I guess it's just another day, Melanie, huh? Just another person arrested right in front of you?*

This place is unbelievable.

"You guys always wear bulletproof vests, don't you? Huh? You always have to wear 'em, right? Am I right?"

When the police lead Keisha out of the unit toward the awaiting squad car Isabel falls into step alongside Mrs. Jackson.

"Mrs. Jackson? Mrs. Jackson, please...please tell me what's going on here. Maybe this is a misunderstanding."

"Ain't no misunderstanding, child." She stops crying long enough to look over her shoulder at Isabel, who stands at the edge of the parking lot. "My Keisha killed her nephew. Killed him dead."

Twenty-Seven

"So that's why I'm asking you what your reaction is to Keisha's being taken away." Isabel focuses just in time to catch Dr. Seidler's question. She has been squinting, trying to read, from across the room, the names of the universities that had bestowed degrees upon her well-trained psychiatrist.

"Isabel?"

"Huh?" She tears her eyes from the framed diplomas. "Yeah?"

"I was asking you what your thoughts were about your friend being arrested."

"I think it's weird." She shrugs.

"Weird, in what way?"

"Just weird, that's all." *I don't want to talk about it right now.*

"I realize you're probably reticent to talk about it, but I think it's a good idea to discuss it while it's fresh."

"Keisha wasn't here for that long, anyway…"

Silence.

"…so, I mean, we weren't really that good friends…"

Silence.

"...it's just that you get to know people, or you think you know them, so quickly here. From group therapy, I guess."

"You had warm feelings toward her, though, didn't you? You expressed that in here once or twice."

"Yeah. I don't really know why, though. There was just something about her that seemed so fragile. But she was tough, too. And that thing she said about someone wanting to control you when they knew what you were all about. She was kind of smarter than she seemed at first."

"What did that evoke in you?"

What did that evoke in me? Evoke?

"Isabel, why are you smiling?"

"It's just...well...*evoke*...it's kind of a word that we're told is a print word. I remember my first year in television my news director got mad at me because I used it in a script. He said, 'No one goes around saying *evoke*.' He told us that and the word *slain* were verboten. Actually, then he added *verboten* to the list, too."

"Okay, well, sorry for using the improper word." Dr. Seidler smiles and turns the conversation back to Keisha. "Why else did you find Keisha so appealing, do you think?"

More silence.

"Let me help you out here, and this is just a theory. Some people believe that we choose our friends, we choose the people we care about, because they remind us of ourselves. Do you think that's the case with Keisha?"

"Yeah, I'm a black girl from the ghetto."

"Look beyond the surface, Isabel. You're quite fragile yourself, right? If you weren't you might not be here. But you're tough, too, when you have to be. Could that be why you felt strongly about Keisha?"

*That and the fact that she gets it. She knows what it's like when
someone takes away your soul. Alex took my soul.*

Silence.

"I don't know," Isabel says. "I want to be by myself for a
while today. I don't really feel like talking anymore."

"Aren't you going over for dinner, Isabel?" Connie is in
early.

"They're already over there, so why don't you sign yourself
out and catch up with them before dinnertime is up."

Isabel dutifully writes *dinner* on the board and wordlessly
leaves the unit.

The smell of cooked beef assaults Isabel as she opens the cafeteria door. She picks up a wet plastic tray and slides it along
the three steel rods that outline the salad bar.

There he is!

Isabel's heart starts beating twice as fast. There, sitting off
to himself at the end of a rectangular table in the corner of
the dining hall is the little boy Peter.

Anthill Peter.

She throws some iceberg lettuce into her foam dish, adds a
couple of cherry tomatoes and Thousand Island dressing and
approaches him. He is concentrating on his mashed potatoes
and does not hear her.

"Hi," she says, clearing her throat. "Can I sit down?"

Peter looks up at her and then from side to side, to check
to see that it is him she is addressing. She smiles.

"I was wondering if I could join you."

Nothing. Back to the mashed potatoes he goes. He is not
eating them, he is pushing them around on his plate.

"I'm not scary or anything," she tries to reassure him. "I
promise I won't bite."

Stupid comment! Maybe he's here because he was abused. Oh, God, maybe he was bitten even, by a monstrous adult who looks like me and who lured him in with companionship...with dinner.

Nothing.

"Okay, well, see you around."

Good going, Isabel. Smooth move. Blown off by a mute nine-year-old.

Isabel chokes down her wilted salad off by herself, away from Ben, Melanie, Kristen and the rest. In between bites she steals glances at Peter, who is still pushing his mashed potatoes around.

She thinks about what Dr. Seidler said earlier, about what it might be about Peter that makes her want to befriend him. What he "evokes" in her.

Peter is now at the trash can throwing his untouched plate of food away.

Now. Do it now.

Isabel gets up, waits a beat and throws away the remnants of her salad. As Peter's group files out she falls into step alongside the mysterious boy.

"Hi, again," she says softly, trying to sound distracted, like she does not care if he answers her or not. "Told you I'd see you around and sure enough...I'm seeing you again!"

The little boy is studying the pavement ahead of each step.

"My name's Isabel."

Nothing.

"Okay, well, that's strike two." She fakes a baseball umpire's cadence: stee-rike two.

"Bye," she calls out. When she looks up from the pavement she looks directly into the gardener's kind face.

"Sad boy," he addresses her as he sprinkles fertilizer on a bed of hungry marigolds. "Umm-hmm, sad little boy."

Isabel considers his words.

"Aren't we all?"

The gardener looks up from his work, cocks his head to one side and gives it thought. "I suppose we are, I suppose we are." Sprinkle. "But you can't let it crush you. No, ma'am. Can't let it crush your spirit." Sprinkle. "You've got to feed your spirit...fertilize it. Umm-hmm."

Isabel walks away.

Twenty-Eight

Isabel

"Isabel!" Kristen calls her over to the smoking deck. "Come sit. We were just talking about boyfriends."

Isabel is confused. The only other person on the deck is Sukanya.

Either it's a freaking miracle or Kristen is crazier than I thought.

"I was asking Sukanya here if she has a boyfriend," Kristen purred, "and then we were scoping out the men."

Sukanya's vacant stare indicates that the conversation has been entirely one-sided.

Curious, Isabel lights a cigarette and pulls up a chair.

"Do you have a boyfriend?" Isabel asks Kristen through her exhale, mindful of the trauma surrounding Kristen's first sexual encounter.

"Not exactly," Kristen begins. "I'm bipolar, you know."

In the years that followed the Incident, Kristen's mania that had begun with self-mutilation grew and soon she was craving outside stimulants to increase the buzzing sensation she would get when the roller coaster climbed to the peak of her bipolar illness.

Kristen became an alcoholic.

When she was happy she was so euphoric she would go on binges at a bar two blocks away from her apartment. Not only would she gulp down whatever she thought to order, she would order rounds and rounds of drinks she couldn't afford for everyone around her. So pleased was she that others were happy to indulge her sick generosity that the mania would intensify and soon she would be so drunk she could barely remember her own name. The bartender knew her well, and while he knew it was probably irresponsible for him to allow her to carry on as she was, he also knew her father was extremely wealthy and paid all of Kristen's bills.

More than once Kristen left the bar, numb with drink, accompanied by men who were faceless to her. More than once Kristen found herself disheveled and lost, wondering whose semen was dripping down the insides of her thighs. That's when the flip side of her bipolar disorder would introduce itself. Kristen attempted suicide four times.

"Mom, I'm fine, I swear."

"Kristen, please don't do this. Please."

"Mom, seriously. My doctor said that ultimately this is my choice. *My* choice, Mom. I feel *great*. I hate having that poison in my system. I hate it."

"It's a lifelong illness, Kristen," her agitated mother said. "Are you even paying attention to me?"

"Yes, Mom." Kristen was decidedly not paying attention to her mother. Her mind was made up. No more medication.

"Kristen, please keep taking your pills. Honey, please. I'm begging you."

"Okay, Mom. Whatever you say," Kristen said, parroting the only words she knew would appease her mother.

Kristen reached for the bottle of medication her mother was holding for her. She pretended to gulp them down but instead let them rest in the twin wells under her tongue, to be spit out the minute her mother looked away.

And so Kristen stopped taking the pills that were working overtime to try to save her from herself.

"What about you?" Kristen is aware she has monopolized the conversation. "You've mentioned you're separated in group. You're still wearing your ring, though. It's beautiful, by the way."

Isabel looks down at her left hand and twists her wedding band around on her ring finger.

"Thanks."

"What's he like?"

"You know what you need?" Casey chomped on her hot pretzel.

"Have you not been listening to me? I know what I need, I just don't know how to get it," Isabel answered.

"Bells and whistles," Casey said. "You need fireworks. A little garter-belt sex never killed anyone. Let's go get you outfitted."

"What's next? Light some candles and listen to Yanni? I'm a freaking cliché."

"Don't you ever watch Lifetime? Connie Sellecca slips into a negligee and bam! She gets laid."

"*Lifetime?* Please tell me I did not hear you use Lifetime, Television for Women, as your reference guide to a good sex life."

"You're missing the point. Let's focus," Casey said, squinting into the distance. "There's a lingerie store up about three blocks. We'll hit it first. Giddyup."

"Ugh." Isabel sighed in frustration as she dragged behind her friend. "I hate this. I just don't see why I have to parade around in some costume to get his attention. We're in the honeymoon stage. Why do I feel like we're a middle-aged couple trying to recapture the magic?"

Casey walked fast and made no comment. Isabel scurried to catch up.

She cleared her throat while they stood at the curb waiting for the light to change. "I'm sorry I haven't called you back, Case."

Casey stayed silent.

"It's just, well, Alex takes up so much time, and then it's late and I know you're in bed and I don't want to wake up Michael and…"

"…and the dog ate your homework?" Casey interrupted. "Jesus, Iz, what's with all the excuses? I know he doesn't like me, you don't have to dance around it. I'm not Forrest Gump, you know. I get it."

Isabel watched the electronic walking man turn into Don't Walk as they missed another chance to cross the street.

"Hey, that's fine. I don't need to be his best friend. I just miss you, kid. That's all. I miss *you*."

"I miss you, too, Case." Isabel's tone was pleading. "Just give me some time. He just *needs*. He needs—oh, I don't know—he needs me, I suppose. He needs to know he's number one with me, you know? I kind of don't mind it. I mean, it's flattering in a way."

Casey raised a skeptical eyebrow.

"No, it's just he's so-o-o into me. He knows everything I do, everything I like, everything I want—"

"Except sex…"

"I'm going to ignore that. He does, though. He's just so focused on me. I just need extra time so I can focus on him like he wants me to."

"Focus away. You can have all the time in the world, kid. I want this to work for you."

"Since when are you supportive of me and Alex? I thought you didn't like us together."

Casey turned and faced Isabel. "*You* like you and Alex together, right?"

Isabel tentatively nodded to Casey. "Yeah?"

"Then that's enough for me."

Isabel paused and watched Casey cross the street before running to catch up with the best friend she'd ever known.

"One more thing?" Isabel looked uncomfortable.

"Don't tell me. You want *me* to have sex with him instead of you?"

Isabel laughed and then turned serious again. "It's just… well…don't mention to Alex I was with you today, okay?"

"Oh, my God, Isabel."

"It's no big deal! It's just that I told him I had a meeting downtown—I didn't tell him I was seeing you—and I don't want him to think I was lying to him."

"Perish the thought."

"So you won't say anything?"

Casey's face was filled with pity. "I won't say anything, Isabel."

When they reached the boutique with a window display swathed in yards of pink fabric and lace, Casey took her friend by the shoulders.

"Okay, now. You can do this. Think *9H Weeks*. You're Kim Basinger. Go get 'em, you little sex kitten."

"This is so pathetic."

"Come on, sport. Buck up. Let's go."

Isabel fiddled with the volume on the stereo but it was hard to adjust since the dial was so sensitive. If someone sneezed near it it would move. Finally she found the right level—somewhere between "Oh, did I leave the stereo on? I must've forgotten, I listen to Sade all the time" and "Hey, lover, come on over and make yourself comfortable." Between obvious and desperate.

She turned to the mirror and pulled at the garter belt.

When she heard him come in she panicked, turned off the music and threw her terry-cloth robe over her half-naked body.

"You're home early," she called down from the bedroom. She checked her look in the mirror and headed for the door.

"Hi," she said.

"Hi, yourself," Alex answered. "You almost ready? Our reservations are for eight." He eyed her skeptically.

"I was thinking…" *Sex kitten. 9H Weeks.* "We could take it easy…" *Take off the robe. Good.* "Relax…" *Why is he making that face?* "And play dinner by ear…" *Oh, God.* "What do you think?"

Alex's look made her reach for the robe she'd tossed in a mock-careless way onto the overstuffed chair.

"What?" she asked, already embarrassed and defensive.

Alex gulped. It was the first time Isabel saw him speechless. "I made these reservations a month ago. It's really hard to get in. Let's just go, okay?"

He was already out the door.

Twenty-Nine

Isabel

"Isabel? Where are you?" Alex hollered as he walked through the front door of their apartment. "I've got news."

"I'm in here," Isabel answered, her tense shoulders involuntarily relaxing at the sound of Alex in a good mood. She had gotten home from work early and was flipping TV channels, comparing the lead stories on the different network newscasts.

"I got the backing," Alex announced.

"What? Oh, my God." Isabel leaped from the couch into Alex's arms. "Tell me."

"Terry called me into his office about an hour ago—can we turn this off?" His tone was more demanding than inquisitive. "He said the Australians came through. Apparently they're sure they want to open a place here in the States and they liked my proposal."

"Wow. That's unbelievable! Just like that…" Isabel was happy to see him so excited. He'd been in a foul mood for weeks.

"Yeah, well, I guess they thought it was a good idea." Alex, pleased with himself, plopped down on the couch next to Isabel. "It's going to be rotten hours—that's the only drawback. Just until the crowds even out."

"So what kind of time will you need to spend there? You'd be the boss, the owner, right? You can go in whenever you want."

"They only want to do it if I can be hands-on at the bar, you know, on the floor, getting to know the regulars."

"And hands-on means you've got to work every night?"

Isabel knew he needed her to be happy for him. But she pressed on.

"We'll never see each other, you know."

"Here's what I was thinking about that." Alex leaned forward excitedly. "I was thinking you could get a morning job and then we'd both be on the same schedule and we'd have the entire day together."

"Honey, I'm so happy for you. Really. But I've just gotten the 5:00 p.m. slot and it'll look great on my résumé. The networks won't even glance at me if I don't have evening newscast experience. But just because I don't want the early shift doesn't mean you shouldn't move forward with your own place. It's what you've always wanted." Isabel was trying to keep it light but couldn't resist adding, "I just worry that we'll never see each other."

Alex was quiet for a moment. He hunched forward in his seat, bowed his head and placed his fingertips together as if he were praying. When he looked up Isabel felt a chill.

"Why do you have to spoil it? Why do you have to be so negative about something I'm so happy about?"

Isabel and Alex had an unspoken rhythm to their disagreements. Isabel could push him—but only to a point. She was always the one to back down first. When she had insisted she didn't want to eat barbecue for dinner she'd had a CD thrown at her, nicking her forehead and causing blood flow. Sensing that a mood swing was imminent, Isabel abandoned her doubts.

"You're right, you're right. I'm sorry. I am happy for you. And we will see each other—I was just playing the devil's advocate. I am so proud of you." Isabel hugged Alex. Within seconds he went back to being enthusiastic.

"But we haven't really talked in weeks!" Isabel leaned on the bed as Alex closed the curtains to block out the bright noonday sun.

"Isabel, give me a fucking break!" he snapped. "Are you completely deaf? I told you I'm taking a nap. Get out!"

Alex pulled his eye mask from the bedside table and slipped it over his head.

"But…"

"'But' nothing, Isabel—*Jesus Christ!* I'm exhausted. Can't you just let me catch up on sleep? Jesus."

"I knew this was going to happen." Isabel wouldn't let up, even though the eye mask was firmly in place. "I knew we'd never see each other. I'm just trying to talk to you for five minutes. Aren't you even wondering what I'm doing home at this hour? Aren't you in the least bit curious?"

"Don't fuck with me, Isabel." His stock warning. He sat up in bed and pushed his eye mask up to his forehead. "I'm going to sleep now. When I wake up, we'll talk—hell, we'll do an Irish jig, I don't give a flying fuck—but right now I am going to sleep. Get out of this bedroom!"

"But I need to tell you something."

"Get out."

Isabel backed out of the unnaturally dark bedroom into the sunny living room. She surveyed the room filled with pricey decorations they could not afford. They were living beyond his means and Alex didn't seem to care. But that would have to end. As she fixed her stare on the huge mainframe computer Alex had just spent thousands of dollars on, she knew his spending would be curbed by sheer necessity. He wouldn't like it, though, and Isabel shivered at the thought of breaking the news.

"You *what?*"

"I lost my job," Isabel said, humiliated at having to repeat it.

"What'd you do?" Alex sneered in an accusing tone of voice.

Isabel looked up, shocked. "What do you mean 'what'd I do'? It's not my fault, Alex! The station just got sold and the new owners are cutting back. They want to bring in their own people. Everyone's been speculating about this for months— ever since the sale."

"Yeah, but why you? How come they fired *you?* I've been telling you to stay on your toes. What've I been telling you? I specifically told you that you need to look good and do good—"

"I always do my best…"

"Was I finished talking? I don't think I was finished talking yet, do you?"

"You know what? Fuck you, Alex."

Alex was still. Isabel gulped hard.

"I was fired. It wasn't my fault. I know you're going to say I'm playing the victim again—blah, blah, blah—but I don't care. I'm not a victim. It wasn't personal and I know that. So just get over yourself."

Alex stared at his wife.

Alex took a step forward. "'Get over myself?' Is that what

you just said? Get over myself? What, may I ask, is that supposed to mean?"

Isabel took a step backward.

"I don't have the energy for this right now, Alex—okay? Please?"

Alex took another step toward her and Isabel knew it was time to back down.

"Look, I'm sorry," she said, careful to stick to the script of their arguments.

"Yeah, you're sorry. You're sorry," he interrupted. "You deserved it, you know that? The more I think about it, the more I realize you deserved it. Why? Because you don't have the hunger. Deep down inside you know that Mommy and Daddy will cushion your fall so you aren't hungry for the paycheck. Some people have to work for a living, you know that?"

"Alex, please…"

"Please? *Please?*" He slapped Isabel so hard across her face that she fell to the floor.

"Did you honestly think you could talk to me that way and get away with it?"

Thirty

"This year the world will lose 2.3 million people to the AIDS epidemic, and nowhere is there a greater toll than here in sub-Saharan Africa. The statistics are staggering: in Zimbabwe at least one in five adults has the AIDS virus, in Zambia the infant mortality rate due to AIDS has increased twenty-five percent, and here, in Botswana, nearly thirty percent of the entire population is HIV positive.

"Even more frightening is this week's announcement from the World Health Organization that we could see an explosion in AIDS cases to the tune of forty million within two years."

Isabel Murphy, ANN News, Botswana.

"Alex? Can you hear me now?" Isabel shouted into the satellite phone.

"Isabel? Is that you? I can barely hear you!" he shouted back.

"Sorry, honey. I'm afraid this is as good a connection as we're going to get. I'll talk loudly."

"That's okay. I can't believe you could even call out. How is it there? Are you okay? God, I miss you so much."

"I'm fine. I'm fine. It's unbelievable here. Hell on earth. It feels like another planet." She looked at the lean-to the crew was huddled under to escape the burning midday sun.

"I bet, I bet. When're you coming home? Have they told you yet?"

"That's one of the reasons I called…."

"Isabel? I think I lost you. Isabel? Are you still there?"

"Alex! I'm here. Sorry. I'll shout. I called because they want me to stay on and go over to Zimbabwe next week. It's really great, actually. Doctors Without Borders is letting us travel with them while they go distribute protease inhibitors to these makeshift clinics…"

"So you're going to miss our counseling session again?"

"…these people, most of them, anyway, don't even know what AIDS is or why everyone in their family is dying…"

"I take that as a yes. I'll call Dr. Bauman and let her know we'll have to reschedule again."

"What'd you say? I missed that."

"I said, *I'll call Pat Bauman and reschedule.* You're out there saving the world and I'm just here…walking the dog…waiting for my globe-trotting wife to remember she has a husband."

"Aw, Alex. I'm sorry. It's just this one story—"

"It's always 'just this one story.'"

"Alex? Sorry, but I've got to go. The doctors we're hooking up with just got to our camp and I've got to go meet them. I'm sorry."

"Yeah, whatever."

The phone went dead before Isabel could say goodbye.

Thirty-One

"You're the one who wanted me to go to therapy in the first place!" Alex pointed at Isabel. "I can't believe you're resisting this."

"I'm not resisting couples counseling—wait! Just listen to me for a second. I'm not saying we shouldn't go to couples counseling, I'm just saying that I don't feel comfortable going to the doctor you see for *individual* therapy. Why can't we find a neutral person? Someone whom we'd *both* feel comfortable with?"

"We can." Alex had calmed down. "If you don't like Pat. But let's just try this for now—okay? For me? This is hard for me, this therapy thing. I don't want to have to get into all my stuff again with someone new. Pat knows me now. It's easy with her."

Isabel looked down at her ragged cuticles and chipped fingernails. "Fine. I'll try it. But I don't think it's right. I'm telling you that straight out. It's not right. I can't believe Pat even suggested it."

"She didn't. I did."

★ ★ ★

"Isabel, before our time is up I wanted to approach you with an idea," Pat said. "As you know, I have been seeing Alex for a period of time. It's been, what, Alex? Seven months? Well, I know this is somewhat unorthodox—you two coming to me for couples therapy on top of my work with Alex—and I hear that you don't feel entirely comfortable with this arrangement. So I'm proposing that you come to me as an individual—just for a session or two—so I can get a more rounded picture. You're shaking your head. Would that not be acceptable to you?"

"I don't think any of this is acceptable." Isabel tried to stay as measured and calm as the therapist as she addressed her husband. "Alex, this *is* unorthodox. Pat doesn't even know me—"

"That's exactly why she wants to meet with you one-on-one," Alex interrupted. "Isabel, you said you'd give this a shot. You said you'd try it."

Isabel looked at her husband, whose beseeching look matched that of Pat's.

"Fine," she sighed. "I'll try it."

"I appreciate your coming in, Isabel." Pat motioned for her to take the seat opposite the desk. "I do think that this will inevitably help me to help you and Alex both work through this difficult time. If I may, I'd like to start out by asking you some questions and, since it's our first visit one-on-one, I may scribble some notes down, if that's all right with you."

Suddenly you care if something's "all right" with me? Why start now?

"That's fine."

"Okay, well, to begin with, what would you say your major problems with the marriage are? This is probably a good place for me to point out that whatever you say to me in here will not be repeated to Alex either in my individual sessions or in our couples sessions."

"My major problems with the marriage?" Isabel considered the question. "Where do I begin? I mean, we covered some of this in our session last week."

"Yes, we did." Pat looked up from her notepad. "But what I'd like to hear is your perspective on the marriage, on your relationship with Alex. We touched on it last week but we didn't go much beyond the surface."

Isabel shifted in her seat. "The sex stuff's thrown me for a loop. I mean, like we talked about, I'm in my prime and Alex has the drive of a ninety-year-old. And it's not just sex drive, because I know there are pills he could take or whatever. It's something more than that. It's deeper than that—like he clicks off whenever it comes to intimacy. Like he's not even there. So that bugs me. And Alex says he doesn't see what the problem is. No, that's not right: he says it's *my* problem. That I place too much importance on sex. Oh, and he hates that I can remember how long it's been since we last made love. He says I keep score."

"Do you?"

"No! I don't keep score as much as I just feel like it's been forever since we had sex and then I check the calendar and I see that—"

"Ah. So you *do* keep track of your lovemaking."

"That's not what I said! I was just—"

"You just said that you checked the calendar, correct? So you make notations of when you and Alex are intimate?"

"No. That's the thing. I keep track of social things on my calendar. Dinner with Marty and Alice, for instance. And, if Alex and I had sex when we got home that night I remember it. So I don't keep track, really. Not the way you and Alex are suggesting."

"Me and Alex. You put me and Alex together as a united front. Is that how you see us?"

Duh.

"Yes. I told you that. Well, I told Alex. That's why I don't think it's a good idea to get counseling from you for our marriage—because I feel underrepresented in our session."

"So why did you end up doing it? Coming in with Alex?"

Isabel picked at her thumb again and pushed down against the speck of blood. "I was scared not to."

"What are you scared of?"

Isabel looked up from her hands. "What am I scared of? Alex, of course. What else would I be scared of?"

"You're scared of Alex?"

"Ah, yeah." Isabel was bewildered at Pat's naiveté.

"Why?"

"Why am I scared of my husband? Are you serious? You seriously do not know why I'd have a reason to be afraid of Alex?"

The therapist was still.

Pat could not be this good an actress.

"Let me see if I am understanding this. He's been coming to you every week for seven months. Every single week. And he's never once talked about how he gets violent with me?"

"Excuse me?" Pat was trying hard not to appear astounded.

"You two have never discussed his violent rages? How he's made me bleed? How I end up in a different motel each time because I'm embarrassed to go back to the same place twice wearing my sunglasses at night? He's never told you any of this?"

Nothing.

"Oh, my God. I feel sick." Isabel grabbed for her purse on the floor and stood up to put her coat on. "I feel physically ill."

"Isabel, wait." Pat scrambled to think of what she could say.

"Wait? Wait for what? For you to do your fucking job and figure out why your patient is coming to you in the first place? Wait for my husband to kill me? Jesus! No wonder the fights haven't gotten any better! He's been lying all along. He hasn't dealt with any of it. I think I'm going to throw up."

Isabel ran out of the office, through the lobby and out into the fresh air. She stopped on the sidewalk and sucked in the air as though she'd been suffocating.

Thirty-Two

Isabel

Isabel was as lost in her depression as an Australian shepherd dog would be without a herd of sheep. It can be a thing of beauty to watch the dog gracefully circling a confused herd. Speeding up, slowing down, sidestepping and charging forward—the dog's every movement is intense. Lying deep at the instinct's center is the simple, involuntary need to please.

"Isabel, you seem a bit subdued today," her therapist remarks. "Is there any particular reason for that?"

Just tell me what you want from me. Tell me who to be and I'll be it.

Daily meetings with her therapist, her psycho-pharmacologist, the nurse on the unit and then group therapy with Larry...Isabel is sick of it. It's draining to appear to absorb all the good intentions of the mental health care professionals surrounding her. Outnumbering her.

It's brainwashing when you think about it: people telling you you're a valuable person, you shouldn't think of dying as an option, you're

*worth more than that… It's like they hope that by osmosis you'll feel
better about yourself. You'll be infused with the intense desire to live.*

Why isn't it working?

"She had it all…a successful career as a television reporter for a
major news network, a marriage and a good circle of friends…find
out what went wrong…Sunday at eight only on Lifetime, Television
for Women."

"Isabel, I think we need to revisit the medication issue,"
Dr. Seidler is saying. "Have you given any thought to what
we discussed earlier? You seemed pretty upset. I've tried to
talk about ECT with you every day this week and each time
you shut down. Isabel?"

Isabel stares at the Native American weaving hanging above
the doctor's desk. She hears every word as if she is underwater.

"I want you to know that I feel our options are becoming
limited. With electroshock therapy we would take very few
risks and see the most benefits. What do you think?"

*Sometimes, if you stare at something long enough you can almost
hypnotize yourself. Kind of like sleeping with your eyes open.*

"Isabel? Are you okay? Isabel?"

The vibrant colors in the wool decoration blur together.

"Isabel? Do you understand that as your doctor I can act in
your best interests if I believe your personal safety is in jeop-
ardy? In other words, I don't necessarily need your approval
to move forward, and I am starting to feel like that is an option I may actively explore…."

She sure uses the word option *a lot. How many times has that
been? Two? No, three. Maybe it's two.*

"Can you hear me, Isabel?"

That voice is so grating.

"Isabel?"

Thirty-Three

"Who should we start with today?" Larry opens up the session by slowly circling the room. Under normal circumstances that would be annoying enough, but with a group of anxious mental patients it is maddening. Some nervous, others paranoid, all twist uncomfortably in their chairs to keep Larry in sight. In the end, he stops behind Ben's folding metal chair. The others exhale in relief.

"Ben?"

"Um, what, Larry?" Ben sits bolt upright as if he hadn't done his homework.

"We haven't heard from you in a while. Why don't we talk about where you are these days."

"Where I am, Larry?" Ben has an unnerving habit of repeating his conversation partner's name with each reply. "I'm here in the session, Larry." While Ben is serious in his bewilderment and in his literal interpretation of the question, the rest of the group laughs.

Larry is gentle. "What I mean to ask, Ben, is, how are you feeling these days?"

"Oh! I'm fine, Larry. Just fine." Larry waits for more. "Um, I'm looking forward to finding out about my next stop, though. They tell me they're still waiting to hear whether I got a bed at Strawbridge Ranch."

"Why don't you tell the rest of the group about Strawbridge."

"Sure!" Ben is relishing this time in the limelight. "Strawbridge is, like, a halfway-house-type place. It's cool, though, 'cause we get to work on the ranch—milking the cows, feeding the chickens and stuff. Not wild animals but tame farm-type animals. It's great! And I hear they have great food there. Unbelievable food, Larry. I talked to one of the nurses and she said they've got the best blueberry pancakes. I don't know how often they have them. Maybe once a week or something…but blueberry pancakes! I can almost taste them now!"

Melanie laughs again. Ben is getting so revved up that spittle is forming in the corners of his smiling mouth.

"That's good, Ben. Good. Let us know when you hear about the bed."

"I will, Larry. I will definitely." Ben is a little disappointed to see that his time is over and Larry is moving on to someone else.

"Melanie? What about you?" Larry has turned to Melanie because she is still laughing about Ben's pancake reverie.

"Well…" Melanie, it is clear to Isabel, is feeling good today. Her animated elation points up Isabel's empty numbness. Melanie surveys the room to make sure everyone else finds Ben as amusing as she does and then decides to proceed. "I was just wondering. I mean, we all talk about why we're here and all Ben ever talks about is a bed at Strawbridge. We never have talked about why Ben is here."

The room is silent as everyone looks from Ben to Larry

and back again after this daring faux pas. It is as if Melanie has thrown a gauntlet down.

"That would be up to Ben, Melanie. It's up to all of you to decide what to share with the group."

"Yeah, but you always push us. The other day Isabel didn't want to talk about herself and you made her. And you've done that with me before, too."

"You're right, Melanie, but keep in mind—I am a professional. I am trained to know when to push someone and when to let them be. It is entirely up to Ben to share what brought him here. Ben? Do you have anything you'd like to say?"

Ben looks surprised and pleased to find himself the subject of debate. "Um. Well, I don't have a problem talking about it, Larry. If Melanie wants to know that's fine with me." He straightens his thick, square glasses and shifts in his seat.

Melanie, too, looks a little surprised that it has been this easy to get Ben to talk.

"I guess it started with the arrest. You may have heard about it…I'm the guy who got arrested because they said I was making terrorist threats to blow up my school." Ben says this with veiled pride.

"Why were you making threats to blow up your school?" Larry ventures, knowing the answer.

"*I wasn't making threats to my school!*" Ben yells. So quickly has he gone from childlike enthusiasm over a breakfast item to adult rage over life's inequities that everyone in the room looks startled. Larry does not check his volume. He calmly looks at Ben.

"Sorry, Larry. I wasn't making threats to my school," Ben repeats, "I was making threats to my *teacher*." No one looks relieved at the clarification.

"Mr. Rickson. He was my ninth-grade teacher. He turned

the letters in to the police. He's the one that smeared my name and told them I was a terrorist. I just, like, wrote to him. I wrote him a few times."

"How many times did you write to him, Ben?" Again, Larry seems to know the answer to his question.

"I don't know. A lot of times, I guess. Maybe twenty. Thirty, maybe. I don't know. But the point is—"

"And *why* did you write to him, Ben?"

"Why? Why did I write to him, Larry?"

"Yes." Larry is stroking his beard.

"I wrote to him because he humiliated me. He humiliated me in front of the whole class. He said I was stupid, Larry. You shouldn't do that to a kid, you know? He said I was an idiot. He called me 'idiot' when he called on me in class. He made me stand in front of the room and repeat after him 'I am an idiot' in front of the whole class." Ben cannot look Larry in the eye.

"So when you wrote to him, did you tell him that? That he shouldn't have humiliated you?"

"Yeah. I told him that. I told him how mad it made me. I told him how it made me want to kill him or something. I don't know. I said a lot of things in those letters. I know it wasn't good to send them." Ben adds this last sentence half-heartedly, parroting back what he has, perhaps, learned at Three Breezes.

"What happened then? You sent the letters and what happened?"

"I sent the letters. I wrote him at least once a day. I guess he saved them. He let them build up or something, I don't know. The next thing I knew he wrote me back denying that he had humiliated me! He had his lawyer write me saying he had no knowledge of the incidents I was describing and that I better stop writing."

"And?"

"Well, I guess I went a little berserk, Larry," Ben sheepishly admits.

"What did you do?"

"I, um…" Ben looks miserable. His medication has kicked in enough for him to discern between right and wrong and he knows that his behavior had been seriously dangerous. "I, ah…"

"It's okay, Ben. It's safe here," Larry says softly.

"I got all my camouflage on and went to his classroom. I went to my school and went to his classroom."

"Now, this wasn't when you were currently in school, right?"

"No! I told you, Larry! He was my *ninth-grade teacher!* Sorry. Sorry, Larry. No. He had been my teacher eight years ago."

"So then what happened?" Larry looks as if he has not heard this part of the story before.

"I had an old—*used*—grenade and I held it out like I was going to throw it on him. At him. Like I was going to throw it *at* him. I wasn't, though! I mean, it was *used.* Anyone with a brain could've seen that! Who's stupid now, Mr. Rickson? Huh? Who's the idiot now? That's what I said to him. You should've seen him…" Ben smiles with the memory.

"You should've seen that son of a bitch when I walked in. He practically jumped under his desk. I guess I surprised him, too, because I wasn't this size when I was in his class. I've grown since then," Ben says proudly. "Anyway, he was so fucking scared. Oh. Sorry. Sorry for cursing, Larry. He was shaking like a little baby. 'Who's stupid, Mr. Rickson? Huh?

Who's stupid?' I asked him and he just stood there. Practically peed in his pants."

"Did Mr. Rickson call the police then, Ben?"

"No. I don't know who did, actually. After I scared the shit out of Mr. Rickson I went down the hall to the principal's office. I had all my clips on so I looked fuckin' amazing. Oh. Sorry. Sorry for swearing again, Larry. I had all my ammo clips on so I think they were a little nervous there. I think that's why they might've called the police. I wasn't gonna do anything, though. I just wanted them to see that they couldn't push me around anymore. I just wanted them to know that I'm not stupid. I wanted them to know that you shouldn't do that to a little kid. You shouldn't tell a little kid that he's an idiot, Larry. You shouldn't do that."

Larry walks over to Ben's chair and gently places his hand on Ben's slumped shoulder. "No, Ben. You're right. You shouldn't do that. You're not stupid, Ben. You have a mental illness called schizophrenia. You realize that now, don't you?"

"Yeah. Yes, Larry. I know. I'm schizophrenic," he tells the group. "And Wellbutrin! Wellbutrin has saved my life, Larry. You know that? I just felt like saying that. It's amazing this drug…"

"Ben, I'm proud of you." Larry speaks quickly to block Ben from rambling on about his medication, as he is known to do. "This is the most you've talked about the letters in some time. I think we've done some real work here."

Isabel is amazed that Ben, the disgusting yet strangely compelling giant, is the boy she'd remembered reading about.

"Larry, can I just say one more thing?" Ben asks innocently.

"Sure, Ben." Larry looks as curious as the rest of the group—minus Sukanya.

"It's just that…" Ben looks lost for a moment. "It's just

that…well…if it weren't for Wellbutrin I think I'd be dead. I know I'd be dead. I'd be dead, Larry."

Melanie groans out loud and then smiles as she reaches for her bottled water.

"I know, Ben," Larry sighs. "I know."

Just then the door to the living room bursts open and Connie the night nurse appears.

"Larry? Sorry for interrupting but we need your help on something." She gives him an urgent look that says it cannot wait.

"Get *away* from me!" The high-pitched scream can be heard in the living room now that the double doors are open. Larry has ended the session abruptly and disappears around the corner into the unit bedroom area.

"Leave me *alone!*"

Isabel does not think twice about disobeying orders to remain in the living room. She wants to go back to her room. At the edge of the doorway she hears a familiar voice.

"Larry? Larry, please tell them to leave me alone. Please?"

Isabel looks around the corner and sees Connie standing in Lark's doorway with an orderly. The orderly is Nick, Connie's burly son, who is trying to earn money for school by working at Three Breezes during his summer break. He hardly speaks to the patients—as if their insanity is contagious. Isabel is uncomfortable around him—his collegiate air seems incongruous to this place. She senses he is filing away stories about all of them to be retold over beers at the frat house.

"Lark!" Larry shouts.

Connie suddenly turns and runs down the hall in Isabel's direction toward the nurses' station. She looks right through Isabel.

When Isabel turns back to the scene down the hallway, Nick is gone.

"Isabel, please go back into the living room," Connie calls out over her shoulder as she heads back into Lark's room with the "tool kit," a case the nurses always reach for in emergencies. Isabel does not budge. Connie has already disappeared into Lark's room.

Two men run past Isabel from behind, startling her. On their way down the hall she hears a couple of unintelligible bursts of static-heavy commands coming from the radios fixed to their belts.

This doesn't look good.

After a few moments Nick and his mother back out of the room and make way for the rest of the group. Larry emerges, his eyes, sad and preoccupied, focused on the floor as he walks down the hall toward Isabel. His forearm is wrapped in gauze.

Then Lark, an orderly on either side of her bandaged body, is carried out. Isabel watches as the threesome, with its white centerpiece slumping, head toward her. She knows she will have to move to make way for them but she is frozen. She is hypnotized by the jacket.

As the three pass, Isabel feels Lark staring at her but she cannot look. She goes back into the living room as Lark is shut into the padded room. *The soft room.*

"What is it? What's going on out there?" Melanie looks panicked.

"Huh?"

"Earth to Isabel." It is Ben. Smiling Ben. Psychotic Ben.

Isabel looks at everyone as if for the first time.

"Isabel? Melanie's talking to you!"

"Oh, sorry." Isabel is searching for words. "I didn't see anything," she lies.

"Nothing? You must've seen *something*. It had to have been Lark. She was the only one not here for group. Unless it was the new person in Keisha's room."

"I told you, I didn't see anything."

With everyone still gathered at the double doors, carefully following Larry's directive, Isabel moves to the far side of the room and sits in the chair next to Sukanya. The two stare straight ahead into space.

We look like a sick version of that painting with the husband and wife farmers. What was the name of that, anyway? They had a pitchfork. American Gothic! *That's it.*

Slowly and quietly Isabel slips a little closer to the depression always waiting for her just around the corner.

What's wrong with me? What's wrong with me?

Thirty-Four

"What's old is new again at this year's Grammys. On the list of nominees—the Beatles and Eric Clapton. The Rolling Stones are also up for an award. But littered among these familiar names are new ones, and the combination will no doubt make tonight a night to remember."

Isabel Murphy, ANN News, New York.

"When's our first live shot?" Isabel asked Tom. "Do I have time to run to the bathroom?"

"Affirmative," he said, looking at his watch. "T-minus ten minutes and counting."

"Okay. Smoke 'em if you got 'em, soldier. I'll be right back."

"Ten-four."

Isabel went in search of the rest rooms, swimming upstream against the crush of music fans and studio executives hurrying to take their seats before the show began.

"Excuse me. Excuse me," she said, trying to stay polite.

A guard pointed a few feet ahead and Isabel rushed into a stall, conscious of the time.

After washing and drying her hands she headed out of the bathroom while adjusting her dress and walked directly into the back of a man blocking the bathroom exit.

"Oh! Sorry, but can I get through?" she said as the air returned to her lungs. Her mouth dropped open when he turned around.

"Well, hello there!" Alex was theatrically cheerful. "Fancy meeting *you* here."

"Alex!" Isabel looked beyond him toward the camera stand and Tom, but she couldn't see over the bobbing sea of heads. "What're you doing here?"

He followed her glance and turned back to her, his mouth twisted up into a Grinch grin. "I don't want to keep you," he said. "You're in a hurry. We can walk back if you want."

"No," Isabel said a little too quickly, wanting to avoid a scene between Tom and Alex. "How'd you end up here?"

"I have friends, musician friends, who got me a ticket. I thought you might be here." The grin grew.

"What're you...following me?" But Isabel didn't need to ask. She knew he was.

"Naw," Alex replied.

"I have to go now, Alex. Just leave me alone, okay?"

He didn't move or break his stare.

"Did you hear me?" She was almost pleading. "Will you stop following me? You're freaking me out, Alex."

Without saying a word, he stepped aside and ushered her past with a mock chivalrous sweep of his capeless arm.

"There you are!" Tom looked relieved. "They want you early. Get plugged in and talk to the producer."

Isabel passed the clip-on mike up under her dress to her collar and fastened it. She put her earpiece in and turned up the volume. "Hello? Check, check, check. This is Isabel Murphy. Mike check one, two, three."

"Hi, Isabel?" the nervous producer came into her ear. "It's Paula. Can we come to you in about two minutes? I know it's way early but we're crashing here and we need to fill."

"That's fine," Isabel said. "Two minutes it is."

"You're a gem. Thanks so much."

Jesus, what am I going to talk about?

She looked back over her shoulder, scanning the crowd for Alex. Her heart was pounding like a drum against her rib cage. She felt its pulse vibrate in her ears. She knew he was nearby. The prickly feeling on the back of her neck hadn't gone away yet.

Where is he?

Down below the skybox where the reporters were stationed, Isabel saw the legendary rocker on a huge screen set up above the stage, accepting his Grammy.

"One minute, Isabel," the voice in her ear announced.

She quickly leafed through the Grammy program but the words were blurring.

"Thirty seconds."

Calm down. Calm down.

Isabel turned to search the crowd once more for Alex and froze. He was leaning up against the wall, only a few feet away from her. Her eye static mushroomed and she squinted through her anxiety to find the iris on the camera. Her temples were throbbing.

Focus.

She listened to the excited anchor in her ear. "Now we go

live to Isabel Murphy at New York's Madison Square Garden. Isabel? We hear there are some surprises tonight!"

Surprises?

"Ah, yes…" She looked frantically past the camera to Tom, who had come out from behind the viewfinder to search her face with a worried look.

He's mouthing something. What's he mouthing?

"Sorry, Tom," she managed. *Wrong name. Wrong name!* "As you can imagine, it's hard to hear with all this wonderful music in the background. It's pretty loud here."

Tom ducked back behind the camera.

I can do this.

"That's okay, Isabel." The anchor sounded every bit as nervous as Tom looked. "Tell us, what's surprised you so far tonight?"

Alex.

No. Don't think about that. Focus. Grammys.

"Keith Richards." She pushed the name out of her mouth. Tom peered around his camera again.

Dammit, doesn't he know I'm trying to concentrate here? What is he mouthing?

"He *was* slated to perform," she continued as if in a dream, "but for some reason he was a no-show and had to accept his Grammy via satellite…."

Tom left his camera on his tripod and moved toward Isabel.

It's awfully hot in here.

"I think that surprised me the most. Everyone here was talking about how this was to be his first live solo performance ever."

Why is Tom yelling at me?

Maybe I should wrap it up.

The voice in her ear was saying something but she couldn't make out the words above the din of white noise in her brain.

"That's all for now," she squeaked, feeling the sweat trickling down her chest. "Back to you, Tom."

The last thing Isabel remembered before she collapsed was the light on the camera switching off.

Thirty-Five

What is wrong with me? I can't figure out how to wake up out of this stupor.

"Is there something about Lark that touches you?" Dr. Seidler asks. "Can you tell me what you thought when you saw Lark being led away?"

Numb. I felt numb. There's nothing we can do to save ourselves....

But Isabel cannot form her thoughts into words.

"Have you thought about Lark much since that day last week?"

Oh, Doctor, I see you making this big effort to save me...don't bother. Leave me alone. That's all Lark wanted...to be left alone. That's all I want, too.

"Isabel, we need to talk about ECT."

That's right. Try to shock my brain into functioning normally. Try to jolt my body back into reality. That's the solution, isn't it? You want to scramble my brain so it doesn't get sad anymore, so that I can function like a "normal" person. So that this mind-numbing life I live can be tolerated. It won't work...I already know the answer

*to the riddle: life is meaningless. Nothing has any value whatsoever.
Once you know that you can never go back.*

"I think it would do you a world of good. I really do—otherwise I wouldn't suggest it. But I would like to know, I'm going to try to find out, one last time, what you think about it. Can you tell me what you're thinking?"

I am blank.

"That's it, then," her doctor says decisively, watching Isabel closely for her reaction. "I have made an appointment for ECT for you tomorrow morning." She scribbles a note to herself. Isabel feels like she is watching her catatonic self from the ceiling of the small office. Watching Dr. Seidler make the next move on the chessboard.

ThatsitthenIhavemadeanappointmentforECTforyoutomorrowmorning.ThatsitthenIhavemadeanappointmentforECTforyoutomorrowmorning….

"So I want you to get a good night's sleep tonight and I'll see you when you wake up. Don't eat breakfast. We'll go over there *(Over there…over there…send the word…send the word…over there…the Yanks are coming…)* together in the morning."

Isabel goes back to her room.

"Isabel?" The singsong voice of Julie the day nurse. Isabel notes that on the metal clip of Julie's clipboard she has written her name in large block letters with dots on the ends as if she were in college.

She still uses rollers and sets her hair.

"Isabel? Did you forget? We have group exercise now! We're going to the pool, so go jump into your bathing suit! The rest of the group is waiting!" Everything Julie says is punctuated with exclamation points.

They'll be waiting until hell freezes over if they're waiting for me.

"Isabel, you must not have heard me, sweetie…."

You're so chirpy I want to rip your face off.

"No," Isabel says to Julie just before closing the door to her room in Julie's face.

It suddenly occurs to Isabel that Julie bears a scary resemblance to Joanie from *Happy Days.*

It is a leaky-faucet night: the minutes drip by at an excruciatingly slow rate. Isabel lies in bed, nearly paralyzed with fear.

How did this happen to me? How did I end up here? God...I know I haven't gone to church in years and I take your name in vain and sometimes I even doubt your existence so I have no right to ask you anything...but please, please—if you can hear me—please help me. Please keep me from having electroshock. I'll do anything. I really will. I'll talk in my therapy sessions. I'll cooperate with all the doctors here. I'll work on myself—anything. Just please don't make me have electroshock.

Isabel turns onto her stomach to try to fall asleep, but she is kept awake by the sound of her own breathing echoing through the mattress coils.

"Isabel?" A knock on the door. "Isabel? It's Dr. Seidler."

Oh, God. Oh, God, no.

Isabel feels nauseous with exhaustion and the sick realization that her therapist is there to accompany her to electroshock.

"Good morning," Dr. Seidler says, trying not to sound too somber. "I'll wait outside for you to get dressed and then we can get going."

What should I wear? What did Francis Farmer wear?

Like a zombie, Isabel pulls on a pair of shorts and a T-shirt, slips on her JP Todd mules and looks in the mirror.

Jesus Christ.

She opens the door and tentatively steps out into the hallway.

"You ready?" her therapist asks, and without waiting for an answer, starts walking.

"I can imagine you're a bit frightened, Isabel," Dr. Seidler says as they turn onto the path that leads to the medical treatment facility. "I wouldn't blame you, we're always scared of the unknown. But let me just tell you that before we do anything we'll explain how it works and what you should expect so you won't be surprised by anything. In fact, the only surprise will likely be how easy it is."

Easy for you to say.

Isabel stares down at the path as they walk along. Her empty stomach is churning with bile.

"The technician and the doctor overseeing the treatment will be there to answer any and all of your questions."

"What about *you?*" Isabel panics. "Aren't *you* going to be there?"

"I will for the initial meeting, but once you go into the treatment room I'll have to leave."

"Why?" Isabel's voice is urgent.

"You'll be in good hands" is all she says. "Don't worry, Isabel. You won't even notice I'm not there."

They walk along in silence, following the pathway that cuts across the grounds. Dr. Seidler walks at a brisk pace but slows from time to time to allow Isabel, slumped and sluggish with dread, to catch up. The building they are headed toward looks more like a conventional hospital than any other structure at Three Breezes.

As they pass the cafeteria, the door opens and out file small children. There, taking up the rear as always, is little Peter. As they pass each other he looks Isabel straight in the eye for the first time. For that brief moment Isabel feels a tremendous sense of peace.

Don't let this be you, Peter. Don't ever let yourself get to this point.

But Peter is already studying the pavement, searching for the anthills he is so desperate to avoid.

The Medical Treatment Facility is a structure remarkable only in that it has not one piece of ornamentation, not one redeeming decorative architectural element. To Isabel it is a whole other world: nurses she does not recognize clutter the hallways, visitors stand around killing time, the smell of a distant cafeteria permeates every corridor. Having been cloistered in her tiny unit for more than three weeks, Isabel finds it surreal. She quickens her pace to keep up with Dr. Seidler.

"It's just up ahead," says Dr. Seidler, noting Isabel's worried face.

"So many people…" Isabel says, her eyes wide, taking it all in.

"I know." Dr. Seidler sounds apologetic. "I've been telling them for some time now that we need a more private place for some of our treatments.

"Here we are," she says as she holds the door open for Isabel.

The psychiatric wing is much quieter. They turn into a nondescript waiting room and Dr. Seidler motions for Isabel to take a seat. "I'll be right back," she says as she goes through an unmarked door at the far side of the room.

"Where are you going?" Isabel's heart is beating so fast she feels it in her throat.

"I'm just going to let them know we're here. Don't worry. I'll be right back."

Isabel's breathing becomes shallow.

Oh, God. Oh, God.

She scans the room to find something on which to focus her attention but finds nothing. The blank walls are littered with nail holes where pictures once hung. Isabel squints to make out the discolored squares surrounding the marks.

Why'd they take down the pictures? What's so bad about pictures?

"Isabel?" Dr. Seidler is standing in the open door, motioning her to pass through it.

I am Alice in Wonderland...I will pass through this door in the looking glass and I'll become smaller...smaller...smaller...

Isabel has slumped so far down in her chair that her shirt rides up her back. She stands up and pulls it back down. Wordlessly she crosses the empty room, her breaths still short and shallow.

"Hello, Isabel."

This guy looks like that Ghostbusters *actor. What's that guy's name?*

"I'm Dr. Edwards and I'll be treating you today. Why don't you come on into the treatment room so that I can show you exactly what's going to happen."

Not Bill Murray. Not Dan Ackroyd...the other guy.

Isabel follows the two doctors into the treatment room. The smell of ammonia is overpowering.

Harold Ramis! That's who he looks like. Harold Ramis.

Dr. Edwards gets right to the point. "The machine you're looking at is what we use to gauge the intensity of electricity used to treat our patients. I know it looks like a dinosaur but it's state of the art." The doctor is proudly standing alongside his silent, mechanical partner in crime.

State of the art when? In 1960?

"It's quite simple, really. We'll ask you to lie down on this table and we'll attach two electrodes to your temples. Then we will set this needle and flip this switch and the current will be administered. It's very brief. The whole thing lasts a matter of seconds. You might feel a bit of a jolt but it's not painful. In the old days, patients had rubber mallets in their mouths to protect them from biting off their tongues. Now we need nothing of the sort."

"Isabel?" Dr. Seidler is facing her. Isabel feels like she is snorkeling, the muffled words come at her in slow motion.

She turns to face her therapist and watches Seidler's mouth as it moves, imagining tiny air bubbles floating from it with each word.

"See? I told you it'd be quick," Seidler is mouthing, not so surreptitiously checking her watch while reaching out to touch Isabel's forearm in reassurance.

"And maybe feel a bit tired..." Isabel turns to watch Dr. Edwards's mouth move. She nods at everything they are saying. She watches as they talk at her and then to each other.

Smile. Let them see you're a picture of grace under pressure...smile! Hello, I'm Isabel Murphy, ANN News. Reporting live...

Isabel's attempts at twisting her mouth into the shape of something upbeat fail and her smile is more of a miserable smirk. Dr. Seidler looks sad.

Isabel telepathically messages her doctor.

Take me with you.

Failure. Dr. Seidler is gone.

"Okay, Isabel, we'll have you lie down right here," an overweight nurse pats the hospital bed as though it is made of feathers and sitting by a fireplace at a bed-and-breakfast.

"Are you cold? Do you want a blanket?"

Maybe some hot chocolate while I warm myself here by the fire.

Isabel cannot speak. She watches the kind nurse open a cabinet and pull out a light hospital blanket to drape over Isabel's bare legs.

"Now. This jelly might be cold. I'm just going to dab a spot of it on each side of your forehead. There. This will help the electrodes stay in place. They're suction cups so they need a bit of moisture. Now they're in place and we're all set to go." Her touch is soft.

Wait! This is happening too fast! Hello? Can anyone hear me? Wait.

It is as if the entire scene is part of a dream sequence in a movie and someone has hit the fast-forward button on the VCR after watching in slow motion for a while.

I'm not ready for this. Wait…please wait.

"Okay, Isabel," Dr. Edwards is hovering over her head, checking the nurse's work. "Looks like we're good to go."

"Good to go." Harold Ramis with a military background. Good to go. Goodtogogoodtogogoodtogogoodtogogoodtogo.

Thirty-Six

"Okay, so we'll run first then we'll get bagels on Chestnut Street," Alex offered. "Just come running with me. Please?"

The sand is so soft it feels like running in molasses. The waves are too big to run along the water's edge without getting soaked. In the distance, the Golden Gate Bridge seems to remain untouchable no matter how hard they run toward it. The wind is at their backs gently nudging them along.

"Isabel, come on! Try to catch me!" Alex is smiling, calling out over his shoulder, his jog turning into a sprint. "We'll finish sooner! Think bagels! Come on, Isabel!" His words are carried to her by the wind.

I can't keep up, Alex. Wait up.

"Isabel?"

Alex!

"Isabel?"

Where am I?

Isabel squints up at the ceiling.

San Francisco? Did we already get the bagels?

"Isabel? Isabel, are you awake?"

Oh.

Above her Dr. Seidler is smiling, her head distorted. Her lips seem huge to Isabel.

"That must've been some dream!"

It was just a dream.

"Um, yeah. Where am I?" Isabel feels completely disoriented.

"Three Breezes, Isabel. You're in Three Breezes Hospital. Do you know who I am?"

It feels like Alex is in this room. Where did he go?

"What?"

"It's Dr. Seidler," Isabel's therapist answers. "It's time to meet, Isabel. Do you feel up to it? You still seem pretty groggy. Would you rather rest some more?"

"I'm okay, I guess. Can I just throw on some sweatpants, though?" Isabel tries to move her arm and feels sore, as if she has just finished a kick-boxing class.

"Of course. My office, five minutes." Dr. Seidler leaves Isabel to get dressed.

God, I miss him. I miss him so much it hurts.

Isabel pushes her aching body up and leans back against the edge of the bed and cries so hard the bed shakes, knocking the headboard against the wall.

Alex. I don't know why...but I miss you.

"Are you feeling okay?" Dr. Seidler is scrutinizing Isabel and scribbles something on her notepad while Isabel slowly eases into the chair facing her therapist.

"It feels like I've been asleep for days," Isabel tentatively answers.

"You've been sleeping for the past sixteen hours or so. That's completely normal," Dr. Seidler explains. "You may feel tired for the next few mornings. After electroshock therapy a lot of patients feel groggy. It helps if you just succumb to it and sleep as much as you can. Think of it as your brain repairing itself."

"I actually feel pretty well rested."

"Isabel, let me ask you a question. Just now when I woke you up—do you remember what you were dreaming about?"

"Alex. I was dreaming about Alex." The dream was so lifelike that Isabel felt as if she'd just come from running on Chrissy Field along San Francisco's marina. "It was really bright, very sunny. And we were doing the run we did every weekend. We used to drive to the marina and park and run on the beach out to the Golden Gate Bridge. Usually the wind was coming toward us so the run out to the bridge was hard. But in this dream, I remember, it was coming from behind. It was kind of pushing me. Anyway, that was my dream. Pretty boring, when you think about it."

"Not at all. Not to me. Can you think of what the dream may mean?"

Isabel studies her hands in her lap. They look shriveled and foreign to her. Then she remembers the question.

"I don't know. I think I was just dreaming about the past. A good memory of Alex. Of the Alex who was kind, not abusive. When he was happy I always felt elated...like nothing could touch us. That's why it felt like a good dream. What do *you* think it means?"

"You said the wind was pushing you along. The wind is a primal force. Something we cannot control. And in the dream it was *pushing* you. And you noted that that was exactly opposite to what really happened when you went running along the beach. In reality, the wind pattern was opposite of what you dreamed. Do you think that maybe Alex was opposite of what he seemed at first? Certainly, from what you've told me, he was a force that was at times out of control."

"Yes!"

"And yet *control* is at the core of what your issues tend to be about. Alex was too controlling of you, certainly. But in the beginning, maybe you were comforted by his control of situations, since your father so lacked it—probably because of his drinking. It seems to mean something. I didn't mention this to you when I first asked because I didn't want it to color what you remembered, but typically, immediately following electroshock therapy, patients report dreaming about the incidents or people that have affected them the deepest. I find it interesting that, out of everything you've experienced, your subconscious chose Alex. What do you make of that?"

"I don't know." Isabel still feels dreamy and soft from sleep. "I just know that it was nice to remember something good about Alex since he's so scary these days."

Thirty-Seven

"Hurricane Charlie ripped through this tiny town of 877 and obliterated it. In less than an hour it was wiped off the map. But authorities are calling this a success story. Why? Because there were no casualties. None. Look around you and all you'll find is debris. Where houses once stood, there are piles of brick, stone and rotting wood. Where there were once businesses, broken glass and concrete are twisted together with metal. But folks here are happy today. The early-warning system they installed a year ago saved the town's entire population."

Isabel Murphy, ANN News, Puerto Rico.

"Tom, I'm going to go call John and check in," Isabel called over to the photographer while hunting through her purse for her cell phone. "But you know what we need—a wide shot of the main street, closeups of those people over there walking on that debris pile, blah, blah, blah."

"Roger that." Tom was distracted, searching for a blank tape in his gear bag. "We'll have liftoff in T-minus five minutes."

"You're mixing metaphors."

"Copy that. But right now I have to locate a Texas Arthur Peter Elvis. Aha! Have located said target and will now execute your orders, Sergeant."

"Whatever."

Tom straightened back up, tape in hand, eyes locked on something—someone—in the distance. "Incoming." His voice softened so only Isabel could hear him.

Isabel looked up and then followed his line of sight.

"Oh, my God."

Tom stepped in front of her.

"Were you expecting company?" he asked over his shoulder, still locked on his target.

"No." Isabel could not believe who she saw through the tangled mess of a tropical town.

"I've got it covered."

"Tom, it's okay." Isabel halfheartedly tried to shake her fear off and rein in her friend.

"No way, man. No way."

"Well, well, well," Alex said through his Cheshire cat grin, his whitened teeth fluorescent against his tan. "Look who we have here." He sauntered up to them.

"What're you doing here, man?" Tom asked in a belligerent tone.

Alex ignored him, although it must've been hard since Tom was twice his size and blocking his path to Isabel.

"Isabel, could you call off your guard dog?"

"What *are* you doing here, Alex?" she asked, emboldened by Tom's protectiveness.

Alex gave Tom an I-could-take-you-if-I-felt-like-it look, even though he would most certainly have lost in a fight with Isabel's burly photographer. He smiled smugly at them both.

"Can't a man take a little *vacaciones,* as they say here? Great place, Puerto Rico. And, last I checked, a free country."

"You expect me to believe you came here on *vacation.* In the middle of hurricane season. Coincidentally when I'm here working?" Isabel asked. "Who told you I was here?"

"Lots of questions from *la muchacha,*" Alex said.

"Don't be a dick." Tom was impatient. "Get lost, man. She doesn't want to talk to you."

"That true, my darling?"

Isabel winced at the mock term of endearment. "I have to work, Alex."

"My *wife* and I would like a moment to ourselves." Alex adjusted his spine to try for a taller appearance as he spoke to Tom.

"I don't take orders from you, asshole," Tom replied.

"I'll just be a minute, Tommy." Isabel gently touched his back as if to calm him down. "I'm okay."

"I'll be over here." Tom indicated a shady spot about two yards away. "Right here."

When Tom was just out of earshot Isabel turned her attention back to her estranged husband. "What are you doing here?"

"I told you, I'm on vacation."

"Don't give me that, Alex. I know you followed me here. Why?"

He reached out and she flinched. "Easy. Easy. I'm just getting this hair out of your eyes."

Out of the corner of her eye Isabel could see Tom was watching them intently.

"Look, I've got to go." Isabel took a step toward Tom.

"Okay, okay, we'll play it your way. But I must say you've

completely lost your sense of humor." He took a deep breath. "I thought we could talk. Just the two of us."

"Alex," Isabel groaned. "We've been over this a million times. It's over. Let's just move on, okay? Have a little distance?"

"It's not over," he said calmly, the smile instantly vanishing from his face. "Not by a long shot."

"What's that supposed to mean?"

"Exactly what it sounds like. We are not over. This—" he motioned at an invisible string tying them together "—is not over."

"Isabel, we gotta ship out," Tom called to her.

"You better go now." Alex's smile clicked back on. "You wouldn't want to keep your bodyguard waiting."

He didn't wait for Isabel to respond. He walked backward so that he could face her. "Adios."

Isabel felt the hairs on the back of her neck prickle.

Thirty-Eight

"Two o'clock, everyone! Medication time!" Julie consults her clipboard and calls the first name.

"Melanie?"

"Here I am," she calls out cheerfully.

"Okay, Melanie. You know the drill. You're aware of what you're taking, right?" The nurse asks perfunctorily—like a flight attendant mechanically reciting the passenger safety instructions, knowing no one is paying attention. Three Breezes prided itself on its medication regimen.

"I know, I know," Melanie says before tossing the pills into her mouth as if she is gulping down a shot of alcohol.

"Crystal Light or Hawaiian Punch?"

"Hawaiian Punch, please." Melanie's mouth is full of pills so it sounds more like "H'wine Pun, peaz."

She thinks she's so cute, that's what kills me. She thinks everyone thinks she's adorable. News flash, Mel: You ain't all that.

Julie hands her a small Dixie cup, watches carefully as Melanie gulps that down, checks another box on her clipboard and calls the next name.

"Sukanya?"

Sukanya shuffles forward.

"How are you today, Sukanya?" Julie asks as she hands over the tiny cup of pills.

"Are you aware of the medication you're taking?"

Sukanya blinks and the nurse continues.

"Crystal Light or Hawaiian Punch?"

Sukanya casts a glazed glance at the pitcher containing the unnaturally red beverage.

"Here you go."

Sukanya takes the Dixie cup in one hand and the pill cup in the other and starts to turn away. Julie grabs her arm. "Sukanya," she sings in a mock-friendly tone, "you know better than that. You need to swallow the pills here, where I can see you."

Sukanya stares at the fingers wrapped around her forearm until Julie releases her grip. Then she slowly places the pills on her tongue and swallows them down with the punch.

Can we move this thing along?

"Good job. Okay, let's see, who's next? Isabel?"

Isabel moves forward. Like a model patient, she takes her pills in front of Julie and moves away from the doorway of the tiny pill closet. After ECT, this is nothing to her.

"Kristen? You're on deck!" Julie is back to her clipboard, checking away. She does not know that when Kristen pops her medication into her mouth the pills nestle under her tongue. After Kristen turns away from the medication checkpoint, she spits out her medicine.

Isabel has taken only two steps into the group therapy room. There, facing the double doors, is Lark, neatly tucked into the wing chair, enveloped by the jacket.

We have to look at that damn jacket for the entire session?

"Let's start off this group session by checking in with everyone," Larry announces. "Let's go around the room and each of you can let the rest of the group know how you're feeling or what you'd like to work on or, well, I'll leave it to you. Whatever each of you would like to say. Isabel? Let's start with you. How are you today?"

Isabel breaks her stare at the jacket and tries to focus on Larry. Thirty seconds later she looks back at Lark, who appears to be fighting to keep her eyelids open.

"Isabel?"

"Yes?" *Focus.*

"I asked how you were doing?"

Focus.

"I'm not doing too well, if you must know. I hate this fucking place. I don't want to be here. I think this is all a bunch of shit…sitting here, talking about 'what's going on with us,'" she says, mimicking Larry's slow intonations. "I'm sick of it. Sick of it all. I want to get out of here."

"Hmm."

"And furthermore, Lark's sitting in here in that *thing* and it's a little hard to concentrate." She stops and looks back at Lark.

"And?"

"And nothing." She pauses. "Actually…I thought this place trumpeted the fact that all patients are in charge of their own treatment regimens, or however you put it," she challenges Larry.

"Meaning what, exactly?"

"Meaning I have been subjected to a treatment that I didn't necessarily agree to. I thought we were supposed to be able to agree to what kind of treatment we received."

"You're referring, I assume, to ECT," Larry says.

"Yes. I'm referring to ECT."

"What's she talking about, Larry? What's ECT?" It is Ben, who seems slightly agitated.

Great. Just fucking perfect. I'm getting electroshock therapy and Ben the I'm-gonna-blow-up-my-school guy isn't? Great.

"They shock you," Melanie jumps in. "They put a thing in your mouth and they shock you in the head."

"No they don't," Isabel cries defensively. "They don't put anything in your mouth."

Isabel feels her cheeks reddening.

Get those smug looks off your faces: I am not like you, you god-damned nutcases.

"ECT is a very effective form of treatment," Larry intercedes on her behalf. "It's been very successful in the past and I'm sure Isabel's therapist feels it will best suit her needs. Isabel, I hear that you feel upset about this, but I do know that Dr. Seidler has repeatedly tried to talk to you about it."

"Wait a second. Wait just a second. You guys *talked* about me?" Isabel is horrified, picturing a coffee klatch of doctors swapping stories about their pathetic patients. *Five bucks says mine's more screwed up than yours.*

"Now, hold on," Larry says, trying to calm the now un-settled group. "We work in tandem, your therapists and I. I speak constantly with all of your therapists to ensure that we are all up to speed on the issues you're dealing with. It's imperative that we maintain an open dialogue..."

Open dialogue my ass.

"...to better serve your recovery." Larry stops and takes an exaggerated deep breath.

"Let's move on. Lark?"

"Wait! What am I supposed to do?" Isabel is infuriated.

"Seidler told me I'm having ECT again tomorrow—I don't get a choice? That's *not* okay. I am not doing it again."

"Have you told Dr. Seidler that?"

"Yes."

"What did she say?"

Isabel shifts in her seat. "I don't remember," she says sheepishly.

"I think what she might have said was that it is not uncommon for patients to experience anger following their first treatment, but we're confident—" Larry hurries past the word *we're* "—that another session will enable you to achieve the maximum benefits of ECT."

"But...but couldn't there be another way? Couldn't I just promise to work on myself more actively or something? Please? Isn't there any way I can get out of this?"

"Let me talk with Dr. Seidler after this session and see what she has to say."

"Thank you, Larry."

You catch more flies with honey.

Larry takes another exaggerated deep breath to emphasize a subject change.

"Okay. Now. Lark?"

Lark slumps farther down into the tall chair.

"Do you want to tell the group what your situation is, Lark?" Larry asks this while surveying the nervous faces around the room.

"Why don't you do the honors, Larry." Lark slurs her words through the hair that had fallen into her face. She does not try to shake it away, it just hangs there like a veil.

"Lark is in restraints today because we believe she could be a danger to herself and maybe to others," Larry addresses the group.

"And a danger to you, Lar, right?" Lark challenges through her mask.

"Well, if you'd like to talk about that, we can."

Lark's beady eyes dance as she tells the group she bit Larry before being carried away to the soft room. She appears proud.

"Do you think you're a danger to yourself, Lark? Will you sign a contract?"

"What the fuck's a contract?"

"A contract is basically a written agreement between you and your doctors that you will not try to take your life. We write it up in whatever language suits you, but it boils down to a promise that you will not harm yourself for a certain period of time. Feel like signing one? If you do, and if we believe it's in good faith, we'll remove the restraints."

"Fuck you."

"Why are you so angry, Lark?"

"Fuck you, Larry!" Lark has shimmied to the edge of the seat and is struggling to stand up. The jacket ruins her balance and the anger ruins her equilibrium. The combination keeps her tumbling backward into the seat.

"I'm going to have to get an orderly if you cannot control your temper."

"Fuck you, Daddy!"

"Lark?"

"Don't hurt me anymore, Daddy."

Larry stands and quietly moves toward Lark.

"Get away!" Lark spits as she whips her head from side to side until her hair has completely covered her face.

"Lark, what do you want to say to your daddy?"

Lark's breathing becomes forced and shallow, and from behind her hair, she starts to wheeze as she tries to take in air. "Please don't hurt me, Daddy...I can't breathe. Get off. It hurts."

"Do you need your inhaler?"

"Yes," she gasps as Larry reaches for the device tucked beside her in her chair. He holds it up to her mouth and gently calms her down enough to get her to take several inhalations. As Lark's breathing returns to normal, Larry moves away.

"Are you back with us?"

Lark nods, still slumped.

"I want you to know we all support you."

"Yeah, we do," Melanie interrupts. "I know how you feel. I know you hate your dad—I hate my father-in-law. I thought about getting him a gift for Father's Day this year but I blew it off. Screw him. He gets me the cheapest presents for my birthday, so screw him. I love the Sharper Image catalog. That's where I usually got him something but I didn't this year. Besides, I was here. I mean I am here," she laughs, "so I said to Elwin, I said, 'if *your* father—'"

"Melanie? I'm sure Lark appreciates your support. Now, maybe someone else has something to say?"

"Lark?" Kristen practically whispers. "I know we're not close friends or anything, but if you want to talk you can come to my room. I'm not having visitors this weekend so I'll be around." Kristen begins to cry.

"Why are you crying?" Larry moves toward Kristen.

Boy does he have his hands full today.

"I don't know. I don't know."

"Are you sad that you're not having visitors?"

Isabel feels envious. Her parents are visiting for the first time, and while part of her is excited about it, the other part dreads it immensely.

Kristen blows her nose. "It gets so lonely here on the weekends."

"Yeah, and the food's not as good." Ben nods in agreement.

"I hear that," Larry says. "Things are slow on weekends on purpose. We feel time off from group sessions and individual sessions can be useful for patients. Sometimes it can give you time to think, time to write in your journals, time to process everything.

"Getting back to Lark, though. Isabel? It looked like you wanted to say something."

With Kristen sniffling, Melanie seething and Lark bandaged up in restraints, Isabel can think of only one thing to say.

"Hey, Lark, if you want to inhale my secondhand smoke this weekend, I'm all yours."

She hopes that behind the wall of dirty hair Lark is smiling.

"Isabel, Dr. Seidler and I spoke on the phone a few minutes ago and I wanted to talk to you about our conversation."

Isabel's heart is speeding up as she searches Larry's face for clues.

"What'd she say? Do I have to go in again tomorrow? Because I've got to tell you, I'm just going to refuse it. I'll get on the phone with my attorney and I'll sue this place for malpractice if I have to—"

Larry is holding up his hands as if to say "I surrender." "Hold on, hold on. Let's not get ahead of ourselves here. Calm down."

Isabel's stare is unblinking.

"Now. Dr. Seidler told me that you and she talked about this—that electroshock is one of the most effective forms of treatment—"

"Blah, blah, blah," Isabel interrupts. "I don't fucking care how effective it is. I'm not doing it again."

Don't cry. Do not cry.

"What you're experiencing here is a common side effect of the treatment—wait! Before you interrupt me again, let me tell you that many patients experience aggressive irritability following their first treatment. That's precisely why Dr. Seidler is recommending a second round. To curb the irritability and to therefore receive the top benefits of the treatment."

"By irritability you mean belligerence," Isabel shoots back. "You, this place, no one allows any of us to stick up for ourselves. The minute we do it's off to the soft room." Her arms sweep a large arc of frustration in one direction and then another. "Or it's 'Hey, have some more ECT. It'll shock the *irritability* out of you.'"

Suddenly Isabel is overcome with exhaustion. Larry is watching her carefully.

"You know what? I give up," Isabel says as she collapses into a nearby chair. "You and Seidler...you know I don't have the energy to fight...so forget it. I give up."

Larry moves a chair close to hers and sits forward in it. "It's fear you're really feeling, isn't it? Not irritability. Not anger. Fear. Am I right?"

Silence. Isabel looks down at her lap.

"I can imagine you're scared."

"You can imagine? What? You can imagine what it's like to go from having everything to having nothing? To being treated like an infant sometimes and an inmate others? I can't even count how many times I've traveled, alone, mind you, to foreign countries to cover pretty dangerous stories—wars, even. And yet I can barely take two steps out of the unit without someone telling me to sign myself out.

"I've interviewed heads of state, presidents, CEOs, you name it—all of whom treated me with dignity and respect—and now I can't even shave my legs without some lesbian nurse ogling me.

"I've had to become an expert on dozens of subjects, different cultures and a handful of medical breakthroughs, and yet I am not allowed to request that electrodes *not* be taped to my temples. Don't tell me you can *imagine* what I'm feeling, Larry. You have no idea what this feels like."

It is Larry's turn to look at his lap.

"You're right," he says without looking up. "You're absolutely right. I have no idea what it's like to be in your shoes."

Then he looks up, straight into Isabel's frightened eyes.

"But I think, then, that it's safe to say that you, Isabel, have no idea what it's like to be in my shoes."

Isabel tilts her head ever so slightly. *Touché.*

"You probably don't realize how frustrating my job can be. How tough it can be to see patients suffer, to not be able to reach them, help them. And yes, it is equally difficult to see some patients make significant strides—" he gives Isabel a knowing look "—only to sabotage themselves by refusing the very treatment that is helping them."

Silence.

"Just give it one more shot, Isabel. Then, if you don't want to do it anymore you can take it up with Dr. Seidler. One more time."

Thirty-Nine

The knock on the door is loud.

"Time to go, Isabel!" A man's voice. Isabel sits up in bed, alarmed.

"What?" she scrambles out of bed and jumps to the door. "What is it?"

She opens the door a crack and pokes her head out. An orderly is checking his watch.

"I'm here to take you over to the medical facility," he says briskly.

Shit. "Um, I'll be right there." She closes the door and frantically scans the room. The window.

I could fit through it… I could climb out the window and run away. Shit. They'd find me. Plus, where would I go? Goddammit.

Reluctantly, she crosses over to the small chest of drawers and pulls on a pair of shorts, looking at the window as she buttons them up. She takes a deep breath to counterbalance the shallow ones.

One more time. One more time.

"Okay." She closes the door behind her and follows the

orderly down the hall and out of the unit. They walk in silence. Isabel concentrates on synchronizing her steps with the orderly's.

Left. Left. Left, right, left. Left. Left. Left, right, left.

"The jelly's cold, remember," the nurse describes each step of the process. "I just...have...to...fix...the...suction...cups... to...each...side. There! We're all set." The nurse backs away and Dr. Edwards moves in to double-check that everything is in place.

Isabel watches Dr. Edwards fiddle with the dial of the electroshock machine.

Who you gonna call? Ghostbusters!

Forty

"The investigation into the crash of TWA Flight 800 is becoming, as you might imagine, a massive operation. Later today the Coast Guard will be joined by the navy's USS *Grasp*, up from Virginia. The rescue-and-salvage ship will do much of the heavy lifting of the fuselage and it will provide divers, whose top priority will be to hopefully locate the plane's two black boxes. At this point it is highly unlikely there are any survivors."

Isabel Murphy, ANN News, East Moriches, Long Island.

The helicopter blades beat so much sound into the air Isabel had to shout into her cell phone.

"Sorry! Can you say that again?! I can barely hear you!" She yelled, hoping the helicopter would pass before John started to talk again.

"This is…so be sure not to…okay?" Goodman's voice was fading in and out.

Isabel kept moving inland from the beach, trying to get

better cellular service. "John? If you can hear me, I'm going to call you back from inside the car!"

Another news helicopter was coming up the coast.

It had been sixteen hours since Flight 800 went down off the coast of Long Island. As the day wore on, the number of reporters standing awkwardly in the sand, sweating in their blazers and good shoes, increased exponentially.

It had been fourteen hours since a phone call woke Isabel out of a deep sleep.

"Isabel?" The voice was thick with urgency.

"Yes?" Isabel answered, trying to sound awake. It was one-thirty in the morning.

"Ah, Isabel, this is John Goodman from ANN. Sorry to call at this hour."

John Goodman?

Isabel had interviewed with him the week before, just days after moving from San Francisco to New York.

"That's fine. What's up?"

"Isabel, we have a situation here," he began. She could hear a lot of noise in the background. "A 747 has gone down some-where off the coast of Long Island." He sounded exhausted. "It had just taken off from JFK."

Isabel was wide awake by this time and was scrambling for the TV remote control so she could see what the networks were already reporting.

"Oh, my God" was all she could say when she finally switched on CNN and saw an animated graphic showing a plane nosediving into the water.

"Yeah, it's pretty bad," Goodman agreed. "Isabel, we're gonna need you to do some TV for us. I'm not gonna lie. We're up the creek staffwise right now. We've got someone out on Long Island, but we're gonna need someone to relieve her in the morning. I'd love to have the luxury of trying you out before something as big as this but I don't, so I'm calling you to ask you, can you do it? Can you go live for us?"

"Yes." Isabel didn't even pause to think about it.

Fourteen hours later, Isabel knocked on the door of the van the network had rented and shyly asked if she could make a phone call from inside, though the hum of the generator was almost as loud as the helicopters.

"John? It's Isabel. Sorry about that. There's such bad service out here on the beach."

"It's like this—" he wasted no time "—you're live at the top of the next hour. I want you to know that we've been pumping a source at the NTSB and we've got a good lead right now. They won't go on record, but you can get away with sourcing it as someone high up in the investigation. They're saying—you there?"

"Yeah." Isabel licked her dry lips and reminded herself to breathe. "I'm here."

"They're saying it might have been linked to the center fuel tank. Apparently they've had problems with center fuel tanks on 747s but they haven't drawn much attention to it. Got it? You can go with the info, just don't source NTSB."

"Got it."

One hour later Isabel's producer told her she was clear and congratulated her just as Isabel's cell phone rang.

"Mom?" she answered, knowing her parents were the only ones, besides work, who had the number to the cell phone the network had assigned her.

A man's voice chuckled. "Nope. It's not your mommy. But after that live shot I wanna be!"

It was John Goodman again. Isabel tried not to sound disappointed. "Why's that?"

"You were on fire! White-hot! They were only supposed to stay on you for about forty-five seconds and instead they kept you for double that. Wrightman *never* does that—if anything he dumps out sooner than he says. Welcome to the network, Murphy. Consider yourself hired."

Isabel felt the flush of the compliment for a moment, but then went back to the only thing that had been on her mind for the past hour.

"Thanks, John. I appreciate it. Hey, by the way," she said, trying for nonchalance, "you wouldn't happen to know if there's a network affiliate in Trenton, Vermont, would you?"

"Let's see. Hmm. I just got out my affiliate guide and it looks like the folks of Trenton, Vermont, will be getting their news from NBC and ABC. We don't service that market. But who the hell cares about Trenton, Vermont? You got the biggest cities in the country scratching their heads asking 'Who is this Isabel Murphy?' and you want to know if they saw you in *Trenton, Vermont?*"

"Not all of Trenton, really. Just one person."

Isabel's heart felt like it was collapsing.

Goodman was uncharacteristically curious. "Who's in Trenton?"

Isabel watched her foot draw circles in the sand. "My father."

Forty-One

"Good morning!" Dr. Seidler scrutinizes Isabel on her way into the office. "How are you today?"

Isabel knows this is not an empty question that can go without its inevitable reply just as Dr. Seidler is well aware of all that is riding on the electroshocks to which her patient is being subjected. Isabel ends the suspense with a single word.

"Good," she says.

"Really?" Dr. Seidler is relieved. "Tell me more."

"I don't know how and I don't know why, exactly, but I feel good. Right this second I feel pretty normal. I don't want to jinx it, though, so maybe we shouldn't talk about it."

Her therapist nods.

"Of course, now, you know why I'm asking you this, but I wonder what you were dreaming of last night?" Dr. Seidler asks. "Do you remember?"

Not only does Isabel remember, her dreams were so vivid, so real, that she is sure that is part of the reason she feels better.

"Work stuff, mostly," Isabel answers. "I dreamed about stories I've covered and a couple of different places I've been. It's weird, though. I thought dreams were supposed to be kaleidoscopic, maybe based on things from real life but then distorted in sleep."

"Sometimes. Were yours fairly reality-based?"

"Yes!" Isabel is glad her doctor isn't surprised by this observation. "Is that normal? These dreams I had last night, after ECT, were exactly as they were in real life."

"That's to be expected. Electroshock therapy is meant to treat people who have retreated, for lack of a better word, too far into themselves. That can take on many different characteristics. In some it might be a retreat due to severe depression, in others it could be paranoia or paranoid schizophrenia, although that takes treatment to an entirely different level on the whole. Dreams immediately following the administration of ECT are attempts by the brain to begin functioning in reality again. Think of it as your brain reminding you who you are and where you've been. That's why you're having these dreams. Or, I should say, that's probably why your dreams so mimic reality."

"So here's the big question. Do I have to keep getting ECT?"

Isabel braces herself for the reply.

Forty-Two

Calm

Calm down. Calm down.

Isabel repeats the mantra in the shower. *Calm down.*

Back in her room she towel-dries her hair and sifts through her clothes for something that does not smell, something that will cover her unshaven legs.

Hi, Mom. Hi, Dad. Guess what? I'm undergoing electroshock therapy! Aren't you proud of your baby girl?

Isabel stands in front of her metal mirror. Glass mirrors are not provided at Three Breezes. Waves of acid gnaw at her stomach lining.

Work's tough these days, Dad? Aw. Poor thing. Sometimes? When the nurse applies the suction cups to the sides of my forehead? They don't quite stick and she has to apply more cold jelly. I hate it when that happens, don't you?

Nearly two hours before her parents are supposed to arrive, Isabel has already washed and dried her hair and cleaned her neat room.

I've got good news and bad news. The good news is the doctors think my treatment is working beautifully. The bad news is the treat-

ment is…drum roll, please…electroshock therapy. How 'bout them apples?

"Isabel?" Someone is knocking on her door.

"Come in."

Lark appears in the doorway.

For a moment, Isabel sees her as her parents will see her: a strung-out mental patient in tacky polyester clothes.

"What's up?"

"Want to smoke?" Lark asks sheepishly.

"Sure." Isabel is relieved to have a distraction. She has been so anxious about her parents' visit she had barely slept the night before. Now time seems to be dragging.

It does not occur to Isabel until they are pulling their plastic deck chairs together that Lark is anxious, too.

"How's it going?" Isabel asks.

"Fine," Lark grunts, preoccupied with getting some secondhand smoke into her system.

"You doing okay?"

"Yeah, sure, whatever." Lark leans in for Isabel's exhale.

Wouldn't it be funny if Mom and Dad turned the corner right now and saw me practically making out with Lark?

"My parents are coming in a couple of hours."

"You glad about that?"

"I guess," Isabel admits.

"You can be happy about seeing your parents, you know," Lark says, cracking what for her amounted to a smile. "You don't have to hide it on my account."

"It's weird how nervous I am. I feel like I've been in a cave or something."

"Yeah. I know the feeling."

* * *

Isabel signs herself out so that she can await her parents' arrival. Around the corner, at the edge of the small parking lot, she positions herself on the low rock wall so that she can see both points of entry. She checks her watch every thirty seconds.

I bet they're turning into the hospital grounds right...about...now.

Isabel stands as the black Range Rover turns into the lot.

"Mom." Isabel nervously and woodenly hugs her mother. Over her shoulder she looks for her father.

"Oh, honey."

"Where's Dad?" Isabel knows the answer before it is spoken.

Forty-Three

Honey

"Honey, he wanted to come." Isabel flinches as her mother runs her hand through Isabel's hair. "I can't get over how much better you look. Rested."

"Mom, don't. Okay?" Her voice cracks as she gulps back tears.

"Oh, Isabel. Your father would have been here if he could have, you know that."

"Don't make excuses for him, okay?" Isabel's voice is raised. "Why are you always making excuses for him? He 'would have been here if he could have'? What? Something came up that was more important than visiting his daughter in a mental institution? Do you hear how absurd that sounds?"

Katherine is nervously motioning to Isabel, moving her hands in a downward signal, universal for "lower the volume."

"Isabel, please keep your voice down. I know this is upsetting."

"No. No you don't." Isabel waves her mother off and starts heading for the unit. Katherine hurries behind her. "All my life this has happened." Isabel spins around and faces her mother.

"For years I've heard 'your father would have been here if he could have.' Years. And you know what I've realized? It's bullshit! He's probably too hungover to come. This whole 'he wanted to come' thing is bullshit!"

"Language," her mother warns. "Watch your language, young lady."

"Oh, give it up, Mom. Look around you. You think anyone here cares about *language?*" She mimics her mother's tone.

"Isabel, I'm still your mother and I am saying it bothers me, okay? So please refrain from using bad language around me."

"Oh, please." Isabel pauses and then her words are deliberate, her tone measured. "You know what? Stop. Don't. No more excuses for Dad. No more trying to make it okay that he has missed out on my entire life. No more dancing around his drinking. Don't shake your head, Mom, I'm sick of it. Is he on the wagon? Is he off the wagon? I can't ask you because you just will not talk about it. I want us to talk about it. Can't you do that?"

"I didn't realize I was always making excuses for your father. I…I will try not to do that from now on."

"He's had one big long hangover for the past thirty years! It's bad enough that he hasn't been there for anything that's been important in my life…."

"Now, I will say this and don't interrupt me. I'm not making excuses for him, but I will say that your father has always been there for the important things in your life—"

"Mother, I *will* interrupt you. I know exactly what you're going to say next. He's been there for the plays and the graduations and the dances. Right? That's what you were going to say, right?"

Her mother nods, not sure where Isabel is leading her.

"But, Mom, you know what I've realized? The important

things are what happens in between the plays and the graduations. On the way to the dances. That's real life. The rest is all
for show. This—" Isabel extends her arms in a Julie-Andrews-
on-top-of-the-mountain gesture "—this is real life. Three
Breezes is real life. It doesn't have a pretty set design or offer
me a diploma or have a great band, but it's real. That's why
I don't want to hear excuses anymore. Do you understand?"

After waiting for what Isabel has said to absorb, waiting
for it to make sense, Katherine nods and answers truthfully.

Isabel takes a deep breath and then exhales. "What'd you
bring me for lunch?"

Katherine looks relieved. "Chinese chicken salad."

"From Ella's?"

"From Ella's."

Isabel leads her mother over to the nurses' station, knowing she has to sign her in as a guest.

"Julie? Where's the sign-in sheet?"

"Oh, hello, Mrs. Murphy!" Julie beams. *Of course chipper
Julie is going to be insufferably chipper in front of mom.* "Nice to
meet you! We're all so fond of Isabel." *Yeah, right.*

As Katherine signs in on a clipboard Julie adds, "I'm going
to need to go through those bags you brought."

Isabel had forgotten.

*Shit. The bag check. Damn. Nothing says "picnic" like a nice
little security check for deadly weapons.*

"Smells great," Julie says. "This is fine. I'll have to hold
on to this Snapple, though. Otherwise, no problems. Enjoy
your lunch!"

The Snapple is in a glass bottle.

Isabel leads her mother back outside.

"Let's sit over here, away from the building a little." Isabel points to two Adirondack chairs several yards away under a maple tree.

"Can we do that?" Katherine looks around nervously. "Is it okay?"

"Mom, I can go anywhere on the grounds so long as I sign out and check in at the nurses' station every half hour, okay?"

"That's great!" Katherine tries to sound super enthusiastic.

"The food looks great." Isabel, too, is trying to smooth out the tension between them.

"Now, Isabel," Katherine begins in a tone that only mothers can effect, "don't get mad at me, but I brought a lot extra in case anyone else is hungry. Maybe your friends…" She trails off, looking at Isabel hopefully.

"My friends? The other patients, you mean?"

"The other patients, yes. Do you think that'd be okay?"

She thinks I'm the old Isabel…making friends…running for class president…being team captain…anchoring the evening news. She doesn't see I'm a nobody. A nobody in a mental institution. These people…these people aren't my friends. These people are other failures. Other nobodies. Just let me go, Mom. It'd be much easier for all of us.

"Isabel? Where's Lark—she go to the bathroom or something?" Julie is consulting her clipboard in front of the Adirondack chairs.

"How should I know?"

"She's not having lunch with you and your mother?"

"No. Why?"

"Could she join us?" Katherine looks eagerly at Isabel and then addresses Julie. "Please join us as well, dear, we have more than enough food…."

"Julie? What's up?"

"She signed herself out on the board as having lunch with you two and I'm a little late on my checks." Julie wheels around before finishing her sentence and runs back into the unit.

"I'll be right back," Isabel tells her mother as she heads toward the unit.

"Okay!" Katherine calls after her. "But please invite your friends to come join us for lunch if they can! It's good Chinese chicken salad!"

Back in the unit the nurses have scattered and are simultaneously going door to door, calling out names louder than usual. Isabel stands to the side of the nurses' station.

"I'll call central." "We need to fan." "Who did the last check?" The nurses and orderlies are talking all at once. Within a minute, security is on the premises.

"Isabel? Can we help you?" Julie asks distractedly, knowing Isabel is there for voyeuristic reasons.

"No, I'm fine."

"Well, then, we'll need you to clear out of this area for now, to make some room."

"I'm worried about Lark," Isabel says.

"Lark? What's wrong with Lark this time?" Ben stumbles around the corner so quickly that Isabel almost tumbles backward.

"Nothing's wrong with Lark," the nurses answer in unison while trying to usher Isabel and Ben and Melanie, who has walked up with an inquisitive look on her face, out of the way. But trying to shoo Ben away is like trying to move an elephant with a fly swatter.

Isabel remembers her mother and turns to go back outside. Melanie evaporates as quickly as she materialized and Ben lumbers back into the living room.

"Sorry about that, Mom," Isabel says as she drops back into

the chair a minute later. "Lark's a patient. A...*friend* of mine. They can't find her. I'm sure they will, though. Anyway..."

Katherine looks alarmed. "Does that happen often? People wandering off?"

"No. They're pretty strict about checking our whereabouts all the time. This is the weekend, though, so that's probably why it lapsed. They'll find her."

"Ah."

So, where were we? Ah, yes.

"Mom? Remember how you were asking me on the phone this week about my treatment and I told you I'd tell you when you came to visit?"

"I've thought of little else." Katherine gives up her attempt at nonchalance and is now perched daintily on the edge of her seat.

"There's no easy way to answer that question except to just spit it out. So here goes—I had electroshock treatment."

Katherine is quiet.

"Mom? Say something. Say anything."

Katherine is looking out to the woods beyond the unit. She clears her throat. "I must say I never thought I'd have a daughter who would have to have something like that done to her." She says the word *that* as though it smells.

"They made me do it." Isabel is defensive. "My doctors said it is the best thing for me."

"Is it? Is it the best thing?"

Maybe it is. Maybe it is.

"I...I don't know." Isabel is trying to find words.

"Doesn't this all go on your record? Oh, my Lord, anyone can access your medical records, Isabel. Anyone."

"It's not like I've committed some crime, Mom." Isabel shakes her head.

Katherine looks at her daughter. "I just never thought my little girl—"

Isabel speaks up before her mother finishes: "I'm not your little girl anymore, Mom," she says. Katherine looks away again. "I'm not this happy little girl who does everything that's expected of her."

Silence.

"Look at me, Mom!" Isabel pleads with Katherine. "I've screwed everything up. My marriage is over…."

Katherine winces. "Don't say that…you two could still work things out…."

"It's over. And maybe that's for the best. My job's on the line—in fact I'd be surprised if I still have a job after that whole—"

"They'd be lucky to have you!" Katherine interrupts again.

"Mom! Listen to me. I'm trying to tell you…I'm trying to show you who I am. You can't seem to see me for who I really am. You want me to be perfect."

"Is that so bad? For a mother to want a perfect life for her daughter? Do the doctors here program you to blame everything on your parents? Talk about your clichés, darling."

"Oh, give me a break, Mom. I'm not blaming you for anything and you know that. It's just that I wanted to be perfect for you. But I'm not perfect. And here I am." Isabel opens her arms across like a hostess on *The Price is Right*. "This is where it got me."

Katherine looks hard at Isabel. Then she looks at her own hands. "What do you want me to say?"

"Just tell me why."

"Why?"

"Why is it so important for me to be perfect? What's in it for you?"

"I don't think I like your tone, Isabel Murphy."

"Just tell me—" she pushes harder "—why does my success mean so much to you?"

"That's bad syntax, dear," Katherine says, adjusting her Hermès scarf. "Honestly, I don't know what they taught you in college."

"Mother! Are you even listening to me?"

"There's no need to raise your voice, Isabel. I'm not hard of hearing yet."

"Then why aren't you answering my question? I'll ask you one more time. Why do you need me to be perfect?"

With nothing left for Katherine to fiddle with, her hands flutter back to her lap and she looks out to the field below. Isabel waits for her answer.

"All your life you've craved him." Katherine speaks softly at first. "'Is *Dad* going to be there? Where's Dad? Why can't *Dad* take me to camp?' It's been a bottomless pit. You've always wanted him, needed him so much...."

Katherine trails off. After waiting a few seconds Isabel gently encourages her mother to say more. To solve the riddle for her.

"And?"

When Katherine turns back to Isabel her eyes are full of tears. "What about *me?* I was never enough for you, apparently."

"Mother! That's not true." Isabel, astounded, moves closer to her mother, to soothe her, comfort her.

"You don't know what it's like to see your child completely *deflate* when she turns the corner and sees that it's only you picking her up. To watch as she scans the crowd for the person she really wants to see," Katherine dabs at her mascara with her linen handkerchief. "You don't know what it's like to be there day in and day out for your children, knowing they don't care about you; they only want their *father* to be there."

"But why has this made you want me to be perfect? Why have you expected me to be this happy little achiever?"

"Don't you see?" Katherine looks at Isabel. "I wanted you the way you want your father."

Isabel is breathless with the revelation.

"I guess I've been hard on you because it's killed me so to be rejected by you over and over, year after year, while you wait by the window for your father to come home from work. I know I've expected a lot of you and your brothers. But it was that or become a wreck hoping for your love."

Mother and daughter are both looking out across the grounds.

Katherine is first to break the thick silence. "I don't know what else to say, really." She straightens her posture and carefully folds her handkerchief, smoothing out the wrinkles, and puts it back into her purse.

"Say that you'll love me if I'm not perfect. Say that you'll still love me if I'm a failure at everything…because I pretty much am."

"Oh, Isabel. I do love you. I may not have heard you when you said you weren't perfect…that may be true. But you haven't heard me when I've told you that, no matter what, I love you. I always have. I always will. But Isabel…and this is important…this may be the most important thing I've ever said to you. It shouldn't matter what I think. It doesn't matter what I think. *You* have to love *yourself*. Even if you're a failure. You have to love yourself."

Isabel feels the goose bumps of recognition tingling up her arms. She thinks of Dorothy at the end of *The Wizard of Oz* when Glinda the Good Witch tells her she hadn't needed to make the trek to the Emerald City—she had had the power to return to Kansas all along: she simply had to click her heels together.

There's no place like home. There's no place like home.

Forty-Four

It is the first thing Isabel and her mother notice when they open the door to her room: a single sheet of paper placed neatly in the center of her hospital bed.

"This is weird." Isabel picks up the paper. "It's four poems."

Katherine reads the titles over her shoulder. "'Loneliness,' 'Sleep,' 'Death.' They're so sad."

The fourth is a short poem titled "Lark's Song."

My song is not easy to hear.
Melody.
Music, not.
My song is my voice.
My voice is not easy to hear.
Perhaps that is why no one listened.

The poem is followed by five words in tiny writing: "Don't be afraid of laundry."

"What on earth does that mean?" Katherine asks.

Isabel drops the paper and, without a word, hurries out of her room and down the hall of the unit.

It's too late. I know it. It's too late.

Isabel turns the corner just as the orderly is slamming up against the locked door. It moves but is not quite open. The orderly stands back and then hurls himself up against it once more, pushing it wide enough to slip in. Isabel is directly behind him. She hears nurses coming in their direction.

"Where's the light switch?" His voice, full of urgent frustration, is close to her in the darkened laundry room.

"It's on the right, I think. Not the left," Isabel answers as she tries to reach around the door. There is something blocking her way.

The light comes on and Isabel screams.

Lark is hanging from the metal air duct. Her face is purple, her eyes bulging and bright red with broken blood vessels. She had tied her sheets together and moved the dryer directly underneath the pipe so she could step off it into oblivion.

Forty-Five

Isabel

"Isabel? I was wondering if you would like to read my journal." Ben is standing in front of Isabel, who is sitting in the Adirondack chair looking out over the grounds.

Maybe if I don't answer him he'll leave me alone.

But Ben is not adept at interpreting subtleties. "I know you can hear me, Isabel. Here's my journal." He shoves the notebook at her. "Read it and get back to me."

Ben walks back to the unit. Both his arms hang down at his sides. Isabel watches him go.

Fundamentalists should look at Ben and then try to argue that we did not descend from apes.

Dear Diary:
Herein lies my journal, which I will revisit at least once a day for the duration of my life…

She turns the page.

I would like to begin by addressing the nature of wild animals. They make me very angry. They do not even attempt to adapt to the man's world. They don't even care about you. When you break your arm, they don't care. When your feelings are hurt, they don't care about you. If you miss a train, they don't care about you. In short, they don't care about you....

Isabel flips ahead through the pages, all of which are crammed with Ben's nearly illegible scrawl.

I have come to believe that Northerners are evil. Especially New Yorkers. But Northerners in general. They don't care about you. Southerners, now that's a different story. Southerners are the only truly great people. They really care. The food they cook is the best, by a long shot. They must care about you if they're cooking like that for you.

Why does Ben want me to read this, for God's sake? I don't give a shit about this twisted journal.

"Isabel?" Connie the night nurse is smiling apologetically as she approaches Isabel.

"Larry's here and wants everyone to get together in the living room for an emergency group session. We need you to come inside now."

"I don't want to go to group. I want to stay out here," Isabel replies.

"I know, sweetie, but Larry says it's important for everyone to be there."

"Yeah, yeah, yeah. He wants to talk about 'how Lark's death affected us.'" Isabel mimics Larry's somber tone. "I don't feel like talking about it. Sorry, Connie, but I'm not going."

Connie crouches down in front of Isabel's lap.

"Honey, we know you saw Lark. You were the only patient to see her like that. That's an incredibly traumatic thing.
Larry really wants you to come talk to him."

"What's there to talk about? Lark killed herself. You guys
all screwed up. All the bed checks, the flashlight checks, the
sharps closet. All of that and you can't keep a patient safe in
broad daylight right under your noses. Larry wants to take the
heat off the staff—no offense to you, Connie. I don't want to
hear it. I just want to be alone."

Isabel gets up and walks down a sloping hill into the middle
of the field below. Connie goes inside presumably to get Larry.

Larry pushes through the unit doors and heads straight to
Isabel, who is sitting cross-legged on the grass.

"Larry, don't even waste your breath," Isabel calls out to
the therapist, who is trudging down the hill. "I know you
want me to come to group and I'm not going to, so you can
just turn around."

"I just want to talk with you for a second, Isabel. Is that
okay?" Larry is trying to sound nonthreatening. "After that,
if you want to come to group, fine. If not, no problem."

Yeah, right.

Larry exhales as he plops down beside her on the grass.

"I'm not going to beat around the bush. You're a smart
woman. You know why I want to talk to you. I'm worried
about you witnessing something like Lark's suicide. That can
be a jarring thing to see, even for a professional. I wonder
what you thought when you saw her?"

I didn't think anything. Not one single thing.

"Nothing." Isabel shrugs.

"You realize, don't you, that you are probably still in shock.
That was a horrible thing to see."

"I don't know. I just really want to be by myself, Larry. I don't have anything to say."

"Okay. I'll leave you alone for now. One more question and then I'm out of your hair, so to speak."

"Yeah?"

"Were you aware of the extent of Lark's mental illness?"

"What? Don't you have doctor-patient confidentiality to think about? Should you be telling me stuff about Lark? Jesus."

"You didn't hear me. I am not telling you anything about Lark. I am simply asking if you knew the depth of Lark's illness. Did you?"

"No," Isabel replies. "Not like you knew about it, I'm sure. We weren't close friends, Lark and I, if that's what you mean."

"Okay. Well, I suppose, then, if you didn't know how deeply troubled Lark was then you couldn't have been expected to save her, right?"

"Point taken."

For a few moments neither of them say a word. Isabel tries to concentrate on an industrious line of ants carrying specks of dirt away from their M*A*S*H unit.

"Isabel, I'm going to be direct. You're going to have to decide whether this forces you to sink or whether it helps you swim. None of us can decide that for you. There are a lot of Larks here at Three Breezes. There always have been and there always will be. You are not one of them. You are in the unique position to be able to help yourself. Many of the patients here will never be able to do that. This is tough to hear, I know, and please don't mistake my bluntness for a minimization of your pain. But I sense that deep down inside you know you don't belong here much longer. *You* can lift yourself up. Lark was never going to be able to do that."

Tears are falling down Isabel's cheeks as she turns to Larry.

"Maybe you could've helped her. Maybe I could have," she cries. "She could have lifted herself up…."

"Never," Larry says gently.

He stands up, stretches and shades his eyes from the sun. Isabel looks out across the field and wipes her nose.

"Goodbye, Isabel."

She twists around to watch him make his way back up the hill to the unit. Waiting for him on the smoker's porch are Ben and Kristen, who, Isabel can just make out, is scratching at her wrist. As Larry approaches them Ben jumps to his feet and claps his hands together like a child at Christmas. They follow the therapist inside and the door shuts tightly behind them.

Forty-Six

"What're you doing?" Isabel asks Kristen.

"Shh! Keep your voice down. Want one?" Kristen whispers over her shoulder while reaching into the vending machine for a Snapple.

"No."

"No one's going to find out," Kristen says defensively as she shakes the bottle of iced tea and breaks the safety seal. "I do this every day and no one's said a word yet. They don't even know. Plus, the dollar-feeder thingy is broken. Score!"

"You don't pay for it?"

"I watch the nurses doing it. How come they get to do it and I can't?"

"Well, let's see," Isabel says in a purposely patronizing tone, "for one thing, it's in the *staff* cafeteria. Emphasis on *staff*. You know. People who are actually *paid* to be here. Get it?"

"Little Miss Goody Two-Shoes," Kristen laughs as she takes a swig of her drink. "I always finish it before it's time to get back to the unit."

"What an accomplishment," Isabel mutters.

"Who are they to say that we can't have something good to drink?"

"You're a regular Norma Rae."

"Who?"

Isabel turns and walks away.

Larry's right. I don't belong here. I've got to get out of here.

Thirty minutes later she signs herself out for a walk.

Without planning on it she finds herself outside Peter's unit. There she settles on a large rock and watches the door, wondering what Peter is doing on the other side of it.

Maybe he's coloring something. Maybe he's reading. Harry Potter? I hope so...I hope he has some way to escape his madness.

"I want to get out of here," Isabel says as she sits down in her therapist's office. "How do I go about doing that? Seriously. Tell me."

Dr. Seidler smiles. "It's about time."

"How do I do it?"

"First things first," Dr. Seidler begins. "Let's talk about how you've come to this decision."

"I had an epiphany...I woke up on the right side of the bed...I had a good dinner...I don't know." Isabel does not want to go into detail. Her mind is made up. "Just tell me what I've got to do."

"Okay. Let's do this. Your outside therapist, Mona, and I have talked—remember I've been telling you about our phone conversations—and we both think it might be a good idea for you to ease back into life by going to your session in the city this week. Then you can come back here."

"Commute into Manhattan?"

"That's right. A field trip. That way it might not be such a shock to your system."

"Then you'll sign the papers to let me out? For good, I mean. If I pass this test?"

"This is not a test. I think it would benefit you to go slowly, that's all."

"Okay, I'll do it. Where can I get the train schedule?"

"There's a schedule at the front desk—I'll get it for you by tonight. It's really easy. The nurses will call a taxi for you that will take you to the station and the train goes right in to Grand Central. You go to your appointment and then hop back on the train and come back here. You up for it?"

"Yes."

They trust me? How do they know I won't stop at Duane Reade and pick up razor blades?

"I think you'll do just fine, Isabel," Dr. Seidler smiles. "I think you're ready. In the meantime, I wonder if we can talk about what that last day at work was like for you. The day before you came here. What happened after—" she cleared her throat "—ahem..."

"After I wigged out on live television?" Isabel snorted.

"Speak," said John without looking up, so accustomed was he to multitasking that his colleagues knew not to wait for his full attention.

But Isabel was unable to obey his command. She fixed her stare on the crown of his head, which was bent over his laptop, which fought for space with a Chinese carryout container balanced on a heap of folders in the clutter of his desk.

"You snooze you lose," he muttered, reaching for the phone while clicking on his keyboard.

Isabel simply stood there. After a moment, in an attempt at watering her incredibly dry mouth, she cleared her throat, hoping the phlegm would help cancel out the sick taste in her mouth.

After a curt phone call, John hung up. "What?" he glanced up at her, looked back down and then brought his head back up as though he couldn't quite believe what he'd seen when he first saw her standing there. After that his head did not move.

"Talk to me." For once, she had John's full attention.

Still, she could not form the words.

Focus. Focus.

"Can we—ahem—sorry," she coughed. "Can we close the door?" she whispered.

John went over to his office door and batted down the coats slung over the top of it. Wordlessly he clicked it shut and motioned for her to sit down.

Isabel perched on the edge of the chair and looked down at her knees.

"What's going on, kiddo?"

Kiddo.

"Whatever it is, we can fix it," he said kindly.

Isabel took a deep breath and then dove in. "It's like this…" But the words stopped their outbound journey.

"You can do it," John coaxed.

You can do it.

"I need a medical leave of absence and I need it to start now."

"Now, as in…?"

"Now as in right away. Tomorrow."

John did not bat an eye. "Whatever you need. Take whatever you need."

Isabel had been unprepared for his unconditional support. "But…but I know this is leaving you in the lurch and I don't want—"

"Isabel—" John's voice a deep mix of gentle and gruff "—your health is more important. Can you still pull bulletin duty tonight? If you can't just say, but it might be hard to get someone else in here since it's Labor Day weekend."

"Yeah, yes."

"You sure?"

No.

"Yes."

"Good," he said. "Then your leave will start tomorrow."

"You haven't even asked why," she said.

"If you'd thought it was important for me to know, you would have told me. Now, go. Do what you need to do."

Her eyes filled up with tears and she looked away from him. Silently but with great effort she stood up and turned to the door. As she reached for the handle she straightened her shoulders, took another deep breath, cleared her cheeks of tears and, for one last time, put the mask back on.

"He didn't ask you why you needed the leave?" Dr. Seidler asks.

"No," Isabel answers. "He didn't even look curious about it. It was like he sensed that I couldn't talk about it—whatever 'it' is or was."

"Interesting."

"What?"

"I'm wondering how that made you feel. Sitting there in his office—you were obviously at a real low point. What did you think when he told you to take whatever time you needed?"

Isabel's mind wandered back to the day that now seemed like it belonged to a parallel universe. "I remember thinking that if I let John down I wouldn't be able to live with myself. I remember thinking I'd just go home and do it."

"Do it?"

"Kill myself."

"Because you disappointed John?"

"Well, let's be honest here, I'd been planning it, anyway. But I thought that if John said I was leaving him in the lurch I would do it sooner rather than as I'd planned it."

"You didn't want to disappoint him."

Isabel nods her head in agreement.

"Well. What I find interesting about this is that that is what one might feel about one's father. A lot of people would try to keep from disappointing their *fathers,* not their *bosses.* It seems like you thought of John as a father figure—someone who looked out for you, cared about you. Yes?"

Isabel nods again.

"So when you went to him, obviously at the end of your rope, so to speak, and he stepped up to the plate, giving you unconditional support without even asking you what it was all about, that was healing for you. That was indeed something a father would do. And John did it. He came through."

"Yeah. But then again, I *did* look pretty strung out. Maybe that's why he didn't ask me any questions."

"See? Even now you're hedging. It's like you can't believe someone could offer you their support when you most need it. It's like you don't trust it."

Isabel thinks about the doctor's words. She imagines Dr. Seidler as a gardener, an oversize trowel in her hand, digging into the soil of her soul. Peering into—what? Compost? The cynical part of Isabel wonders. And what would she plant in the space she'd created? What would grow—flourish, even?

"I want to trust it." Isabel's voice is one decibel higher than a whisper. "I want to."

"Then why don't you? What would it be like if you just

felt the warmth of someone reaching out and throwing you a lifeline at a time when you're gasping for air? You don't have to answer. Just think about how wonderful that would feel. To have someone be there for you when you most need it."

Isabel feels a tiny seed dropping into the hole deep inside her and knows it will flower. Someday.

Forty-Seven

Twenty-four hours later Isabel is sitting on a train.

Why is my heart beating so goddamned fast? I've been taking the train for as long as I can remember. This is a piece of cake: there's no room for error, really. I'm in, I'm out. So why do I feel faint?

"This is the 2:10 train to Grand Central. The 2:10 to Grand Central." The conductor's loud voice is a vise tightening on her stomach walls.

Jesus. Maybe I'm not ready after all. This is happening so fast.

"Going all the way in?" The conductor is standing in the aisle clicking his hole punch impatiently.

"Excuse me?" Isabel tears her head away from the station that is rapidly shrinking in the distance.

"Going to Grand Central, miss?"

"Oh. Yes."

"That's $5.75."

Isabel fumbles for her wallet and feels confused searching through the bills.

Should I give him a twenty or a ten? Maybe I'll need change once

I get into the city. I do have exact change but maybe I should hold on to the smaller bills.

"Miss? That's $5.75 please."

Isabel nervously hands him the twenty.

"You got anything smaller?" The conductor is annoyed at having to change the bill.

"No. Sorry," Isabel lies.

He sighs and hands her back the change and moves on to the next passenger. Isabel realizes she has been holding her breath. She exhales.

Calm down. Calm down.

Forty minutes later the voice booms through the cars: "Grand Central Station. This is Grand Central Station, folks. Last stop." Isabel tightens her grip on her purse straps, which have remained on her shoulder for the entire ride.

"Grand Central Station." The voice is echoing in her brain as she follows the crowd of people up the platform into the main terminal. Once there Isabel stops and looks around as if she is seeing the monumental structure for the first time.

I look like a tourist from Iowa wandering through Times Square. All that's missing is that ugly coin purse thing that straps around my waist. Has there always been an echo in here? I never noticed it before.

Isabel inches through the bustling station toward the door she is most accustomed to using. At the Vanderbilt Avenue exit taxis wait for commuters, and at this hour in the afternoon there is a long line of hungry drivers.

I have plenty of time. I don't know why I took such an early train. Maybe I should save money and take the subway. A cab would be ridiculously expensive. I've got time.

She checks her watch for the sixth time.

Right now they're in afternoon group, she thinks as she goes back in to the station and follows the signs for the subway.

She has not taken into account that she is unfamiliar with this particular subway line. Her confusion is magnified.

Calm down. Calm down.

The subway map, with its colorful maze of lines, blurs together.

Jesus. I don't know where I am. Where am I on this map? Okay, calm down. I can do this. I take the subway all the time.

The deafening sound of an approaching train drowns out Isabel's thinking. Passengers pushing through the turnstiles and running past her to jump on board make her head hurt. A sense of urgency surges through her. She steps onto the train.

"Excuse me, sir? Is this the four or six northbound?"

The man looks the other way and pretends not to hear her. Isabel's panic increases as the doors shut and the train picks up speed.

"Excuse me, is this the four or the six northbound?" she asks a well-dressed woman.

"What? No. This is the six express downtown. The next stop is Police Plaza." The woman sounds indignant.

She thinks I'm a mental patient. She knows I'm staying at a mental hospital. Oh, God, I've got to get off this train. Stop! Stop the train!

Isabel's frantic eyes search the map bolted to the door of the subway car.

Jesus, how do I get out of here?

The train lurches back and forth as it snakes through the underground canals. Isabel hangs on to the strap above her, but with each jarring motion her arm pulls out of her shoulder socket. Instead she grips the greasy bar in front of her.

Focus. Focus. Once I get downtown what line am I going to take?

"Next stop, City Hall. City Hall next stop." But the announcement is warbled and all Isabel can pick up are the words *stop* and *hall*.

The train slows as it pulls along the dimly lit platform. City Hall signs are emblazoned every few feet along the way.

When the doors open Isabel gets off the train and feels herself jostled by the other passengers hurrying to get off before the doors close and the train heads across to Brooklyn.

For a few moments, Isabel stands completely still, clinging to her purse.

What do I do?

The platform empty, she follows signs for the exit. Her footsteps echo as she carefully makes her way through the darkened tunnels to the turnstiles. The smell of urine and cigarettes increases her sense of frightened isolation.

Nearing the end of the tunnel Isabel sees sunlight streaming down a dirty staircase. She breaks into a run.

The sun makes her bare arms tingle after the dampness of the underground corridor. She hails a cab and gratefully climbs inside.

"Central Park West and Ninety-sixth, please."

"It's so good to see you, Isabel!" Mona presses her hands together in a prayer position and beams at her patient.

Isabel takes one step into her therapist's office and bursts out crying.

Mona guides Isabel toward the couch. Silently, she strokes Isabel's back and waits for her to speak.

"I can't do it" is all Isabel can squeak in between breaths. "I shouldn't have come."

"Okay, first take a few deep breaths," Mona says. "Deep breath. Good. That's good. Now. Can you tell me what happened?"

The words come tumbling out. "I got so turned around. I got lost. Everything's so crazy here. I used to love this city. I knew my way around backward and forward. I've forgotten *everything*. I don't belong here anymore. I shouldn't have come."

"I can imagine how scary this must have been for you. Keep in mind, you've been at Three Breezes for about a month. That is quite a different, very controlled environment. New York can be overwhelming to anyone, Isabel."

Isabel's heart slows down with each deep breath. Mona's voice soothes her.

I'm okay. I'm okay.

"The bottom line is, you made it!"

"So now it's a triumph simply to arrive at my destination?" she sniffs.

"Yes. For today, for what you've been through these past few weeks—it's a triumph." Mona motions to the Kleenex, which Isabel dutifully uses.

"Do you want to talk about Three Breezes?"

Isabel vehemently shakes her head as she blows her nose.

"Well, we have to start somewhere—so I wonder, have you been able to think about the Alex question? Why you've stayed with him?"

They had worked on it nearly every session for months before Three Breezes as if it were a riddle: why—how—does someone stay with someone who hurts her?

Isabel looks up from the balled-up Kleenex in her hand. She remembers her mother's words: *you have to love yourself, Isabel.* Suddenly it is clear.

"Because I hated myself..." She trails off for a moment and then begins again. "I didn't hate myself because I stayed with him. I stayed with him because I hated myself. How could I have expected anyone to treat me well when I wasn't treating myself well?"

Isabel let the words wrap around her like a fluffy hotel robe. For a brief flash she sees her life as an outsider would see it.

"That's it." Isabel hears a rushing sound in her ears. "I figured it out. It's so simple."

"It's a beginning, that's for certain," Mona smiles. "The big question is do you still hate yourself?"

She looks Mona straight in the eye. "No. I don't believe I do."

The sound of a breakthrough.

Forty-Eight

"Can you tell me where to find the information booth?"

"Huh?" Isabel turns her head to the voice.

The tall German college student is standing too close to Isabel and is speaking loudly.

It's like two Seinfeld *episodes in one: a close talker and a loud talker. Who was the close talker again? Come on, you know this. Close talker. Close talker. Judge Reinhold!*

"The information counter. Can you tell me where to find it?"

Isabel stares at him.

"You do not know." The German answers for her and moves toward a commuter smoking just outside the entrance to Grand Central.

Isabel snaps awake.

"In there," she calls after him. "Down the steps, in the middle of the room. You'll see a round clock on top of it."

"Thank you," the German replies as he pushes through the heavy doors into the terminal.

Isabel waits a beat and follows him in, scanning the huge departure board on her way down the steps.

Once onboard the train she collapses into a vacant seat by the window and closes her eyes until the conductor enters the car collecting fares. Without hesitation Isabel pays with exact change.

She sleeps the entire ride.

"Where to?"

"Three Breezes Hospital, please," Isabel answers the cab-driver.

"Going to visit someone?"

"Yeah," Isabel replies, embarrassed to admit her connection to the place.

"You got it," the driver says, turning onto the road that leads to the hospital. "To the Nut Hut."

Forty-Nine

Isabel

Isabel pulls the folding chair up to the phone in the unit kitchen.

"Hi, Isabel. Goodman here. I'm calling to see how you're doing. Haven't talked to you in a while. I don't know if you're checking your messages, but in case you are I wanted you to know that we handled the, uh, situation so you don't have to worry. I'm still not sure whether you got the message I left a couple of weeks ago, but in case you didn't, I wanted to let you know everything's fine. I spoke with HR to make sure your leave of absence forms got through. They got them so it shouldn't be a problem. Call me, though, if you can. Bye."

"Isabel? Hi, it's me. I know I'm not at the top of your list to call back but I wanted you to know how sorry I am. I've been calling you and I keep getting the machine. Are you out of town? I thought this time I'd leave a message in case you're picking them up. Um, I want you to know I'm getting help. Just like you said to do. I'm getting help. Don't write me off, okay? Please?"

★ ★ ★

"Damn. The machine cut me off. It's me again. I know you don't believe this but I love you, Isabel."

"Isabel, this is Ted Sargent. We would like to have a meeting with you at your earliest convenience. Call my assistant, if you would, to set up a time. Her name is Deborah and she's at extension 5421. Thank you."

"Isabel? Hi, it's Michele from work. Um, I just wanted to give you a heads-up that Sargent was up here looking for you. Not to worry you but he looked pissed. After I told him you were on sick leave he went into John's office and they shut the door for, like, ten minutes. Is everything okay?"

"Yes, Isabel, this is Deborah, Ted Sargent's assistant. He asked me to call you to set up an appointment to meet with him and someone from Human Resources. Please call me at 5421. Thank you."

Isabel hangs up the pay phone and fixates on the square metal numbers on the keypad. The longer she stares the fuzzier the numbers become.

Fifty

"It happened again."

"What happened again?"

"I had an episode on my trip to the city," Isabel says. *Please don't tell me this means I'm back to square one.*

"Was this one like the time at work. When Diana died?"

"Yeah, kind of. Actually, not as bad."

"Not as bad?"

"No. Well, I don't know."

"Tell me what happened."

Isabel is fighting to stay focused on the session.

"What are you thinking right now? Can you tell me?"

"I'm really trying *[focus]*…I'm trying not to blur everything together. It's so comfortable *[focus]* to stare at one spot. I just want to think for a second." Isabel is mesmerized by the floor in front of Dr. Seidler's feet. She is silent for five minutes.

"I feel numb again."

At least I'm saying this out loud. That's got to count for something, right?

"Was that what happened in New York? You felt numb?"

"Kind of—" still staring "—it was kind of like I was in a coma or a trance or something. I heard everything going on around me but I couldn't move a muscle."

"Before that did you feel panicked? Worried at all? I spoke to Mona this morning and she told me that you were disoriented when you got to her office. You had gotten lost. Can you tell me what happened?"

Isabel pulls her eyes from the floor to the window, where they settle on the peeling bark of a birch tree just outside the doctor's office.

"I'm just trying to get to the root of what appear to be extreme panic attacks," Dr. Seidler explains. "In some cases they might be termed psychotic panic attacks."

"But I'm not violent or anything." *Psychotic, psychotic.* "I'm not psychotic."

"It's just another word for 'acute' in this case. I didn't mean to imply you were violent—I certainly don't believe you are. Again, was this one as bad as the others?"

"Um, no. I don't think this was as bad. But that's probably because I didn't know anyone. When it happened at work I was on the air. I was in a newsroom surrounded by people I know."

Isabel remembers the messages left on her answering machine.

"It looks like I'll probably get fired for that last one. I just called in and checked messages. They want to fire me."

Isabel's eyes sting with tears.

"I'm so sorry. Are you sure, though? Maybe you misinterpreted the calls?"

"I'm sure."

Silence.

"It's trite but true, Isabel. New beginnings come from other beginnings' ends."

"I know, I know...when one door closes another opens," Isabel sighs. "Blah, blah, blah."

"I want you to know that this is very treatable. We can prescribe something that can help curb the panic. Millions of people suffer panic attacks. There is a very effective medication I would recommend—it's Xanax, actually—that could greatly diminish your attacks, if not help them disappear altogether. That, along with working on what triggers the panic in the first place, can be a terrific course of treatment. I don't think this hinders your efforts to leave here."

Isabel looks alert. "Really?"

Dr. Seidler smiles. "Really. I can prescribe something today and we can see how it works. I want to make sure I get the dose right since you're already on Serzone and Zyprexa. Many times Xanax can help boost the effectiveness of antidepressants, so that's what we'll hope for."

Isabel brightens for the first time. "So even though I had another attack you still think it's okay if I leave? This isn't a setback?"

"Not at all. As I said, acute panic attacks are more common than you would think, and people aren't institutionalized for them. I'm most concerned with your coping mechanisms mixing in with your depression. That is and will continue to be the struggle you have to concentrate on. The panic attacks— I'm confident we can successfully address them so they won't pose any more problems for you. I would have been surprised if your trip into New York went smoothly. In a way, this was to be expected."

Isabel takes her time walking back to the unit. The footpath veers off to the right, and for the first time, she decides to turn toward the art studio, knowing the patients on her unit do not have art class until later in the day.

She crosses the grassy field and stops outside the door to the studio, careful to listen for any signs there is a class underway. Hearing nothing, she tries the door. The smell is elementary school: papier mâché and turpentine. She lets the door close quietly behind her and looks around at the watercolors hanging on every wall of the room. Sunlight floods in from a huge window, warming the clay figures left out on counters to dry. She absentmindedly lets her hand alight on many of the pieces: an ashtray, a vase, a bust of an elderly woman.

Just as she is turning to go, Isabel hears something and stops. Muffled grunting sounds seep out from behind a closed door opposite the front of the building. She listens for a moment, straining to make sense of the sounds. The grunting quickens and mingles with a woman's sighs.

I'll be damned! Someone's having sex in here.

Isabel reaches for the doorknob and hesitates.

What if it's a doctor or something? I don't want to see that. But, damn! I can't leave without finding out who's in there.

Isabel's curiosity is overwhelming. She is barely breathing.

Isabel turns the knob and gently eases the door open, trying to make as little sound as possible. Standing just out of sight, Isabel peers inside.

There, lying on a table in front of the kiln is Kristen with Nick the orderly, Connie's son, standing between her legs.

Oh. My. God.

Isabel shuts the door and runs out of the studio, knowing that within seconds Nick will pull up his pants and race after whoever discovered them.

She crouches behind a hedge on the side of the building. She cannot run directly to the unit because, even with a head start, she would not have time to cross the field without being recognized.

"Hel-lo?" Nick calls, trying to sound casual, friendly. "Who's there?"

The voice is getting louder. *He's getting closer.*

Isabel holds her breath.

"Hello?" Nick calls out again.

There is a sound of a door opening and closing, followed by the sound of hurried footsteps on the path. The steps are heading away from the art studio.

Kristen.

Isabel can feel the pulse of her heart beat in her throat. She knows she has to make a move but is not sure where Nick is.

"I know you're out there," Nick is saying. "I can explain if you'll just let me, whoever you are."

His voice is coming from farther away.

"Come out, come out, wherever you are!"

He's circling the building.

Isabel makes a run for the back door to the cafeteria. The door opens easily and she slips inside.

Another unit is in the middle of lunch so she grabs a tray and cuts in line in front of the vat of institutional mashed potatoes, careful not to look over her shoulder when she hears the same door open and close. There is so much noise and activity in the lunchroom Isabel fits in undetected.

Nick scans the room, crosses it and goes out the front door.

She shuffles along in the line of patients and then ditches her tray at the salad bar and leaves.

Looking both ways before cutting back across the field and onto the main footpath that leads to her unit, Isabel consciously slows down, to look as if she is just coming from her doctor's appointment, in case Nick doubles back.

Within seconds she reaches the smoker's porch and there, calmly taking a drag of her cigarette, is Kristen.

Why do I feel like I'm the one who's done something wrong?

Kristen has not seen Isabel approaching and jumps in her chair. "Oh, hi. You startled me." She puts her hand to her chest.

"Sorry," Isabel says. "Didn't mean to scare you."

"That's okay. Want to join me?"

I don't want to join you. You're on the southbound train and I'm heading north...directly out of here.

"I've got to go to the dry erase board and let them know I'm back from Seidler's office." Isabel heads to the door, grateful for an excuse to escape the wreck that is Kristen's life.

Just before it closes behind her, Kristen calls out. "Isabel? If you see Nick, um, that orderly? Could you tell him I need to speak to him?"

Without turning around Isabel says "sure" and goes inside.

Fifty-One

"Have you seen my baby?" A disheveled girl accosts Isabel minutes after she walks back into the unit, shoving a tattered picture at her.

"Huh?" Isabel steps back.

"My baby. Look at my baby." The girl slurs her words as she sways her considerable weight from one leg to the other. She looks like she is fifteen years old.

Isabel glances at the photo. "Cute. You new here?"

"Isn't she an angel?" The young mother ignores Isabel's question and teeters off toward the main door. "She's my precious baby." Before she reaches for the horizontal bar that, when pressed, opens the metal door, the nurse, who has been following behind her, steps in front of it.

"Cindy, you can't go outside. Back to your room now."

Isabel watches the obviously heavily drugged new girl stagger back to her room.

"Did you see Nick?" Kristen had become too impatient waiting outside.

"Oh, um, no. I was just talking to that new girl…the one

who's in Keisha's room. I haven't gotten to the dry erase board yet."

Kristen is already off, wandering the halls for her secret beau. Isabel watches her make way for Cindy, who is also wandering, weaving uncertainly.

"Hi!" the new girl calls after Kristen. "Have you seen my baby?"

Kristen does not even glance over her shoulder.

"Everyone, this is Cindy." Larry speaks loudly to get the group's attention. "She is joining us for the first time today."

"Hi, Cindy," Melanie chirps.

Cindy smiles groggily. "I was wondering if everyone here has seen my baby." She looks down and seems surprised to find that her own fist is clutching her cherished photo, crumpling it. She stares into her lap and appears to will her fist to release the picture—to no avail.

"Why don't you tell us a little about your baby girl, Cindy," Larry suggests as he settles back into his chair, crossing his arms against his chest.

"Her name is Angel," Cindy dreamily considers the assembled group.

"Where is she now, Cindy?" Larry asks.

"Now?" Cindy seems confused by the question.

"Where is Angel now?"

"Hmm," Cindy's thinks. "Let's see…" As her mind trails off, she turns to gaze out the window and then upward toward the sky.

"Cindy?"

Isabel studies Cindy's tangled hair, her bad complexion and her pudgy arms.

What a whack job.

"Yeah?" She slowly turns her head back toward the sound of Larry's voice and then appears to remember the question. "Oh, yes. Angel. She's in heaven now."

Silence.

"How did she get there?" Larry asks. Isabel shifts in her seat without taking her eyes off Cindy.

"Huh?" Cindy seems bewildered again.

"Do you remember what happened last week?" Larry hints.

"Last week…"

"You were found holding your baby in a plastic bag. Do you remember that, Cindy?"

Ben moans and Melanie starts to cry. Cindy contemplates the sky again.

"Angel suffocated to death, Cindy. Maybe you could tell us a little bit about that," Larry says, continuing to prod his new patient. She seems incapable of listening.

"You with us, Cindy?"

"Not really." She smiles at Larry.

"Okay. Well." He looks at his fingernails. He surveys the room and then he takes in a deep breath and releases it.

Congratulations, whack job. You've rendered our fearless leader speechless.

"Did you kill your baby, Cindy?" Ben startles the group with his angry question. He is glowering at the new girl.

Cindy cocks her head to one side but continues to stare at the sky.

This is like Wimbledon, everyone looking from Ben to Cindy and back again. No, it's a courtroom—Ben's the prosecutor, Larry's the judge.

"I'm talking to you, Cindy!" Ben shouts. "Did you kill your baby?"

Objection, your honor!

"Ben, let's calm down a bit, okay?" Larry stands up and walks across the room toward Ben.

"I can't calm down, Larry." Ben's face is the color of a Christmas scarf. "I just want to know. Did she kill her baby?"

Larry hesitates and then turns abruptly to address the new-comer.

"Cindy, Ben is asking you a question."

Overruled. The witness must answer the question.

"Angel belonged with other angels," Cindy says softly, her eyes never wavering from the clouds. "I wanted her to be with the other angels."

"What the fuck does that mean, Larry?" Ben demands. "Does that mean it's okay for her to kill her baby?"

"Beyond the obvious reason, why is this touching such a nerve with you, Ben?"

"Because it just is, Larry. Does she think it's okay to kill her baby? She doesn't even seem upset about it. She thinks it's okay to kill her baby or something. What's going on?"

"Cindy? Would you like to talk to Ben, here? He's got some questions he seems to want answers to. Can you help us out?" Larry tries again to pull Cindy back from outer space.

Cindy whispers, "I just wanted her to be free."

"What about the baby's father?" Ben asks, his voice crack-ing. "Did you even think about him? What about the baby's father?"

"Okay, Ben, that's enough," Larry cautions.

Cindy crosses her arms and slowly rocks her body back and forth in her chair. Ben is steaming; the group is spellbound. Cindy starts to suck her thumb.

"Let's move on," Larry says as he pulls an empty chair into the middle of the circle. "Ben? Why don't we talk about what you're feeling right now. What if you direct what you have to say to Cindy to the chair instead."

"What I'm feeling right now?"

"Yes."

"Pissed off. I feel pissed off, Larry. I mean, this girl comes in and talks about killing her baby like it's okay to do that, you know? Doesn't that piss you off?" Ben addresses the rest of the group.

"Doesn't anybody else see that this is fucked up?" he asks again.

"I do." Tear-streaked Melanie throws support to her friend.

"Ben, in this group we try to talk without judgment," Larry says. "Can you see that you're passing judgment on Cindy right now? Maybe we can instead figure out what bothers you the most about Cindy's situation. Do you understand what I'm saying?"

"I guess," Ben sulks. "It bothers me that she didn't want her baby. That she thought she could just throw her away or something. Like trash."

Cindy is gazing at Ben.

"A baby's not trash, Larry! You don't throw a baby away just because it's not easy for you! You can't do that."

"Does that remind you of anything, Ben?"

With the back of his hand Ben wipes away the spittle that invariably forms in the corners of his mouth.

"My mom used to say that she wanted to throw me away and start over. She used to tell me that all the time. That if I wasn't careful she'd just throw me out with the trash. I didn't mind it so much when she hit me, but the trash thing, that killed me. I used to be so scared about that, you know? I used to pray that I'd get really big so that I couldn't fit into a trash bag. One summer? One summer I grew. I got, like, six inches taller. I was so relieved. I knew then that I wouldn't fit in the bag. Even one of those big Hefty bags for leaves and stuff? I knew I wouldn't fit into that. Until that summer I really thought she'd do it. Throw me out."

Ben hangs his head. Larry puts his hand on Ben's giant shoulder. In the corner of the room Melanie is sniffing. Cindy's eyes are dry.

"Medication time!" the nurse calls down the corridor two hours later.

Within minutes the ragged group forms an uneven line in front of the pill station.

"I hate this," Kristen mutters to Isabel.

"Why?" Isabel looks at her and wonders about Nick.

Kristen holds her hand up to Isabel's ear and whispers behind it. "It's poison, you know. They're trying to poison us."

"What?"

"Come on, Isabel." Kristen becomes impatient. "Don't play dumb. You know they're poisoning us. They don't want to have to bother with us. It's Darwinian."

She used to seem so normal.

"I read this article about how the pharmaceutical companies try out new drugs on mental patients without telling them. That's what's going on here. That's why they're always so nice to us at medication time. They don't want to piss us off or we'll refuse to come. Why do you think they watch us swallow the pills?"

Isabel has a blank look on her face so Kristen continues her paranoid rant. "I'll tell you why. Because we're freaking guinea pigs, that's why."

"Kristen?" The nurse calls.

"Here!"

"Hawaiian Punch or Crystal Light?"

"Hawaiian Punch, please," Kristen answers sweetly.

As the nurse hands her a Dixie cup, Kristen turns and throws Isabel a conspiratorial smile.

She's not swallowing. I knew it.

Isabel watches Kristen closely. It looks like she is washing the medicine down with the punch. But Isabel steps out of line and watches Kristen duck into the bathroom around the corner.

What a freaking cliché.

Fifty-Two

Isabel

"Isabel? Ted Sargent again. I'm told that you are under the weather and I'm sorry to hear that. However, we do need to schedule a meeting sooner rather than later. I understand you don't feel well, but business is business. So please call my assistant, Deborah. We'll be waiting to hear from you."

"Isabel, it's John. I'm not gonna lie to you, kiddo. Sargent wants to reevaluate your contract. I've tried talking to him, but he's a shithead and won't listen to reason. I'm calling you because he keeps calling up here looking for you and people are starting to ask questions. My advice? Fuck him. But you may want to make it easier on yourself and return his call. I thought you should know it doesn't look good. Fuck. I hate this phone call. Call anytime. Bye."

"Hi, this is a message for Isabel. Isabel, this is Jack Cartwright with 'Page Six' of the *Post*. I'm hearing a lot of rumors about you and your future at ANN, and before I write anything up I wanted to speak with you. Hear your side of the story. You know the drill. Give me a call. I'm at 212-555-8765. Thanks. I need to hear from you by the end of the day. Deadlines, you know."

"Isabel, Michele again. Sorry to keep rambling on your machine but I thought you should know that this guy from the *Post* is calling people here in the newsroom and asking questions about you. I'm not saying anything, but he did ask to speak with me. Thought you should know. Call me. Bye."

"Yeah, Eagle One, this is Eagle Two. Checking command post. Looking for signs of life. I got your back, soldier. You know that, right? I'd take a damn bullet for you. Okay, that's a ten-four."

"Isabel, what *is* this shit? I just got a call from the *Post* asking me about our divorce! What the *fuck* is going on? Have you filed? This is totally fucked up. *Now* I can see why you won't return my phone calls. Payback's a bitch, right? Well, two can play that game. I'd suggest you call me back before I retain a lawyer and sue you for libel. You want to screw me? Well, come and get it. Try me. You better call me back. I'm going to go before your shitty machine cuts me off. You have it programmed to do that or something? I wouldn't put it past you."

I'm offended by that. My answering machine is top of the line.

Fifty-Three

Isabel

Isabel starts running every morning. For thirty minutes she follows the road that loops around the grounds and within days she is jogging it twice. The running is cathartic, a way to sweat out the toxins of the cigarettes smoked the previous day; a way to escape the commotion in the unit; a way to regain her focus on the outside world. Sometimes, if she starts early enough in the day, she happens on deer, grazing on the dew-soaked lawn. She stops and watches the graceful creatures, feeling a sense of magic, as if they are symbols of good luck.

"You're looking well today," Dr. Seidler remarks with a trace of surprise. Isabel walks in, still sweating from her run.

"I'm feeling pretty good, actually," Isabel answers. "Just being able to run again, to sweat even, is really helping me." *That and a few shocks to the brain.*

"How do you think it's helping you?"

"I just feel better. I can't explain it."

"You know about endorphins—I certainly think you're feeling that—but I think it's also a healthy way to get back in the game, so to speak. To get back into a regular routine…"

"Yes." Instead of staring off into space, as she often does during their sessions, Isabel focuses on her therapist. She feels like she is seeing Dr. Seidler for the first time.

"What are you thinking about right now?"

Isabel waits a beat and then answers. "I was thinking that up until now you've looked kind of blurry to me. Like when you look through a camera and something's just a touch out of focus. But today I'm getting a clear picture. It's weird."

Dr. Seidler smiles and sits back in her chair. Isabel relaxes, too, and eases back against the sofa cushions.

"That's a good sign, Isabel. That's a very good sign."

Fifty-Four

"Wa-hey, there! Beautiful day for a run." The gardener smiles broadly at Isabel as she approaches the flower bed he is weeding.

During runs, Isabel practices deep breathing in through her nose and out through her mouth. She enjoys concentrating on the mechanics of the run: feeling her legs move back and forth, pumping her arms in concert with her legs all the while conscious of her breathing technique. She also thinks about her mother's advice: love yourself. The words float above her every step:

love.your.self.love.your.self.love.your.self.

"It's a great day!" she calls back to him.

"That's right. Ev'ry day's a lovely day."

Love.your.self.love.your.self.

Fifty-Five

Kristen

Kristen crosses the deck of the smoker's porch with a smile stretched across her face.

"You'll never guess what I'm doing tomorrow," she says to Isabel, who is tilting her head back to soak in the warm sun. She shades her eyes so she can get a better look at Kristen.

"What?"

"Guess!" Kristen is beaming.

"Oh, for God's sake, just tell me—I'm no good at guessing games."

"I'm going to visit my brother! I got a pass to go to Long Island and he's sending a car here to pick me up. A Town Car. You know—one of those limo wannabes? It's coming to pick me up in the morning and then it's going to wait for me all day and bring me back at night. It's all arranged. Can you believe it?"

Isabel closes her eyes, lets her arm fall back down and resumes sunbathing. "No, I can't believe it," she says wearily. "Good for you."

"*That* sounded real sincere." Kristen is miffed at Isabel's lack of enthusiasm. "What's wrong with *you?* By the way, Melanie's on a mission to steal your mattress so you better watch out."

"What?"

"Melanie's big kick today is that her back hurts because her mattress is old. She thinks it's a conspiracy against Jews, that you have a better mattress than her. I'm just warning you."

"Whatever."

"Wanna know a secret?" Kristen asks. "Can you keep your mouth shut?"

It takes all Isabel's energy to tilt her head back upright and shade her eyes once more. "What?"

"I may not come back tomorrow night." Kristen is gleeful. "My brother's cool. He'll back me up if I tell him I don't want to come back here."

"Aw, Kristen." *I do not have the energy for this.* "Are you sure that's a good idea?"

"What're you, my mother all of the sudden? Just be happy for me. This is what I want to do. They're always telling us to be 'true to ourselves—'" she takes a long drag of her cigarette "—I'm just following doctor's orders."

Kristen looks pleased with herself.

"Okay, first of all I've never heard them say 'be true to yourself.' And second of all, I know you aren't taking your meds."

Kristen looks like Isabel slapped her. Isabel stretches her legs out in front of her so they can get some sun.

"What?" Kristen recovers and tries to act as if she has no idea what Isabel is talking about.

"Look, I won't tell anyone your little secret." Isabel is too tired to continue much longer.

Kristen hardly makes a sound as she steps on her cigarette and walks away.

★ ★ ★

"Kristen! Someone's here for you!" Ben hollers down the hall toward Kristen's room. He sees Isabel turning the corner. "Isabel, did you know Kristen's got a day pass?"

"Yeah." A part of her knows Kristen is caught in a down-hill spiral and wants to reach out to help her, but the other part feels beleaguered. *I have to concentrate on saving myself…I can barely do that…I can't save Kristen, too.*

"I wonder where she's going." Ben is excited about the flurry of activity Kristen's day pass has inspired. "Do you know where she's going?"

"Long Island." Isabel answers Ben over her shoulder as she signs herself out for a walk around the grounds so she won't have to be confronted with Kristen's smug determination to ruin her life.

"Walk," she writes in the taped-off square next to her name. Then she fills in the time: "9:00," even though it is 8:55, buying thirty-five minutes of freedom before she has to check back in.

Isabel turns abruptly and leaves the unit when she hears the sound of Kristen's door shutting and footsteps coming toward her.

Outside it is muggy and overcast. Coming from the freezing air-conditioned unit into the sticky air feels, at first, like sinking into a warm bathtub. Isabel rubs her bare arms as she follows the path to the parking lot. There, idling silently, is Kristen's sinister escape module. The windows are tinted so Isabel cannot get a look at the driver, but as she walks past she glances into the car through the clear glass of the front windshield. The driver is staring directly into her eyes. It un-nerves her so she quickens her pace up the gentle slope of the driveway.

Isabel knows Kristen is right behind her so, to avoid the awkwardness of a furtive farewell, she breaks into a light jog around the corner and out of view of the road she knows they will take.

On cue, the car slowly turns the corner and gently makes its way over the speed bump that separates the unit's parking lot from the main driveway. Isabel watches the car pick up speed then slow down at the front gate, pausing for oncoming traffic.

After its taillights blend into the stream of cars hurrying past, Isabel begins to run, sprinting at first and then tapering off into a slower pace. The air is thick with clusters of gnats but she does not mind.

Fifty-Six

Isabel

"Isabel, telephone!" Ben bellows down the hall after dinner.

Isabel had been writing in her journal. "Booth or kitchen?" she calls back.

"Hey! Keep it down, will you?" Regina yells from behind her closed door.

Isabel ignores her and asks again as she heads toward both pay phones. "Phone booth or kitchen, Ben?" Since Ben does not answer she checks the kitchen first. A visitor is in the middle of a conversation on that extension. Around the corner she sees the light beaming from the booth.

"Hello?"

"Isabel?" The voice is unrecognizable.

"Yes? Who is this?"

"It's me," the voice sniffs. "Kristen."

"Kristen, what's wrong? Are you on Long Island?" Isabel sits forward on the hard metal folding chair that barely fits inside the collapsible booth door.

"Um, no." Kristen is crying.

"What is it? Where are you?"

"I'm in the hospital."

"Oh, my God. Are you okay? What happened?"

"The driver," she sobs. "He was bad. He was a bad guy. Bad."

"What? What'd he do?"

"We ended up at JFK." Isabel strains to hear Kristen, who sounds as if she is sneaking the phone call. "When I got in he asked if I minded if he smoked in the car and I said no. Then I asked him if I could bum a cigarette and he handed me back one. There was something in that cigarette, Isabel. I just know it. I could taste it."

"Was it pot? Was it a joint?"

"No, not like that. It was like a menthol, but not really. I felt a head rush after two drags. Anyway, I kept smoking. I knew I shouldn't have but I thought, what the hell. Then I think I must have passed out or something because the next thing I know we're circling the airport. I told him I wasn't going to the airport, I was going to Long Island, and he just started laughing and saying for me to be quiet. That I didn't know what I was talking about." Kristen starts sobbing harder.

"Calm down. It's okay, Kristen. Just calm down." The words are empty, but Isabel does not know what else to say.

"Anyway—" Kristen takes a deep breath "—anyway, he told me to get out of the car, that the ride was over. He made me get out of the car at JFK!" Kristen dissolved into tears. "When I got out of the car I realized my shirt was on backward and two buttons on my jeans were undone. I turned around but he was gone."

"Jesus. What'd you do?"

"I wandered around for a while, I don't know how long. It was so scary. I haven't been out of the hospital in a long time." Isabel remembered her own confusion in Grand Central. "All the loud speaker announcements. It was frightening. Then some cop in the terminal came up and asked me if I needed directions. I must've looked lost or something."

"Then what?"

"I started to tell him what happened and then I started crying so he took me to this customs room—some weird room with nothing in it but a table and two chairs. The light was really bright. That's all I could think about, how bright the light was. Anyway, I started to tell him the whole story and he asked where the car had picked me up and when I told him he left a few seconds later to make a phone call." Kristen is sobbing too hard to continue.

Isabel waits.

"The next thing I know a different cop, at least I think he was a different cop, came in and asked me to follow him and they put me in an ambulance. I hadn't even finished the story yet!"

"But, Kristen, it's good they took you to the hospital. You said yourself the guy was a bad guy. They wanted the doctor to check you out, make sure you're okay. Maybe they think...well, maybe you were taken advantage of. Sexually assaulted..."

"Isabel, you aren't hearing me!" Kristen raises her voice. "I'm not in a regular hospital! I'm at Bellevue. They took me here because I told them I'd come from Three Breezes."

"Oh, my God."

"Yeah. And I have no idea how I'm going to get out of here. They gave me some pill and *made* me swallow it. I have no idea what they made me take. They don't believe me about the driver, either. I can tell. They think I made the whole thing up."

"What about your brother? He lined that car company up— can't he talk to the police? They can track down the driver through the company. They keep logs of who goes out on which pickup. In the meantime, can't he get you out of there while they look into it?"

Kristen's sobs turn into a hacking sort of laughter.

"What?" Isabel is bewildered. "What's so funny?"

"Oh, Isabel," Kristen sighs.

"What? Tell me what is so funny!"

"I didn't think you bought it."

"*Bought it?* What do you mean?"

Kristen starts laughing again.

"Kristen, what? What're you laughing about? Is it this story? Are you kidding about this story?"

"No, not *this* story." Kristen is impatient. "The *other* one."

"Kristen, what the hell is going on? What are you talking about?"

"I don't have a brother, Isabel!" she laughs triumphantly.

Kristen pauses to marvel at her own cleverness. "God. I thought *you* of all people would have figured it out, but I guess not. I guess I should thank you for cheering me up. I thought I'd never smile again after this whole disaster."

There is silence between them while reality takes hold.

"How'd you get your day pass?" Isabel's stomach lurches as she tries to piece together the puzzle. "Your doctors signed off on your pass—how'd you arrange that?"

"Listen, I don't have time to go into all that right now. I'll tell you later," Kristen says, the smile in her voice gone. "You've got to help me. Please. I don't know how I'm going to get out of here but I've got to."

Oh, now I'm supposed to help you?

Kristen's self-destruction simultaneously scares Isabel, sickens her and fills her with frustration. What frightens her the most about Kristen's determination to ruin her own life is the realness of it. *How long before I start to unravel? How long until I have a relapse?*

After a moment Isabel decides to put some distance between her sick friend and herself. *I am not like you. And I cannot save you.*

"Kristen, even if I wanted to help you I don't know how I could. Why don't you call your doctor?"

"My doctor there, you mean?"

"Yes. Your doctor could talk to the people there and get you transferred back."

"I don't want to go back on medication, Isabel. I'm not going back on that stuff. It's poison. They can't make me start taking that again. Besides, I don't need it anymore."

"Are you listening to me? Call your doctor. You should be talking to your doctor, Kristen. Okay?"

"Okay." Kristen takes several deep breaths. "Okay. I'll call my doctor."

"Good."

"Thanks, Isabel." Kristen sounds genuinely grateful.

Isabel hangs up the phone, leans back into the folding chair and closes her eyes.

"Isabel?" Ben is standing outside the phone booth.

"Yeah?" she answers as she stands and flattens herself against the door frame so that she can squeeze past him without coming into contact with his perpetually sweaty frame. She holds her breath against his smell.

"Sorry to bother you," Ben says nervously, oblivious to Isabel's attempts to circumvent his imposing body.

"Excuse me! I'm trying to get by here."

"Oh, sorry." He moves to the side.

"What is it?"

"Have I told you about Wellbutrin?" He smiles hopefully.

"Yes, Ben," Isabel sighs, and walks away. "I believe you have."

"It saved my life, Isabel. It's that simple." Ben follows Isabel down the hall. "I just can't say enough about it. Wellbutrin. It's amazing."

"That's great, Ben. Well, thanks for walking me back to my room. I'm going to be shutting the door now…."

"Wait! Isabel?"

"Bye, Ben."

"Isabel!" Ben continues after the door shuts in his face. "I wish you'd just listen to me, Isabel. Why won't anyone listen to me when I talk about Wellbutrin?" Ben knocks a few times and finally lumbers off.

Fifty-Seven

"Hi, this is a message for Isabel. Isabel, this is Deborah in Ted Sargent's office. Just wanted to let you know that we got your message and will plan on meeting on October 2. I'll be in touch on the first to confirm. Until then, hope you're feeling better. If you need to reach me I'm at extension 5421."

"Isabel, hi, it's me, Alex. Look, I'm sorry our conversation didn't go very well. I still get so upset hearing your voice. Please call me back. I promise I won't lose my temper again. I need to talk to you. I do love you, you know. Bye."

Fifty-Eight

Isabel

"Isabel?"

"Yeah?"

"It's Kristen. Sorry to wake you up in the middle of the night. It's just that there's only one pay phone here and there's always a line for it."

"What's up?" At the sound of Kristen's voice Isabel goes from groggy to wide awake. "Are you still at Bellevue?"

"Yeah. Isabel, you've got to get me out of here. Please? Please help me get out of here...."

"Kristen, I have no idea how to get you out of there. In case you forgot, I'm in a mental hospital, too. Did you call your doctor yesterday?"

"Yeah, and he wouldn't do anything. He said he'd handle it and I haven't heard word one from him. Listen, I can't talk long," Kristen whispers urgently into the phone. Isabel pictures her cupping her hand over the mouthpiece. "They're making me participate in a medication experiment. I don't have time to explain but I want you to know if anything happens to me, that I'm doing this against my will. Got it?"

"Kristen, what are you talking about?"

"I've got to go in a second. Someone's standing right behind me trying to hear what I'm saying. You're a reporter, you can do something about this. They use us for medical experiments against our will. I'm telling you, Isabel, this is a *huge* operation. My doctor said he was going to try to get me out of here but he hasn't called me back and frankly I think he's in on it, to be honest with you. Please help me. Please get me out of here."

Why me?

"Kristen, isn't there *anyone* else you could call? What about your parents? Can't you call them?"

"No! They don't know where I am and I want to keep it that way!"

"Why?"

"I've always been an albatross around their necks," Kristen says in a disgusted tone. "They wouldn't hesitate to write me off for medical experimentation if they thought it would get rid of me once and for all."

Isabel is tired and knows there is no reasoning with paranoia. "I've got to go."

"Okay, I read you. I'm with you. They're tapping the phones, right? You don't want them to be able to record this… thanks, Isabel. You're always one step ahead of me. *God!* I knew you were the *one person* who would understand. I'll call you back later. In the meantime, you'll do what I told you?"

"What?"

"Work on getting me out of here, remember?"

"Goodbye, Kristen."

"Bye!"

Isabel hangs up the phone and looks at her watch. Two in the morning. She thinks about staying up and watching television but instead makes her way back to her room and crawls back into her crinkly bed. Her sleep is fitful and unsatisfying.

At daybreak Isabel changes into her running clothes and tiptoes down the hall to the sign-out board. She heads out the door into the warm fall morning. She puts her head down and watches the pavement as she picks up speed.

"Wa-hey there, my friend." *Sure enough, the gardener.* "Lovely day we got here!"

Is he ever in a bad mood? Jesus.

"Yeah," she answers without meeting his eye.

Fifty-Nine

"I need to talk to you about a day pass." Isabel shifts uncomfortably in her seat. *Tell her. Tell her about Kristen.*

"Sure," Dr. Seidler says. "What's up?"

"I'm getting fired," Isabel says matter-of-factly. "I set up a meeting so they can go ahead and get it over with."

"You mentioned they were calling you." The therapist pauses. "How do you feel about the prospect of meeting with them? Who, exactly, would you be meeting with?"

"Ted Sargent—the head of the news division. He's the one who's been gunning for me ever since the Diana thing. I expect someone from Human Resources will be there as well. They don't know what I've been doing on this medical leave so I'm sure they feel like they've got to be careful, in case I'm in rehab for a drug problem. Wouldn't it be against the law for them to fire me if I was in rehab?"

"Yes, if you had a drug or alcohol problem they would have to hold your job for you if you were making a good-faith effort to be clean and sober. But that's not what we've got here, unfortunately, since you're on contract, and, as you've pointed out, your contract just happens to be expiring."

"So they get rid of me by not renewing. I know, I know. In a way it'll be a relief. I feel like this pressure's been building...I'm so ready to prick the balloon."

"Are you?"

"Yeah. I've thought about it and I've realized that that job, that *life,* is not for me. Plus, I don't want to go back into a work environment that's not friendly. Everybody'd be gossiping about me...speculating about what happened to me, blah, blah, blah. I'd rather have them do it and get it over with. The rest I can deal with."

Across the office optimistically filled with colorful southwestern decor, Dr. Seidler smiles at Isabel. *She's been smiling at me a lot lately...she gay or something?*

"What?" Isabel shifts again in her seat. "What're you smiling at?"

"You," she replies. "I'm smiling because you sound like you're feeling a bit stronger and, if my instincts are correct, more sure of yourself and what you want—or don't want—as the case may be. Is that a safe assumption?"

"Yeah, I guess so," Isabel says. "I do feel stronger. I don't know what's changed, but I do feel a little more sure of myself. Maybe being here in the Nut Hut has actually helped me. Go figure."

Dr. Seidler laughs. "Go figure. A lot of patients can't ever see their way to feeling better. In fact, I'd say that's true more times than not. Many people don't take advantage of the help they have access to here so they remain caught in the grip of their illnesses. Of course, many can't help it—they've been ill for so long or have gone without help for so long that a stay here is too little too late. It's refreshing to see someone like you come along. Someone who is self-reflective and open, for the most part, to receiving help...."

"There's something I need to tell you. Not about me. About another patient here. I feel bad for not having come forward sooner. Because she's in trouble."

"Who?"

"Kristen. Let me start from the beginning..." Isabel tells her doctor everything: about Kristen's not taking her medication, about Nick the orderly, the bizarre car ride that ended at JFK, about Kristen's paranoid phone calls from Bellevue... everything.

"I'm glad you told me." Dr. Seidler is looking up from the yellow legal pad she'd been scribbling notes on. "I'll take it from here, don't worry. You did the right thing coming to me about it.

"Switching gears, because our time's about up. About your day pass. When do you need to go?"

"October second. I'd need to leave in the morning—our meeting's first thing—and then I'm going to meet with Alex to cap off a warm-and-fuzzy love-fest day. I'll probably be getting back kind of late."

"That's fine." Dr. Seidler writes the date down on her calendar. "I'll have the pass for you tomorrow."

As Isabel leaves the session she scans the grounds looking for the gardener, feeling bad she had been abrupt with him earlier in the day. She looks along the tree line, where the manicured lawn meets the woods, at the beds of impatiens circling the cafeteria, and toward the sad structure on the hill where Peter is.

Sixty

Isabel

"Excuse me? Could I speak with Peter, please?" Isabel is nervous. The nurse looks up from her desk and cocks her head to one side.

"I know you!" she says. "You're the jogger!"

"Huh?"

"I see you running on the grounds every time I come in to work. You run right past the employee parking lot." She smiles.

"Ohhh…"

"We've been talking about you…we've never seen a patient running on the grounds before."

"Really?" Isabel smiles weakly.

"I think it's great," she says. "Good for you. Now, let's see where Mr. Peter might be." She swivels in her chair and checks a schedule hanging on the wall behind her. "He's in art. You can go meet him there, if you want to. You know where the art studio is, right?"

Ah, yeah.

"Yes. Thank you." Isabel goes back out the door.

★ ★ ★

Isabel tentatively enters the art studio.

The children are all engrossed in their various projects. The art teacher looks up and smiles. "Hello! Can I help you?"

"Um..." With a not-so-subtle flick of her head, Isabel motions for the teacher to step out of earshot from the children so they can speak privately. "I was wondering if I could borrow Peter for a moment," Isabel asks shyly.

"Well," the young teacher looks apologetic. "You can certainly talk to him, it's not that, but while they're here they can't leave the building. They have to wait here for their escort back to their unit. So you guys could go over there—" she points to an empty table off to the side "—if you want. That'd be cool."

Art teachers are all flower children. That's in a rule book somewhere. All art teachers must look as if they've just stepped off Haight-Ashbury circa 1968.

"Great. Now, I know this sounds weird, but he's not expecting me, so could you come over and let him know it's okay to talk with me?"

"Sure. No problem."

"Thanks. By the way, I'm Isabel."

"Nice to meet you, Isabel." Her face lights up like a dandelion. "I'm Sunshine."

Peter is painting. Other children are talking but he is silent.

"Peter?" He does not look up. "Peter, I'm Isabel. I've tried to talk to you a couple of times. Is it okay if I paint with you for a minute?"

Sunshine smiles and floats away.

No response from Peter. Isabel picks up a brush and dips it into the yellow paint. She starts to paint a huge yellow circle.

"Peter, I'm going to be straight with you." Isabel takes a firmer tone. "I don't know why it is, but I have to talk to you, I have to. So you can just go on painting and pretending you can't hear me, but I'm going to talk to you." Though he has not looked up, Peter's brush has stopped moving along the paper.

"I don't know what your story is," Isabel begins. "I don't know why you're here…and I don't need to know. That's your business. But there's something about you that reminds me of myself when I was your age."

His brush is still. He is listening.

"Did you know that when I was your age I did everything I could to avoid anthills, to make sure no one stepped on them? My brothers would step on them and I could literally *feel* them suffocating under the pavement. I could hear them shrieking for help, I swore I could. I still make sure I step around them. I saw you the other day, I saw you watching out for them, too. That's when I decided I had to talk to you."

Peter's head slowly, ever so slowly, moves in an upward direction.

He's going to look at me!

"You know, I used to feel *everyone's* pain. Animals, insects, people…anyone who was hurt, I could feel it in here." Isabel hugs herself, showing him how deeply she felt. Then she pauses and listens to her own words. "And it made me sad all the time.

"But I've realized…" *What? What have I realized?* "I've realized that if I do that maybe I can't feel my *own* pain. I walk around worrying that I've upset someone, let someone down, made someone mad at me, stepped on someone's anthill…you know? I can't take on everyone else's pain. The ants can take care of themselves, is what I'm saying. Let's face it, they've been here long before us and they'll survive longer than us…"

He's looking up! Keep going.

"…so we have to concentrate on ourselves. On keeping some huge giant from stepping on *us*. Does that make sense?"

Peter's head slowly bobs in agreement.

"Just help yourself, Peter. Don't worry about the ants." Isabel remembers her mother's words. "Just help yourself. Love yourself as much as you love the animals and the insects and you'll get better. You'll get out of this place. I know you can do it. You can get out of here."

Then something strange happens. Something strange and beautiful. Peter lifts his small head and smiles at her.

She strokes his tiny head and hugs him. Hugs him completely.

She holds him for a moment and then releases him.

Without saying anything, Isabel stands up and walks out the door. "Bye, Sunshine." She smiles as she says the name.

"Have a *great* day," Sunshine answers, really meaning it.

Isabel looks back at her friend. Peter is standing motionless, watching her go.

Isabel steps out into the sunlight.

Sixty-One

"Where's my basket?" Casey calls to Isabel after shutting her car door. "By the way, I'm assuming I should lock it, right? Then again I've been trying to talk Michael into a new car for years so I'm gonna leave it open and hope one of your loony friends has the good sense to hot-wire it and go AWOL."

Isabel laughs and inhales the smell of Casey's shampoo as she hugs her. "God, I've missed you!"

"I've missed you, too, kid, but if you don't let go of me your doctor will start saying things like 'Isabel, I find it *interesting* that you chose not to tell me about your homosexual tendencies' and that's about the last thing you need right now, girlfriend."

Isabel links her arm through her friend's, turning her to the unit.

"Now, remember I told you about how weird it is here," Isabel warns Casey. "You sure you're up to this?"

"Are you kidding me? I've been scraping macaroni and cheese out from under the stove for the past three years. This is the most exciting thing I've done in, like…well, ever. Where're you taking me? They gonna do a cavity search on me or some-thing? If so, could you make sure it's a guard who looks like Tom Cruise?"

"Julie, this is my friend, Casey," Isabel says as she reaches for the clipboard to sign her in. "We're just going to be out on the lawn."

Julie looks at Casey's empty hands and then says that would be fine.

"Why'd she look at my hands? She wondering if I'm single? She's cute. For a price I could be."

"I'm insulted. You won't be *my* lesbian lover but you'd take Julie, who still wears headbands? She's checking to make sure you aren't smuggling in any contraband," Isabel answers, open-ing the door to the outside again. "No razor blades, nooses. You know. Just your basic suicide-ward security."

"Honey, I'm less worried about you now than I am about me," Casey sighs, settling into a chair. "I almost put my head in the oven yesterday, I swear. Michael's driving me insane. Come to think of it, I wonder if they have any rooms avail-able here. We could bunk together. Braid each other's hair. It'd be just like old times."

Isabel soaks up Casey's energy as if basking in the sun.

Casey looks at her. "Seriously, you look too thin. Are you eating?"

"Don't start." Isabel senses the conversation is turning se-rious.

"I know, I know. You can take the mom out of the sub-urbs…" She trails off and surveys the grounds. "Pretty nice digs. How is it *really?*"

"If I told you you wouldn't believe me. But it's fine. It's good now, actually. I think I'm doing better."

"You look like shit, if you don't mind my saying."

"You really need to form some opinions, Case."

"What is it? You having trouble sleeping, too?"

"Casey?"

"What, honey?" Casey's face studies Isabel's.

"Um. It's just. Well. I just don't believe you're really here. I can't believe you came to visit me here."

"You can't? You're the best friend I've ever had."

"But…but, I dropped the ball for you. I wasn't there for you when you were having your biopsy." Isabel stops fighting her guilty tears and lets them roll down her cheeks.

Casey takes her hand. "But you wanted to be."

"But I wasn't there for you," Isabel sniffs.

"Look at me." Casey squeezes her hand. "You wanted to be."

Sixty-Two

"Is there anyone who would like to come sit in this chair and start group off tonight?" Larry addresses the group as he paces. "We haven't done this in a while…have someone actually sit in the chair. Any volunteers tonight or shall I pick someone?"

Ben raises his hand.

"Yes? Ben, would you like to sit here?" Larry motions to the chair.

"Um, no. Actually I was wondering why we aren't starting with introductions? We haven't done that in a while, either, and I was just wondering why. I like that part of group. Why can't we start that way?"

"Ben, we all know each other now so it's not necessary. We usually go around the group if there's a newcomer. I hear that you enjoy it so maybe we can do it once in a while. Why don't we quickly go around the room and say our names. Why don't you start?"

"Hi, my name is Ben," he says with pride.

"I'm Melanie," "I'm Isabel," "Regina," "Cindy." Sukanya does not introduce herself.

"Okay, good. Who's in the chair? Who has something they would like to bring up—"

"Larry?" Regina squeaks and then clears her throat to begin again. "I have something I want to bring up with the group."

"Come on down." Larry's Bob Barker imitation embarrasses Isabel.

"It's about Keisha," Regina says.

Isabel sits bolt upright and blurts out, "What about Keisha?"

Larry seems interested, too. "Go ahead, Regina."

"I want the group to know that she's doing well. I don't know if anyone knew this or not but Keisha was facing some, ah, legal problems when she left here. She's overcome those *problems* and is doing really well now. It's not talking out of school to tell the group this since she's not in our group anymore, right?"

"It's okay to let the group know about Keisha's good fortune outside of the hospital," Larry answers. "It's always good to hear about progress toward wellness. If anyone wishes to talk further to Regina about Keisha, why don't you all do that after group. Who'd like to go next? Melanie?"

As Melanie gets up to sit in the chair, Isabel's mind races with thoughts of Keisha.

She checks her watch.

God! Time is dragging by. This is going to take forever.

"Elwin's at his wit's end with me..." Melanie is crying.

Yeah, yeah, yeah...and your parents-in-law hate you...get some new material Melanie.

"...then my mother-in-law told me I wasn't good enough for her son," Melanie continues.

Isabel looks at her watch again.

It's only been ten minutes. Will this ever end?

"...and what's so weird about the mattresses is that I cannot believe it's taken me this long to see that the nurses have it in for me," Melanie sobs.

"Regina? Could I talk to you for a minute about Keisha?" Isabel is so eager for the rest of Keisha's story she practically tackles Regina on the way out of group.

"Sure," Regina says as she allows herself to be led toward the smoking porch, even though she does not smoke. Isabel knows it is selfish, but she is dying for a cigarette.

"It's great news, isn't it?" Regina asks politely while Isabel hunches over the wall lighter.

"Yeah," Isabel says through her teeth, still trying to light up. "Now, back up and tell me everything."

Regina hesitates. "How much do you know about what was going on with her when she left here?"

"I was there when they arrested her, Regina," Isabel replies impatiently. "I know about her nephew."

Regina is relieved. "Okay. Well, my husband's a cop and he told me about this because he'd seen Keisha here when he visited and knew I was friendly with her. You know how she was accused of killing her nephew after she was raped—"

"Yeah? What happened?"

"I guess her lawyer was really good and got all this evidence together that showed that the guys who raped Keisha were the ones that killed the baby. My husband says they left their fingerprints all over everything and that the cops who arrested Keisha in the first place were incompetent assholes, if you'll excuse the expression." Regina looks embarrassed. "My husband has the dirtiest mouth—working on the job, like he does," she explains.

"So it didn't have to go to trial, then?" Isabel looks off into the field as she thinks about how relieved Keisha's mother must have been.

"Yeah. They dismissed the charges and the guys who raped her are now being charged with murder, too. I guess what goes around comes around, huh?"

"Yeah, no kidding." Isabel feels a wave of longing. "Your husband hasn't, by any chance, talked to her, has he?"

"Oh, no. No, he was just keeping track of the case for my benefit. He wasn't part of that investigation."

"Maybe I should call her," Isabel ventures, looking for guidance from Regina.

"I think that sounds like a great idea," Regina says. "You should call her. You could get her phone number from the nurses, I bet. Sometimes they're weird about giving that stuff out, but I bet they'd do it for *you*."

"Why would they do it for me and not for someone else?" Isabel is confused by Regina's comment.

"You're not like everybody else, Isabel," Regina says, blushing slightly. "The nurses'll give you Keisha's number because you can be trusted. You're normal."

Isabel's skin tingles at the compliment.

"There's no such thing as normal, Regina," she says, believing it for the first time.

"Yeah, well, you're as close to it as they come," Regina answers as she rises to return to her room.

Isabel feels a rush of gratitude for this innocent pronouncement. She feels like hugging the shy Regina but knows she will not. She had had little to do with Regina and knows nothing about her. So she calls out to her instead.

"Thank you, Regina."

In the doorway Regina turns back and their eyes lock.

"Thank you for everything," Isabel says.

Regina turns and the door shuts behind her. Isabel puts out her cigarette and walks out into the field to enjoy the last minutes of twilight.

Sixty-Three

"I keep thinking about Alex and the stuff he used to say to me," Isabel tells Dr. Seidler the next morning. "It's weird. Here I am getting ready to go in for this really important meeting at ANN and all I can do is hear Alex's voice in my head. You'd think I'd be more concerned with my career at this point."

"Let's look at that." Dr. Seidler crosses her legs and settles herself more comfortably. "For starters, what exactly have you been hearing Alex say?"

"All that stuff about how I didn't deserve the job I had before this one—the reporting job I lost? I think I told you about that. That's what's going through my head, over and over. Him telling me I *deserved* to be fired."

"Interesting," Dr. Seidler said. "Do you have any idea why this, of all the things Alex said to you, would be the thing that's getting a lot of play in your mind?"

"I don't know," Isabel said. "I can't figure it out."

"Might it be because you're feeling anxious about the ANN meeting, which is—as you described it to me, and correct me if I'm wrong—concerning the possible loss of your job. That, I would imagine, calls up all sorts of feelings in you like dread, sadness, even a little relief. But maybe Alex's words reflect what you are feeling about yourself right now."

Isabel gives it thought.

"I could be wrong, of course. This is only a theory," Dr. Seidler continues. "But I do remember you talking about how low your self-esteem was when you met him, so maybe you felt there was some truth to what he was saying. It's hard, in instances like these, to know which comes first, the chicken or the egg. Your self-esteem was low from the abuse you endured with David—so maybe Alex capitalized on that and, with his verbal and physical abuse, made it worse. Or maybe you were feeling a bit better about yourself but Alex's words and actions knocked you back to feeling bad again. Why do you think you were drawn to such abusive people?"

"I really don't know. But how does this relate to the stuff I have going on in my head now?"

"I'm not sure. I think, though, you seem to be on a precipice. This is still an unformed thought so bear with me, but I wonder if you don't know what to think of yourself. After your relationship with David ended you could have gone either way. You could have found someone the opposite of David, who treated you with respect, someone who showed you only love. Instead, though, you went with Alex, who repeated the patterns of abuse. Maybe Alex confirmed your own self-loathing. In other words, maybe Alex finished the job David started."

"But how come I have been so attracted to this type of guy?"

"You don't know?"

"I don't think I do."

"Let me ask you this, David and Alex—what did they have in common? Besides being hotheaded?"

"Um…"

"Were they intense, would you say?"

"Yes. Very."

"And your father wasn't, right? He was intense about his job, no doubt about it. He was even intense about drinking. But about you?"

"Not in the least."

"Could you have been drawn to that intensity? Could it be that you were craving, starving really, for that kind of attention from a man, since you didn't get it from your father?"

Silence.

"And now you are again at the end of an abusive relationship and you could go one way or another. You could choose to surround yourself with healthy individuals who respect you, or you could find someone who, just as Alex did, takes advantage of your self-doubt."

"But I didn't consciously choose an unhealthy person. Alex seemed like a good, supportive person…."

"Yes, I know. But on some level you had to have seen signs of trouble."

"You're saying I brought this on myself?"

"No! I am in no way saying you deserved this, Isabel. No. Instead, what I'm saying is that we all make choices based on how we feel at a certain time. You were unsure of yourself when Alex came along. In essence, he decided for you how to feel about yourself. He is the one who caused the abuse, Isabel…not you. But now you are trying to find yourself once again and it's very important, at times like these, for you—for everyone—to feel good about yourself, about who you are inside. That will attract good people to you like a magnet. Do you understand?"

"I think so," Isabel replies softly.

"I see in you a strong, smart, lovely person. You need to see that in yourself. That is key. If you value yourself, no one will trample you again."

Isabel felt the way she had years ago when she visited a psychic with her mother at a county fair. The astrologer had read her palm and Isabel had fallen into a trance, her hand tickled as the astrologer's soothing voice washed over her. She rubs her arms and glances at the clock hanging over Dr. Seidler's desk. Their session has ended.

"I know it's time for you to go, but do you have any reaction to what I just said to you?"

"I have to absorb it," Isabel says, not wanting to shake the trance. "It makes sense, I just have to absorb it."

"Very well. Until next time, then."

"Until next time."

Sixty-Four

"Mrs. Jackson? This is Isabel Murphy, Keisha's friend?"

"Oh, hello Isabel. How are you, honey?"

"I'm fine, thanks. I heard the great news about Keisha—is she home?"

"Isn't it wonderful?" Mrs. Jackson sounds elated. "God answered my prayers—He answered my prayers, that's for sure! Let me go get her—she was just getting ready to go on a job interview...Keisha? Telephone!"

Through the earpiece Isabel hears footsteps approach the phone.

"'Lo?"

"Keisha?"

Isabel is surprised at how different the breathless voice on the other end of the line sounds.

"Yeah?"

"It's Isabel. Um, from Three Breezes," Isabel quickly adds, knowing that a last name will not make a difference. She knows Keisha's mother was just being polite pretending to know who she is.

"Hey," Keisha says in slow recognition. "Hey...how you doing? Wow, how's it going?"

"Fine. I'm fine. I heard the news about you, though—you must be doing great. Congratulations!"

"Thanks. Blew my mind, I'll tell you what."

"I bet. I bet."

What do we talk about now? I shouldn't have called.

"What about you? Where you calling from?" Keisha asks.

"Huh? Oh. I'm still here—at the hospital."

"Oh," Keisha says awkwardly. "How's it going there? Kristen still there?"

"No. No, she's not here. I'm probably getting ready to leave soon, too."

Now I sound defensive.

"Great!" Keisha sounds relieved to have something to congratulate Isabel for.

"Well," Isabel says in a tone that signals the end of the conversation. "I just wanted to call and say congratulations. I'm really glad for you." *Say something more.* "Now you can start your life again."

Theirs had been a friendship forged in anguish, suspended in time. In real life it would be impossible to sustain.

"Thanks. And thanks for calling."

Keisha hangs up immediately. Isabel knows they will never speak again.

"Isabel, before we start I have something I want to tell you," Dr. Seidler says gingerly. "You talked to me about Kristen and what's happened to her since she left Three Breezes."

"Yes?"

"I want you to know that, as I told you I would, I have followed up with Dr. Flagg—her therapist here. He told me he had indeed been in contact with Kristen. In fact, he has arranged for her to be transferred back here from Bellevue. She told him to be sure to get that message to you so he asked that I speak with you."

"Wow." Isabel does not know what to make of this news.

"How does that make you feel, hearing she will be returning?"

"When? When is she coming back?"

"That I'm not sure about," Dr. Seidler answers. "I doubt Dr. Flagg knows for sure. There is a lot of paperwork to be completed before she can come back, that and consultations. It could be as early as tomorrow. But the bottom line is she will be coming back. You have an odd look on your face."

Isabel is hypnotized by the raindrops beading on the office window. She watches as one trickles down and melts into another—the two forming a miniature river winding its way down the pane of glass.

"I can't believe she pulled it off," she says, still watching nature draw pictures.

"Pulled what off?"

"Everything." Isabel brings her doctor into focus. "First that whole concoction about her brother. Then getting transferred back here. I don't know. I thought I knew her but I guess not."

"Is that difficult for you? To find out someone isn't who you thought they were?"

"Yeah. It's some kind of weird pattern with me," Isabel says. "Alex wasn't who I thought he was. All that time we had all these problems: with anger, with communication. Maybe it's like you said last time: I took in what I felt about myself at the time. I think that's true.

"Kristen comes along and, at least in the beginning, I think we have so much in common. We're from similar backgrounds, we both had bad luck with our first loves and with guys in general. But then she has this freaky thing happen to her with the limo driver—I still don't know what went on there. It's like her paranoia has totally taken over...."

She trails off and looks back out the window at the rain.

"What about you? You aren't what you first thought you were, either."

"Huh?"

"You told me about the conversation with your mother—she thought you were this perfect daughter and you told her you weren't. But maybe that was you telling *yourself* you weren't perfect."

Yes.

"Is it going to be difficult for you to be face-to-face with Kristen when she gets back here?"

"Kristen? No. I think I've put enough distance there. But Alex...coming face-to-face with him is going to be the toughest thing. I feel if I can just do that I will have conquered the biggest obstacle of all."

"To come face-to-face with someone who betrayed your trust?"

"To come face-to-face with reality."

Sixty-Five

The rain has left the air thick with humidity, and inside the unit it feels more like the middle of August than the end of September. The central air is working overtime and Isabel begins counting the seconds between its blasts in order to bring on sleep. She makes it to one hundred and loses interest.

Outside her room, over the hum of white noise artificially produced by her Hammacher Schlemmer, Isabel hears a series of doors opening and closing. She strains to understand the muffled urgency of a distant conversation that gets louder and then stops altogether.

They're late for the one-thirty check.

Out of boredom and the certainty that sleep is futile, Isabel gets up and turns the noisemaker off. She opens her door and peeks down the empty hallway.

She follows the voices until she can vaguely make out a word or two. Isabel recognizes the raspy intonations of her favorite night nurse. Connie is involved in the dispute, evidently taking place in the soft room.

"No!" she hears a male voice say.

"Wait until the count of three," Connie orders.

"If we…" Another voice trails off before Isabel can identify it.

Around the corner, light from inside the soft room falls in a triangle across the linoleum floor. Shadows slice into it from time to time as figures pass from one side of the room to another. The ebb and flow of agitated voices continues.

"You aren't listening to me!"

"Okay, here's what we're going to do," Connie is saying over the din. "On the count of three we're going to lift the top part off simultaneously. The restraints are in place so this shouldn't be a problem. Fred, you stand on the right and get ready to grab her if you need to."

"She looks pretty sedated," the male voice replies. "Maybe that shot's finally kicking in."

Isabel inches forward and looks over her shoulder. The hall is still empty. Whoever is in the soft room is commanding the attention of all of the night staff.

"Okay, ready?" Connie asks. "One!"

Isabel inches forward.

"Two!"

Isabel takes two more steps toward the room.

"Three!"

As she moves to the edge of the doorway she hears the sounds of metal hitting the ground and the muffled sound of a woman groaning.

Isabel takes a deep breath for courage and forces herself to look into the room. Strapped into a stretcher with a square of duct tape angrily slapped across her mouth, is Kristen. Her eyes are wildly darting from side to side and sweat is beading on her forehead. She looks petrified, like a trapped animal moments before it tries to gnaw its own leg off in order to escape.

Connie and several orderlies have peeled another stretcher off the top of her. While the others are busy cleaning up a mess of medical equipment, Connie crouches at Kristen's forehead and is whispering something to her, trying to calm her down. Isabel feels physically ill and turns away.

It is as if a flash of lightning has illuminated a photo negative of her nightmare and in that one moment, the difference between Isabel and Kristen has crystallized. In that instant Isabel knows they are traveling different roads. She stands there, outside the soft room, and hears Regina's voice. *You're not like the others...you're normal.* She imagines Ben in camouflage marching down the halls of his school. She pictures Sukanya in the laundry room, reciting a Yiddish prayer. She sees Lark's bloated body dangling, lifeless above the dryer.

She walks slowly, mechanically back to her room.

When Isabel closes the door to her room she knows, perhaps for the first time in years, that she is going to live. Before this night the prospect of returning to the "real world" had filled her with anxiety. Now she feels a quiet confidence.

Sixty-Six

"There's nothing more for me to do here," Isabel announces to Dr. Seidler within thirty seconds of the beginning of their appointment. "I'm ready to go home now."

"Wow," Dr. Seidler smiles. "Good. Okay, let's get you home. Tell me about this resolve. What happened?"

"I'm ready to go," Isabel says, completely sure of herself. "I know I've said this before, but this time I mean it. I am truly ready to go."

"Excellent. I think you've done some good work here, Isabel," Dr. Seidler says. "You've made incredible progress. It's my hope that you've also learned some coping skills so when you feel overwhelmed in the future you can better deal with it. There are a lot of options out there."

"I know. I do feel like I've gotten much better about talking things out rather than letting them build up inside. That's been my problem all along. One of my problems. The rest I can continue with in New York, with Mona. That's an ongoing project."

Dr. Seidler has been nodding enthusiastically. "Absolutely," she says.

"So. When can I blow this Popsicle joint?"

"Let me get your paperwork together and prepare you for your official discharge. You should know that I am required to put in a call to your therapist, Mona, just as a courtesy more than anything else. It's just to notify her that you are leaving. You will need to call her to set up an appointment. As part of your discharge we need to be sure that you will have out-patient follow-up care. Just a formality since I know you will continue your work with her."

"I'll call her right after this," Isabel says. "And I'll call my mother to come pick me up. I need to tell her when, though."

"When would feel right for you? I know you have your meetings in two days."

"I can do it from there. Maybe it's best that I get acclimated for a day back home before I go into the office. So...tomorrow? Can I leave tomorrow? That way I'll have Larry's group today and a chance to say goodbye to everyone."

"You're sure about this, Isabel?"

"Positive."

"Then let's make it tomorrow." Dr. Seidler smiles warmly. "Why don't you have your parents pick you up right after our morning appointment so we can say goodbye as well."

"Great." Isabel had forgotten she would also be saying good-bye to Dr. Seidler.

"Now that that's settled, let's talk about what you're going home to," Dr. Seidler says. "Let's try to use every minute we've got left talking about what you'll face when you leave here. That is, unless you have something else you'd like to address before you go?"

"No. That's a good idea."

"There are two pressing issues I feel you need to be especially careful about when you leave here, but I know you don't need me to tell you that. Your meeting at ANN is likely to be stressful, and you'll be facing Alex for the first time in quite a while. How do you think you can best cope with those situations?"

"See, that's why it's best if I go in from the outside, not from here. If I went into the city from here, got overwhelmed again—even if it's only half as bad as it was on that other trip—then went in to meet with my boss, I'd be a basket case. I'd have absolutely no strength to say anything in my defense, even if it were just to save face. I'd be worried that my medication wouldn't be powerful enough to prevent another panic attack and I'd freeze up again right there in Sargent's office. It would be a nightmare.

"Whereas if I leave here tomorrow I can have a night to get used to my apartment and I'll have a fighting chance of salvaging at least a shred of dignity at ANN."

"True." Dr. Seidler is nodding again. "It just occurred to me, what if they don't fire you?"

"Huh?"

"Well, you've been assuming you're going in to face the firing squad. But what if you come clean and tell them you've been getting the help you need in order to deal with the medical problem that had prevented you from doing your job and you feel ready to tackle it again. What if they said, 'Okay, Isabel. Then come on back.' What then?"

"I honestly don't think that'll happen."

"Still…"

"I'm not one hundred percent sure right now. I feel like I can't make that decision in here. Maybe that's why I want to leave. The big decisions of my life right now need to be made at home. I need to be in a different context. Maybe I would go back to ANN. Maybe I could kid myself that I wouldn't let myself get that stressed again or that I know how to deal with stress now so everything would be better. But maybe not. Let's face it, the stress is always going to be there—this is the news business. I just need to figure out whether I want my life to be filled with that. And that's something I can't figure out from an Adirondack chair at Three Breezes."

"Well said. So, what about Alex?"

Isabel pauses.

"In some ways that's a dilemma that's unsolvable. I mean, that train's already left the station. I can't help him. I know that now. I can't be responsible for his happiness."

"He made you feel responsible for his *un*happiness before. How do you know you won't get drawn back into feeling responsible again?"

"I feel like I've been through too much since then. I don't know," Isabel says, straightening herself in her chair. "I don't know how to describe it better, but I just *feel* ready."

"Then let's get you out of here."

Sixty-Seven

"Mom?"

"Honey, hi!"

"I'm leaving."

"What?" Katherine sounds alarmed. "What do you mean? Where are you going?"

"I'm going home."

"Honey—" she calls out to Isabel's father "—pick up the phone! It's Isabel! She's checking herself out of the hospital! Isabel, did they say you were ready for that?"

"They said I could leave when I felt ready and I do." Isabel feels like it is real now that she has told her mother. "Can you come pick me up?"

"Isabel? What's wrong?" Her father sounds preoccupied to her.

She takes a deep breath, bathing her internal organs with oxygen, and releases it.

"Isabel?" Her father is calling out to her through the telephone line. Through years of missed opportunities. "What's wrong?"

Though he cannot see her, she smiles into the phone.

"Oh, Dad—" *there'll be plenty of time to talk about that* "—I'm ready to leave, that's all."

"Of course we can pick you up, honey," Katherine says. "When?"

"Tomorrow. At ten. But if that's not good for you it could be later, I suppose."

"Tomorrow? So soon! It seems a little rushed," Katherine says.

"Why are you leaving?" her father worriedly asks.

"It's time, Dad." Isabel has to sound sure of herself for her parents. She pictures Kristen's wild-eyed return to Three Breezes, trapped between gurneys like a human burrito.

There is a slight pause while her parents struggle to decide whether to ask Isabel more questions or simply take their daughter's word.

"We'll be there," her father says.

"Thanks," Isabel says, hoping this time he means it.

Sixty-Eight

After calling her parents, Isabel's outlook changes. Just as Clark Kent becomes superhuman inside a phone booth, Isabel begins to look at Three Breezes with a form of X-ray vision. With only twenty-four hours to go, she begins to say a mental goodbye.

Melanie is the first person Isabel encounters on her way back to the unit.

"Isabel, I was thinking," she says with a look of intensity to which Isabel has become accustomed.

"Sure, Melanie. What's up?" she says, slowing her pace but not stopping, which forces Melanie to walk alongside her.

"I don't have time to beat around the bush so I'm going to cut to the chase. I need a new mattress. I've talked to them about it over and over and no one pays attention. If you would mention it, they'd listen."

Isabel is filled with an odd feeling of warmth toward this strange woman who is so fixated on the injustice of having to sleep on an inferior mattress that she completely avoids any chance at self-examination.

"You know, Melanie—" Isabel tries not to smile "—I think this will all work itself out in the next twenty-four hours or so. In fact, I'm sure of it."

Melanie's eyes widen. Most everyone has ignored her mattress complaints. "What do you mean?" she asks as her eyes narrow into suspicion.

"I have an idea," Isabel says as she leads Melanie out onto the smoker's porch, as she had done with Regina. "If you sit with me while I have this cigarette, I'll tell you my plan."

Melanie cannot believe her luck. Here is somebody who not only cares enough about her sleeping situation to talk to her about it, she even has a plan! She leaves her suspicion behind and follows Isabel.

Isabel sucks fire out of the wall lighter and inhales smoke into her lungs.

"Here's my idea," she says, exhaling smoke to the side of Melanie. "What if I went to the nurses' station tonight and told them that you could have my room starting tomorrow? You could even be all packed up and ready to move. I'll tell them it's a simple switch."

"You would do that for me?" Melanie is incredulous.

"Sure. It's no problem." Isabel does not know why she does not tell Melanie that she is being discharged in the morning. She feels like being appreciated for what is perceived to be a selfless act of kindness.

"What's in it for you?" Melanie's eyes again convey her skepticism.

"What's in it for me? Melanie. How cynical of you. Why does there have to be something in it for me? Can't I just do something nice for a friend?"

Melanie begins chewing on the inside of her mouth while she considers the authenticity of Isabel's offer.

"I don't get it," she says, her mouth twisted to the side as her teeth work on loose skin. "Why are you being so nice to me?"

"Let's just say I like to leave kindness in my wake," Isabel says, smiling.

"That makes no sense to me whatsoever, but I'll take you up on your offer. You'll really do it? You'll talk to the nurses tonight?"

"Yes. I'll talk to the nurses tonight." Isabel knows Melanie will obsess over this until the morning but she does not care. She is not ready to tell everyone she is leaving. They will treat her differently once that knowledge is shared. It is too painful to watch others leave Three Breezes.

"It's a deal."

Isabel extends her hand for a shake, but Melanie scoffs and walks back to the unit sulkily.

"Hey, Isabel," Ben calls out as he lumbers past her chair on the porch. He is scooping chocolate-swirl pudding from a cup that looks ridiculously small in his huge paw.

"Ben! Come sit with me." Isabel signals to the empty chair opposite hers.

Ben looks surprised at Isabel's hospitality. He eases himself into the plastic chair and scrapes the bottom of the pudding cup with his plastic spoon.

"What's up?" he asks with his mouth full.

"I just wanted to talk with you," Isabel says as she again exhales smoke. "We never get a chance to talk one-on-one, so I thought now is as good a time as any."

Ben moves the last of the pudding around in his mouth and then hangs his head. "Aw, man! You're leaving, aren't you?" he directs his high-pitched whine to his lap.

"Why do you say that, Ben?" Isabel is stunned that he, of

all people, has been perceptive enough to feel such a subtle shift in the atmosphere.

"I can tell. I can just tell. It's true, isn't it?"

"Yeah, it's true. I'm not going to lie to you. I'm leaving in the morning. I was going to tell everyone tonight in Larry's group. God! I'm amazed you figured it out."

"It's not that difficult, Isabel," Ben says with an adult tone of condescension. "You never call me over to sit with you. You always did that with Kristen. Then I saw you do it with Regina the other day. And with Lark, too. You'd sit with Lark. But you always shoo me away. You never wanted to sit with me alone before today, so I figure you must be leaving. Why else would you want to sit with me?"

Isabel is silent for a moment. "You're a very perceptive guy, you know that? You're a smart, perceptive guy. I'm really sorry I never sat with you alone before."

Ben blushes at Isabel's words.

"It's okay," he mumbles, unable to meet her eye. "I know I'm not smart, but I appreciate you saying that."

The same rush of warmth Isabel had felt with Melanie doubles with Ben.

"Ben, I want you to know something." Ben looks at Isabel, noting the change in her voice. "Please listen to me because it's important. I want you to know that you are a good person. Your mother saying all that bad stuff about you—she was wrong to say all that stuff, Ben. She had problems of her own and she took them out on you and you were a kid and that was just plain wrong. I know Larry says we're not supposed to pass judgment on other people's problems but I can't help it in this case. You are a good person with a mental illness that's not your fault."

Ben is staring at Isabel with his mouth hanging open. Puddles of saliva are gathering dangerously close to the rim of his mouth. He is transfixed.

"I know I should mind my own business and I know you have a lot of other things to work on, blah, blah, blah. But I want you to know that you're a good guy. Don't let anyone ever tell you different. Not your teacher, not your mother, no one. And it sounds like you've struggled with a learning disability, from the things you've mentioned in group. That's not your fault, either. You are a good person. If you believe that, you can do anything."

Ben sucks up the spittle as he closes his mouth and looks back down. Then he says softly, "Wellbutrin. Wellbutrin has saved my life, Isabel."

Knowing Ben will need time to digest what she has said, Isabel moves to a lighter topic.

"Ben, it occurred to me that I need to write down the name of that barbecue place you mentioned, in case I ever get that way." She knows this is the highest form of flattery.

A look of true elation spreads across his wide face.

"Aw, Isabel," he sighs, "you gotta try this place. It's called Bobby D's and it is so good I can smell it now, as I sit here talking to you. I'm telling you I can smell it now. You know what they do? They marinate the ribs overnight in this special sauce…"

Isabel smiles, pulls out another cigarette and lets Ben talk her ear off about ribs.

Sixty-Nine

Larry

"Larry, can I tell the group something?" Isabel says, after clearing her throat at the end of what will be her last group session.

"Sure, Isabel," Larry says, knowing what Isabel is going to announce. "You've got the floor."

Isabel inhales deeply and exhales.

"I'm leaving tomorrow."

Across the room Regina softly moans. Sukanya stares into space. No one speaks.

"I wanted to tell you all because I know firsthand how it feels when someone doesn't say goodbye and leaves abruptly," she says, thinking of Lark. "It's unsettling. And this is unsettling for me, too—saying goodbye to you. But I'd rather do it this way than just disappear."

Silence.

Melanie is shaking her head.

Larry finally breaks the uncomfortable silence. "Does anyone want to say anything?"

"I *knew* it!" Melanie shouts. "I *knew* there was something more to your little *room switch plan,*" she says in a mocking voice.

"What are you talking about, Melanie?" Larry looks baffled.

"Melanie…" Isabel tries to soothe her.

"Don't talk to me!" She will not be soothed. "For the rest of your time here, don't talk to me!"

"But…" Isabel tries to interrupt Melanie's melodramatic display.

"But, nothing," she says. "Don't talk to me."

"Okay, all right," Larry says, looking back and forth between Isabel and Melanie. "You two want to tell me what this is all about?"

"Isabel told me that I could switch rooms with her in the morning," Melanie seethed. "I asked her point-blank why she would offer to do something like that for me and she said it was because we were friends. I knew there was another reason for it! I knew it! Now she's leaving. Perfect. Just perfect."

Melanie angrily folds her arms across her chest as if to say with body language, "that's all I have to say about that."

"Isabel?" Larry turns to her.

"Melanie, I'm sorry," Isabel says. "I'm sorry I didn't tell you the truth."

"Why didn't you?" Melanie asks, tears starting to roll down her face.

"I don't know. I honestly don't know. I wasn't ready to say out loud that I'm leaving, maybe. Or maybe I just wanted you to think I was a nice person. I don't know. But I'm sorry, Melanie."

Isabel looks down.

"Isabel, I'm sure the rest of the group joins me in wishing you the best of luck when you leave here." Larry is smiling at her warmly. "Can we all get together and give Isabel a send-off?"

One by one Ben, Regina and finally, somewhat begrudgingly, Melanie get up and stand on all sides of Isabel's chair.

"Okay, guys. Let's all take a moment of silence and think good thoughts for Isabel," Larry says, his voice coming from behind the group.

Isabel looks back down to her lap. She jumps when she feels the first hand on her shoulder but is filled with a tremendous sense of calm as other hands rest on her shoulders and upper back.

I'm never going to see these people again. The thought is, this time, connected with sadness, not with hope.

Before each hand leaves she feels tiny squeezes of support. Isabel swallows back a lump forming in her throat.

"Goodbye, Isabel." Larry's quiet voice breaks the silence. "Good luck."

When Isabel glances up she looks across the room directly into Sukanya's eyes. For a brief second, Sukanya seems to be focused on her, not drifting off into space. When Isabel blinks, Sukanya does, too…and then slowly looks away. Isabel knows that is Sukanya saying goodbye.

Seventy

Rounding the corner, she finds the gardener watering a bed of impatiens. She slows to a walk and stands for a moment watching as he gently moves the hose from side to side over the brightly colored blossoms. There is a contagious serenity about him that casts a spell on Isabel.

Now she has to break that spell.

Alex. Her job at ANN. For the first time in a very long time Isabel is thinking about her future. And for the first time in a very long time, she does not dread it. Lark, Kristen, Ben, Melanie, Regina, Keisha, Sukanya: their faces flash through her brain and then blur. She turns and looks back at the unit and closes her eyes. She knows it is time to leave.

"Hey," she calls out as she resumes her jog toward the gardener. She has never learned his name. Without turning around he answers her. She can tell by the sound of his voice that he is smiling. Is it her imagination or does he sense she is leaving?

"Wa-hey, my friend."

"It's my last day here," Isabel says as she jogs in place, aware that it will force real conversation were she to stand still. She wants to keep this light. She wants to keep moving forward.

"Good news, good news." the gardener nods. He glances in her direction, but his arm continues to wave the hose over the thirsty flowers.

"Well, I'll see you, I guess," says Isabel, unsure of how to say goodbye.

"I hope not, my friend. I sure hope not," he answers as she turns to jog back toward the unit.

"It's a beautiful day, isn't it?" she calls back to him, smiling to herself, knowing his answer.

"Ev'ry day's a lovely day. Ev'ry day's a lovely day."

★ ★ ★ ★ ★

Acknowledgments

It is almost impossible for me to properly convey my gratitude to the following people for their tremendous support—both professional and personal—throughout the four years it took to complete this novel: Laura Dail, Mary Jane Clark, Stuart Horwitz, Susan Pezzack, Amy Moore-Benson, Jodie Chase, Jill Brack, Tres Mills, Liz Flock…I could not have done it without all of you.

And to my parents, whom I love deeply—thank you.

1. Does your opinion of Isabel change at all as you read more about her illness and how other people—Alex, her parents—may have affected or contributed to her mental state?

2. Early on in the novel, Isabel attempts suicide, and we learn that it's not her first failed attempt. Do you think Isabel genuinely wants to die?

3. Many women in abusive relationships have a difficult time acknowledging that a problem exists, and often stay in the relationship rather than leave. What do you think it says about Isabel that she does not leave Alex sooner? What is his role, if any, in Isabel's mental decline?

4. What are your thoughts about Isabel's observations about her fellow patients at Three Breezes? To what extent, if any, do these people seem "crazy" to you?

Are you able to see any similarities in your own habits or actions?

5. In many ways, Isabel is just as normal as the rest of us. For instance, when she first arrives at Three Breezes, she reacts as any of us would at the nurses' violation of her personal belongings. At what points do you see true psychosis displayed in Isabel's behavior and attitude?

6. There seems to be a trend for children to blame their parents for problems they have as adults. How do you feel about Isabel's parents? Do you believe that they honestly contributed to her emotional state, or are they just convenient scapegoats? Do you find their reaction to their daughter to be too harsh, too cold? Or can you sympathize with their impatience and frustration, or find caring in how they ultimately deal with her?

7. Isabel's emotional reaction to her brothers stomping on anthills—imagining the ants inside are trapped and suffocating to death—has a strong parallel to her stay at Three Breezes. In what other ways is Isabel like the ants she tried so valiantly to save?

8. What do you think the author is trying to do by having Isabel find Lark's body, yet another thing she cannot save? Is the discovery a catalyst to the beginning of Isabel's recovery? If so, how?

9. Discuss the dichotomy between Isabel's "normal" life in the public eye as a well-known journalist and

her life as a patient where she has no celebrity, no reputation and no power.

10. The author deliberately does not tie up loose ends when the story is over. What do you think happens after we leave Isabel?

11. How relevant is the title, But Inside I'm Screaming, to your life? What are you screaming about? What would happen if you verbalized that scream?